A Murder and Maggie MacGill

by

Rebecca Lee Smith

A Murder and Maggie MacGill

Cover Art by *Teddi Black*

The Wild Rose Press, Inc.
PO Box 708
Adams Basin, NY 14410-0708
Visit us at www.thewildrosepress.com

Publishing History
First Edition, 2025
Trade Paperback ISBN 978-1-5092-6229-8
Digital ISBN 978-1-5092-6230-4

Published in the United States of America

Dedication

For Ayden and Quinn.
Two beautiful, sweet souls. The lights of my life.

Chapter 1

Jogging past the houses on Victorian Row at one in the morning may not have been the smartest thing I'd ever done, but the sight of those stately old homes rising in the mist never failed to thrill me. It was the kind of gorgeous old neighborhood depicted in the movies I loved, where secrets lurk deep within the walls and the sweet old widow at the end of the street is always the head of the coven.

I reached through Mrs. Grayson's fence and pinched a dead blossom off one of the black-eyed Susans I'd fertilized that morning. I hated gardening, even though I had an annoying knack for it. I only felt slightly guilty I'd spent months digging in the Grayson House dirt, ingratiating myself to the richest, most despised woman in town, in order to convince her to let go of some of that old money she clearly never used and help save the Art Factory, the children's art center my mother had started before she left. Fat chance of that. But I was hopeful.

I came to the end of Langley Street and turned the corner heading for home.

The sudden glare emanating from the house on the hill brought me to a squeaking, stumbling halt. My breath caught hard in my throat. I curled my fingers around the fancy wrought iron fence posts and stared up at Grayson House.

Every light in the old Victorian was on. Blazing

from the windows, whitewashing the shadows beside the rhododendron hedge, illuminating the tiered front lawn like the twenty-four-hour doorbuster sale in a car dealer's parking lot. Mrs. Grayson's housekeeper only stayed until dinnertime, leaving the town matriarch alone in the house until the next morning. Everyone knew that. In a town the size of Wrenhaven, Tennessee, everybody knew everything. And then some.

My first instinct was to call her grandson Stephen. I'd only been going out with him for three months, and although I'd never broached the subject, I was sure he and his grandmother were not on the best of terms. He made the thirty-minute drive over the mountain every other day to check on her, like the dutiful closest living relative he was, but he made it grudgingly. He grumbled and fumed and seemed genuinely put out that the burden of his grandmother's wellbeing had fallen on him. Leaving me to wonder if the only reason he volunteered to be at her beck and call twenty-four-seven was to secure his share of what promised to be a massively large inheritance.

I felt in my pocket for the phone I'd left charging on the dresser and cursed softly. I was notorious for leaving it at home. My brother Jesse thought I should tether it around my neck like a first grader's nametag, and I was beginning to think he was right.

The fact that so many lights were on inside Grayson House at such a late hour was disturbing. On my late-night runs, I'd often noticed a small lamp burning on the table in Mrs. Grayson's foyer and another one upstairs. But nothing like this.

Constance Grayson was old and frail with a weak heart and a mind still unnervingly intact. If she were in trouble, she would call the sheriff, not hobble through a three-story mansion flipping on lights with her cane to attract attention. But then, eighty-six-year-olds didn't always live by everyone else's rules. My grandmother used to play show tunes on her baby grand in the middle of the night wearing nothing but my grandfather's Army blanket and a smile. Insomnia could do a number on anyone.

I glanced behind me.

Shadows from the sycamore trees spread like tentacles across the deserted street. Several new people had moved onto Langley Street in recent months. Mostly families with small children. But even though Wrenhaven was a friendly town, it could be dicey ringing a doorbell at this hour, knowing some folks still kept a loaded shotgun by the front door.

Should I just run the four blocks home and call Stephen? Neither choice was ideal.

Stephen guarded his time alone and would want proof it was a real emergency. Nothing short of a full-blown catastrophe would make it worth his time crawling out of bed, backing his prize Jaguar out of his garage, and making the trek across Blue Wolf Mountain to his grandmother's house for the second time that day.

The tall iron gate creaked as I pushed it open. Except for the lights burning, nothing at Grayson House seemed out of place. But I'd seen enough horror movies to know better than to fall for that one. I took a deep breath and tried to stifle the urge to run.

It wouldn't hurt to try the front door and make sure it was locked. That would be the first question Stephen would ask when I called. If the door was locked, then cool. If it wasn't locked, I wouldn't go inside; I would wake up one of the neighbors and ask them to call the sheriff. Maybe I'd try the friendly looking bungalow down the street. The one with the Wedgewood blue trim and the hand-painted sign in the front yard that said, *Welcome to Our Patch.*

My gaze flicked from brightly lit window to window. No sign of anyone in the house. No one on the porch. One quick peek through the front windows, and I would at least have something to report.

I hurried up the sidewalk, climbed the porch steps, and peered through the thick beveled glass. A round pedestal table holding a Chinese urn sat in the middle of the foyer. A huge grandfather clock stood in its corner. A high-backed red velvet loveseat with matching tufted chairs sat nestled in the crook of the winding staircase. I'd always imagined the inside of Grayson House would be stunningly beautiful, but I never thought it would look like a Dodge City brothel.

I tried the front door. Locked. That was a good sign.

What if Mrs. Grayson was inside and needed help? Maybe she wasn't able to get to a phone. Maybe she was calling for help and no one could hear.

I rang the doorbell.

The long sequence of Westminster chimes played out with my heart doing double-time. I gave Mrs. Grayson a few minutes to respond then knocked on the door.

Nothing.

Now I was getting worried. Maybe she had fallen and couldn't get up. Maybe she'd turned the lights on because she thought she was going blind.

I jiggled the knob and knocked again, banging the wooden crosspiece until the glass shook.

"Get away from that door!"

I spun around.

A blue pickup truck had quietly rolled to a stop in front of Grayson House. A man threw open the door and catapulted from its cab. *"Hey,"* he bellowed. "Didn't you hear me?"

His low growly voice seemed familiar. Too familiar.

"Of course, I heard you. Everybody within a three-block radius heard you." A dog barked, and I gestured impatiently toward the end of the street. "See?"

He looked at me square-on. The bright light from the porch slashed across his face and down his blue button-down Oxford shirt. My heart began to beat in slow, rolling thuds.

He took the porch steps two at a time then stopped in front of me. A gust of wind rustled his short brown hair, swirling it up and down as if it had a life of its own. I stepped back and tried to breathe.

Eli Grayson.

Eli Freaking Grayson.

I would have known him anywhere.

It had been a long time since our paths had crossed, but he hadn't changed. Same broad shoulders. Same lean build. Nothing to set him apart from any other nice-looking, slightly nerdy guy until he unleashed his killer grin. Like the Kraken. Then—and I'd seen it happen more times than I could count—whoever was on the receiving end of that grin might as well chuck everything they knew about life and throw in the towel. Because it was over.

He didn't seem to recognize me, which was a relief but also disheartening since I had never forgotten or forgiven what he'd done. In the last seventeen years, I'd spent hours staring at the ceiling when sleep would not come, wishing that wherever Eli Grayson was, a hole in the ground would open up like the giant maw of some demon bound for hell, slap that devastating grin off his face, and swallow him whole.

And now, in a bizarre twist of fate, I was dating his cousin. Although, I doubted he knew that. Stephen wasn't on particularly good terms with Eli, either. In fact, after three months, I had become painfully aware that Stephen wasn't on particularly good terms with much of anybody.

"I'm Eli Grayson." His deep voice rumbled. I'd forgotten how the sound of it could tear right through me. "This is my grandmother's house. Constance Grayson's house."

"I know. I live four blocks away."

His eyes met mine. They were still that strange grayish-green color like the water in Watauga Lake that could deepen or lighten depending on the sun. I'd forgotten that too.

"Would you mind telling me what you're doing here, trying to open my grandmother's front door at one—" He glanced at his watch. "—seventeen in the morning?"

"I was out for a run and saw the lights on."

"You were running? At one—"

"—seventeen in the morning. It helps the insomnia."

"I'll have to try it sometime." He seemed to relax then, reasonably sure I wasn't there to rob the place, or much of a threat if I was. He shrugged and stepped back to inspect the upper windows. "So what's the deal with the lights? Doesn't it seem odd they're all on?"

"That's what I thought."

"And did you develop a theory to go with that thought?"

"Look, I'm worried about her. Maybe she was afraid of falling in the dark."

"Constance Grayson isn't afraid of anything. Least of all, the dark." He narrowed his eyes. "I talked to her tonight around 7:45, and she was fine—reading and watching TV."

"So she knew you were coming? Maybe she left the lights on for you."

"All of them?" His gaze landed on my face. "I'm sorry. Have we met before?"

That was a loaded question. And one I didn't want to answer.

"We should probably call the sheriff," I said. "I was going to, but—" I stopped, embarrassed to admit I'd gone out alone so late at night without my phone. But it didn't matter. His focus had already moved past me to the concrete planters lining the edge of the porch. He kneeled by the one near the steps and pawed the dirt with two fingers.

"What are you doing?"

"Looking for the front door key." He snapped off a forsythia twig and used it as a rake. "She used to hide the door key in one of these planters. I think it was this one."

"And you believe it's still there?"

"Oh, yeah."

"You've been gone a long time."

"Seventeen years."

"And you show up now? At 1:17 in the morning?"

"It would have been earlier, but a jackknifed tractor-trailer shut down the interstate outside of Winston-Salem for two hours. I told Grandmother not to wait up."

"Where were you coming from?" I knew exactly where he was coming from.

"Kitty Hawk, North Carolina. It's a nine-hour trip, and—*bingo!*" He pulled a twisted wad of aluminum foil from the pot. He brushed off the soil and unwrapped a silver key. "I knew my grandmother's aversion to change would pay off."

"Hey, now. There's nothing wrong with not liking change."

He glanced at me sideways. "One of those, are you? Prefer to let things clack along just like they've always done? Don't like anything pushing you out of your comfort zone?"

"I'm very fond of my comfort zone."

He stood and unlocked the heavy door. It swung open, and we stepped inside.

His gaze flicked from the cobwebs wrapped around the crystal chandelier to the parlor doors to the dark oil painting of a soldier wearing a kilt. The muscle in his jaw clenched and released. "Stephen was right. This place is a mausoleum."

"I don't have a good feeling about this. I think we should call Sheriff Conley."

His gaze remained glued to the top of the stairs.

I stopped being afraid a burglar was hiding behind the drapes and focused on the man in front of me. A man who seemed to be frozen in fear.

The steady tick of the grandfather clock echoed through the foyer like a heartbeat.

We started up the long staircase, then past a sitting room and down a dimly lit hallway. Uneven wood floors creaked beneath our feet. Faded wallpaper curled back at the seams. An amoeba-shaped water stain spread across the dingy ceiling like a sea creature. For someone who supposedly had more money than God, Mrs. Grayson sure wasn't spending it where she lived.

Eli stopped in front of a closed door. His hand curled around the glass knob. Neither the dull lighting nor the disconcerting sandy brown scruff of a day-old beard could hide the film of perspiration on his upper lip. "Dammit," he said.

"Are you okay?"

"I shouldn't have waited this long to come back." He straightened his shoulders and knocked. "Grandmother? It's Eli. I'm sorry to disturb you, ma'am, but all the lights are on, and I—" He looked at me helplessly.

"Try the door."

He turned the knob and pushed it open. The sickly sweet aroma of honeysuckle and menthol floated toward us.

"Grandmother?" He took a few tentative steps into the room and stopped. "Oh, Christ."

I peered around the door.

Mrs. Grayson lay neatly tucked into the middle of her mahogany four-poster bed wearing a high-necked white nightgown. Her half-closed eyes, milky and bloodshot, stared at nothing beneath a thick fringe of mascaraed eyelashes. Her red-lipsticked mouth hung slightly open. Rouged, wrinkled cheeks sank beneath the sharp protruding bones of her face.

I had never seen death before, but there was no mistaking this was it. My eyes stung with unexpected tears. I'd never seen the mighty Mrs. Grayson look so small and still.

"Feel her pulse," I said.

"I—" Eli swallowed.

"I'll do it." I walked around the giant bed. "Mrs. Grayson?" I said softly. "Can you hear me?" Mrs. Grayson's carotid artery bulged in her throat like a twisted rope. I placed two fingers against it and waited, even though I could tell by the cold dry skin that the woman's heart had stopped beating hours ago. "I'm sorry, Eli. She's gone. Do you want me to close her eyes?"

"We shouldn't touch anything until the sheriff gets here." He pulled his cell phone out of his pocket. "I need to call 911. They do have 911 in this town, don't they?"

"Yes, but what about Stephen? Shouldn't you let him know?"

"I'll call him in the morning. Go on home. You don't need to be in the middle of this."

"I'll wait for the sheriff; he might want me to make a statement. Then I'll leave."

Eli nodded, his eyes still fixed on Mrs. Grayson.

I edged past him into the hall and stood for a moment in the shadows. How many times had I fantasized about running into him again? What he would look like. The withering looks I would give. The snappy comebacks I'd fling his way. One for every possible scenario I could think of. Except this one.

I hated Eli Grayson more than any man I'd ever known. But the sight of him standing at the foot of his dead grandmother's bed, holding onto the footboard as if it were the one thing that was keeping him from flying into a million pieces, stirred something deep inside me. Something that resembled compassion.

And at that moment, astonishing as it seemed, I almost felt sorry for the poor bastard.

Chapter 2

I took the long way to Fat Daddy's Bar and Grill, skirting Blue Wolf Mountain instead of going through town. I needed time to think. Time to wrap my head around the faculty meeting I'd just left. My friend Jules had been right when he'd warned me our jobs were expendable, and I hadn't believed him. I'd known Bainbridge Elementary wasn't in the greatest shape financially—I'd been supplying my art students with paper and paint for three years—but I had never imagined that in a town as creative and artsy-craftsy as Wrenhaven, their school would let their art teacher go.

How was I going to tell Pop and Jesse I was out of work? How would either of them survive financially without my help? Pop's house painting business had been going downhill for years, his remodeling services replaced by young do-it-yourselfers who considered HGTV their holy grail. Jesse's fledgling restaurant, Comfort and Joy, was barely breaking even. If it went belly up—and that was a real possibility—he would be out on the street. Well, not the actual street. But he'd have to move in with me and Pop. And Pop's twenty-five-year-old fiancée, who couldn't stand either of us, wasn't going to like that one little bit.

I shook my head. What the hell was going on? First, Eli Grayson shows up. Then I find Mrs. Grayson dead in her bed. Then, two days later, I lose my teaching job.

Was the Universe punishing me for sucking up to a woman I couldn't stand in order to finance my mother's children's art center? Or was it just not my week to shine?

I parked my vintage black Volkswagen beetle, named Velma so long ago no one could remember why, beside Fat Daddy's rail fence and cut the motor. I glanced in the rearview mirror and shuddered. The brief indulgent cry I'd allowed myself in the school bathroom after the meeting had done a number on my face. Black mascara floated on my lids. Dark brown liner smeared the corners of my tear ducts. The soft swell under my eyes looked like I'd polished off two pounds of shrimp. Not only that, but my new haircut made me look like a hedgehog.

I pulled a packet of tissues from Velma's glove compartment and blew my nose. Then, on impulse, grabbed my phone and punched in Stephen's number.

I felt guilty, knowing I should have invited him to come have a drink with us. But Stephen hated Fat Daddy's. And he didn't care much for Jules. And I doubted if the fact that I had just lost a chunk of income my family depended on would garner much sympathy from him. Stephen would point out that I needed a better job anyway. One that paid more and didn't involve passing out construction paper and non-toxic paste to a bunch of snotty-nosed kids. Then he'd stare at the row of TVs above the bar, sip his dirty martini, and complain about the spelling and grammar mistakes on the closed caption scroll.

I opened Velma's door and stretched my legs. The sour odor of rotting garbage drifted across the parking lot from the dumpster. Anger had begun to set in. At the school and at myself. I should have realized my time at Bainbridge was almost over and planned for it. I'd heard the rumors. I knew the Arts were always the first to go during cutbacks. And yet, it never occurred to me that when push came to shove, the school would part with me. I might not have been the warmest, fuzziest teacher ever to set foot in Bainbridge Elementary, but the kids liked me. I told them the truth when they asked the hard questions. I got along with their helicopter parents. How could the school let me go without a fight?

The phone clicked to life.

"Hello." Stephen's velvet voice never made it much above a whisper.

"Hey, Stephen. I know I said I'd drop by after the faculty meeting, but—"

"I was going to call you, Maggie." He sounded like he'd just woken up. I could imagine him sitting on the side of his bed in his big expensive house, all warm and tousled and beautiful. I had never dated a man who could turn heads like Stephen Grayson. Which, I had to admit, was a large part of the appeal. Maybe all the appeal. I was becoming disillusioned with his not so nice personality, and we weren't exactly burning up the sheets behind closed doors, but in public, I was the envy of every straight woman who saw us together.

"I'm at Fat Daddy's." I hadn't meant for that to slip out, but maybe it was for the best. If Stephen and I were ever going to have a real relationship, he was going to have to learn what give and take meant. Sometimes it meant forgoing jazz clubs and martini bars to sit in a drafty old country music roadhouse because your girlfriend's life has just taken a dive.

Two cars and a truck pulled into the parking lot.

Charcoal gray clouds tunneled across the fading sunset like a sideways tornado. The hulking rise of Blue Wolf Mountain loomed on the horizon, mysterious and dark.

"I met someone, Maggie."

"Oh, right. You said you were going to grab a bite after work. Who did you run into? Did they tell you about the faculty meeting?" I got out and walked around the car.

"I met my soulmate."

I stopped beside a red pickup truck and caught a glimpse of the reflection in the tilted side mirror. A woman with panicked brown eyes and a spiky black haystack on top of her head stared back at me. "Your soulmate?"

"At Hooters."

"What?"

"I hate Hooters; it's so pedestrian. But some of the guys from the firm wanted to go, and I was craving chicken wings, and this really hot server came over to our table and wrote her name with a felt-tipped pen on the paper tablecloth. Then our eyes met, and I—"

"—heard violins swell in the background?"

"Well…yes."

I leaned against the front of a truck. "So she's a waitress there? With orange short-shorts and tan pantyhose? With cleavage pushed up to her chin and hot wing sauce smeared on her—"

"This is upsetting you."

"No, I'm just trying to get the visual set in my mind. So when I'm at home later waiting for the alcohol to wear off, I'll have something fun to think about."

"Maggie, please."

"Does this mean you're not going to the Art Guild

Awards with me on Saturday night?" I swallowed. "Does this mean you're breaking up with me?"

"Maggie we were never really together. You know that. We've always been in the friend zone. We were only seeing each other until something better came along."

"You were waiting for something better? Is that why we never—why you never tried to—" I stopped, mortified. "God, Stephen, I wish you'd told me this three months ago. I could be having this conversation with *my* soulmate." My eyes swam. "What's her name?"

"Rochelle. But they call her Rocki. With an *I* at the end."

"Does she dot it with a little heart? Or does she use a smiley face?"

"Maggie…don't," he said tiredly.

"I wish—" What did it matter what I wished? Once a person found their soulmate, all bets were off, right? It was like winning the lottery. Or getting accepted into an Ivy League school with a C average. Or getting hit by lightning.

"Maggie, you called me. What did you want?"

"Nothing, Stephen," I said around the stone in my throat. "Nothing at all."

****

Fat Daddy's Bar and Grill was hopping. Every seat at the horseshoe bar was taken. Country music blared from the overhead speakers. Jeff, the three-hundred-pound bearded bartender, slammed down beers and shots as fast as he could pour them. The tangy aroma of barbecue sauce and fry grease rushed my nose, sending an inconsiderate blast of longing to my empty stomach.

Jules waved to me from a booth in the back.

"Stephen dumped me," I said. "For someone he met at Hooters."

Jules laughed. "Oh, that is just *horrible* news. How will you ever manage without that supercilious prick in your life?"

"Beats me." I tried not to laugh.

"Not to worry, Maggie. If you start to miss him, I can always take you to some pretentious little bistro, order you a drink you'll hate, and criticize what you're wearing. Hey, here's Libby with our drinks. After we both lost our jobs tonight, I figured we deserved them."

I raised my shot glass. "To becoming comfortably numb."

In unison, we licked the rim of salt, knocked back the tequila, and bit the lime.

Jules signaled for another round. "I'll miss teaching with you. This is the second school I've been bumped from due to budget cuts. Next, I'm going to look for a private school that has lots of money to burn and wants to burn it on Music Appreciation."

"How can you always be so optimistic?" I asked.

"Just lucky, I guess."

"And why did Bainbridge wait so long to cut the staff? It's the middle of summer. Most of the job openings for next year have already been filled in other schools."

"Maybe they didn't have a choice. How about you, Maggie? I know how much the Art Factory means to you. Any chance it could become your fulltime job?"

"I doubt it. The rent's gone up again. I'm not sure the center is even going to make it."

"That's a shame. Some of those kids are special needs. I've seen you work magic there." He dropped his voice to a spooky rumble. "You…are…The Art Whisperer."

"That's me." I laughed.

"Maybe you need to sell some of those seascapes you have stashed in your loft. They're amazing, and I'm sure there's a market for them. Or you could travel. What happened to that beach trip you swore you were finally going to take?" He shook his head. "Thirty-five-years-old, and never seen the ocean."

"Pop's got two bruised ribs and a broken ankle. I can't leave town until he can manage on his own. I don't mind helping him paint houses—I've done it every summer since I was sixteen—and I don't mind helping out Jesse at his restaurant. Even if it is a snooze. At this point, I could slap semi-gloss on woodwork and bus tables in my sleep."

"I can always float you a loan," Jules said.

"Now, you know I can't let you do that," I said softly. "But thanks."

Libby brought the second round.

I glanced up. Eli Grayson stood beside the bar, watching me.

A trail of heat pricked my spine. I swallowed the second shot and shivered, then closed my eyes and waited for the amber liquid to stop scorching a path down my throat. "The guy at the end of the bar—"

Jules turned around. "Oh, yeah. He was at the faculty meeting tonight."

"You're kidding. I didn't see him. That's Eli Grayson. What was he doing there?"

"He was standing in the back, looking like he wanted to be anywhere else. Somebody said he works for the consulting firm that oversaw the cutbacks."

"Eli Grayson got us fired?"

"He's coming over," Jules said. "Now, you have to admit, he is kind of hot. I mean Stephen looks like a movie star, but his cousin looks like he owns the movie studio. He's loosening his tie like James Bond after a hard night at the casino. Definitely more Sean Connery than Daniel Craig. Maybe he's gay." Jules sighed. "Is there a god? Could this man be my date for New Year's Eve?"

"I don't think he's gay," I said. "Just an asshole."

Eli ducked under a swinging lamp and stopped beside our booth, wincing as Carrie Underwood blasted a high note from the speaker above us. "Hi," he said.

"Hi," I said, deciding to be polite. "This is my friend Jules."

"You were at the Bainbridge faculty meeting tonight," Jules said.

"That's right," Eli said. "I'm the representative for The Grayson Group, my family's consulting firm." He turned to me. "Look, I don't mean to intrude, but is there somewhere we could talk? It's important."

"I am—*was*—the art teacher there. And Jules is—*was*—the music teacher. And you are the ill-informed person who recommended that our jobs be eliminated. Right?"

"I…I guess I am," Eli said.

"You're Stephen Grayson's cousin," Jules said.

"Do you know Stephen?" Eli said.

"No, but she does." Jules pointed to me and coughed. "Well, not in the Biblical sense."

"Stephen and I dated for a while," I said.

"You're kidding," Eli said. "When did you guys break up?"

I picked up my phone and glanced at the time. "Eighteen minutes ago."

"And on that note, I am outta here." Jules tossed a wad of bills on the table. "I'm paying for the shots and the appetizer since I forced them on you."

I laughed. "Gotta use that trust fund for something, right?"

"You know it, babe." Jules shook Eli's hand and grinned. "Nice meeting you, Eli. Even if you are Stephen Grayson's cousin and the asshole who got me fired."

Eli slid into the booth across from me just as Libby appeared with a platter of baked potato skins dripping with melted cheese. "The guy who was here—Jules— did he leave already?"

"Yeah, Libby, he had to go." I scooped up the money on the table. "But he left this to pay for his drinks. My check is separate."

Libby's eyes widened in disbelief. "All this? Really? Gee, thanks."

Eli waited for her to leave. "That was a nice thing to do."

"It's pretty obvious she has a crush on Jules, so I thought it would soften the blow when she finds out he's not interested."

"How do you know he's not interested?"

"Because he's dating a soccer player named George."

Eli laughed. "That would be a reason."

"That's what I thought."

I had begun to sound like Dolly Parton. Which was troubling since I counted on the theater diction courses I'd taken in college to squelch my east Tennessee accent long enough to get me through a two-drink minimum.

He looked at me closely. "I've blocked out a lot of things that happened when I stayed in Wrenhaven, but I hardly ever forget a face. I'm sure I've seen you before."

"You said you wanted to talk to me. You said it was important."

"I think my grandmother was murdered."

"Whoa!" I shook my head. "Are you serious?"

"Oh, yes. Dead serious."

Even with two tequila shots hustling their way through my bloodstream, I felt an icy chill skitter across the back of my neck. "Then you need to tell the sheriff."

"I did tell the sheriff. He doesn't care. Or maybe he thinks I killed her."

"Did you?"

"No," he said quietly. "Everyone in my family hated the old crone. Including me. But I did not kill her. I was tied up in a three-mile traffic jam on the interstate. I told you that." He sipped his beer. "When I talked to her on the phone the night she died, she sounded strange."

"Strange how?"

"She usually bellows into the phone, but that night she was whispering. Like she was afraid someone might be eavesdropping on our conversation. She said that when word got out what she'd done, it would make a lot of people angry. At the time, that didn't concern me. I assumed she was referring to something she'd put in motion at The Grayson Group."

"But now you don't think that was the case?"

"The Grayson Group has an acting board of directors, which Grandmother maintained complete control over. I've contacted them, and they assure me she hadn't made any recent changes in company policy. Nothing that would make anyone angry." He leveled his gaze at me. "So why did she sound frightened? And why was she whispering?"

"It wasn't Florence skulking in the hallway. She would've already left for the day."

"Maybe this is nuts, and I'm just imagining it."

"What did Sheriff Conley say? Will there be an autopsy?"

"Yes. Conley said the results should be back by tomorrow, then she'll be cremated."

"What does Stephen say about this?"

"I haven't told him I suspect she didn't die of natural causes. If I do, he'll think I'm crazy. He thinks I'm crazy anyway."

The lamp over the table threw geometric shadows across the sharp planes of his face. I opened my mouth and then closed it.

"Say it," he said. "Whatever it is, just say it."

"Mrs. Grayson was eighty-six years old and in very poor health. Florence said she had been diagnosed with advanced congestive heart failure. At best, she only had a few months left to live."

"I know, but that's *months*, not hours."

"Through the years, she's also made quite a few enemies in this town. She used her financial power and privilege to rule it with an iron hand, and not always in the nicest way."

"But you liked her."

"I—"

"Florence said you and my grandmother were friends. That you work in her garden. That her garden was an unholy mess until you started taking care of it, and now it's a showplace. She said she used to serve the two of you tea on the side terrace. Sounds like friends to me."

"We were acquaintances with a couple of common interests. But we were never friends. I'm an art teacher, not a gardener. An art teacher you got fired today from a job she loved."

"Did Grandmother pay you?"

"Of course not. I never asked for money, and she never offered. I only did it on the off chance I might be able to get to know her, and convince her to—" I sighed. "You know, gardening is a great stress reliever. You should try it."

"That's what I use my father's fishing boat for."

We sat in silence for a few seconds, until I decided it was time to go. I fumbled in my purse for my billfold.

"I'm sorry your job was eliminated," he said. "But I didn't have a choice."

"Sure you did. Everyone has a choice. That's what life is: One choice after the other."

"I weighed the pros and cons very carefully."

"Right." I shook my head, then looked him in the eye. "Eliminating music and art before anything else has become so common, it's chilling. I would respect you more if you had tried to compromise, offered Jules and I part-time without benefits, something like that. At least made an effort to hang on to a little bit of culture for the kids' sake."

"My job is saving schools that have been financially irresponsible from going bankrupt."

"At the expense of the children who go there?"

"I made an informed decision." He took a breath. "I'm sure what you do is important. But you teach art, not science or math."

"Do you even know what goes on in an elementary

art class? Life is lot more complicated now. It's scary and unpredictable. Bullies are everywhere. Predators too. Kids have to grow up fast if they're going to survive in the world we live in, and art class is a forty-minute island of calm in a day that, for some kids, is like jumping into a shark tank. It helps identify behavioral problems and learning disorders. It expands a child's imagination, and exposes them to cultural diversity. It gives them confidence—especially the ones who are struggling academically—and shows them a way to blow off steam without resorting to violence. And it teaches them *not* to run with scissors."

"You're pretty verbal with two tequila shots under your belt."

"Three. I knocked back the one Jules didn't drink when you dropped your napkin."

"Smooth move."

"Hey, Frankie!"

"Over here, Tom." I waved to the bartender.

"Your dad called. He says your phone keeps going to voicemail."

"Thanks." I grabbed my purse. "I must have turned it off at the faculty meeting and forgotten to turn it back on. I've been a little distracted."

"Did the bartender call you Frankie?"

"He did." I tucked a few bills beneath the glass pepper shaker. "It's a nickname some jerk gave me in high school. Some of my old classmates—like Tom— still call me that."

"Frankie," he said again, shaking his head. "No. You can't be the same girl who—"

"Can't I?" My eyes met his. "It's a shame you don't remember me, Eli, because I remember you like it was yesterday." I laid my phone down and began to unbutton the front of my shirt. "Maybe this will help."

The blood drained from his face. "No," he whispered.

"You told all your buddies I looked like Frankenstein." I pulled my shirt apart, revealing the vertical heart surgery scar running above and below my no-frills flesh-colored bra. Even though this scar was tame compared to the red gash Eli had gawked at in high school when he and his friends snuck into the girls' locker room, it could still clear a kiddie pool. The scar Eli had seen had healed and faded and morphed into a delicate quarter-inch line of silver-white skin. But it was still there. And unless I sprung for some pretty fancy plastic surgery, it would always be there. "Do you remember me now?"

"I-I…"

"I'm going to take that as a yes. And thanks for encouraging all your friends to call me Frankie too. It was such a nice thing to do."

He sat in stunned silence while I buttoned my shirt.

"I'm sorry. I was a kid then. I was trying to act cool in front of the other guys."

"You were seventeen. That's not really a kid. And telling a girl who has barely recovered from her second open heart surgery and is as self-conscious about her chest as only a seventeen-year-old girl can be, that she looks like Frankenstein, is unforgivable."

My phone rang in my hand.

Pop.

"What's up, Pop?" I scooted out of the booth.

"Someone's outside the window, Maggie. I can hear them scratching on the glass."

"Wait, *wait!* Slow down! What do you mean, you heard something outside? Are you on the sofa? Where's Trude? Are you alone in the house?"

"Trude had to leave. We just got back from the ER. I slipped and fell, and they had to recast my ankle." I got up, without giving Eli a backward glance, and made my way through the crowded bar to the front entrance. Cold air gusted down from Blue Wolf Mountain, cutting across the back of my neck. "Are you coming home soon?" he said in a small, shaky voice that sounded nothing like my father. "The pain pills are wearing off fast, and—"

"Hold tight, Pop. I'm leaving Fat Daddy's now. I'll be there as soon as I can."

I pocketed my phone and wove my way through Fat Daddy's parking lot. Locating my little VW nestled between a slew of monster trucks wasn't easy until I remembered I'd parked it near the dumpster. I skirted a red pickup and stopped short.

My poor Velma looked like she'd been pulled out of a swamp.

Buckets of cheddar cheese nachos, half-eaten burgers, barbecued chicken wings, and fries—oh, so many fries—all scraped from dirty plates, had been dumped like a giant clump of seaweed on her hood. The windshield was strewn with takeout containers and greasy napkins, all of it smeared with heaps of Fat Daddy's Famous Tennessee chili, clearly past its prime.

I stared at my car, not sure what to do. I had to get home. My father was waiting for me with a broken ankle and two bruised ribs, worried that someone was outside trying to get in. I had to get home *now.*

I glanced down and noticed the gash on Velma's

front tire. *Dammit to hell.*

This hadn't been done by a half-blind line cook who had tried to dump the night's food scraps into the dumpster opening and missed. Or by some pissed off busboy who had cleaned off one too many tables and never seen a tip. This had been done on purpose. By someone who either hated vintage Volkswagens or me.

And I was betting on the latter.

Chapter 3

Eli was suddenly behind me. "Do you want me to call the sheriff?"

"Who would do this? Who would vandalize my car like this?"

"I'll give you a ride home. You've drunk too much tequila to drive anyway. I'm parked over there." He pointed to the beat-up blue pickup he'd been driving the night we discovered his grandmother's dead body.

"Nice truck," I said, climbing into the cab. "Where'd you find it? Propped up on cinder blocks in somebody's front yard?"

"I found her at the Kitty Hawk Bait Shop. She's a rescue."

"Kitty Hawk, North Carolina?" I sighed. "I bet it's beautiful there. I've never been to the beach, and I've always wanted to go."

"Just a lot of sand and saltwater." He glanced at me. "You'll get there someday, Mountain Girl. But right now, after hearing how worried you sounded talking to your father on the phone, I need to get you home."

"You're making it awfully hard to keep hating you."

"That's the plan."

It crossed my mind that I might be hitching a ride with a murderer—Hadn't he just told me he despised his dead grandmother?—but I couldn't let myself think about that right now. Or what had happened to Velma.

Not until I got home and made sure Pop was okay.

The other thing I didn't want to think about was the fact that almost everyone in town knew the little black Volkswagen bug with a peace symbol sticker on the back left bumper belonged to me—Maggie MacGill.

When we arrived at my father's house, the only 1920's Craftsman bungalow painted yellow in a sea of beige and brown ones, and where I still lived, everything seemed quiet. We found him sitting in a wheelchair in the living room, his right leg encased in a new white plaster cast, balancing an aluminum cane across his lap like Jimmy Stewart in *Rear Window.*

"What happened, Pop? That cast on your ankle was a lot smaller when I left here at four o'clock."

"I fell again. Trude had to take me to the ER, and they recast it. Damn thing's up to my knee now."

"What were you doing up?" I asked. "You're supposed to stay off that foot."

He peered at me over his wire-framed glasses. "I had to pee, Maggie. I'm sixty-nine years old, and I had to pee, okay?"

"So where is Trude?" I glanced around, knowing full well Trude had ditched my father and gone somewhere else. Somewhere more fun. Gertrude Claussen was my father's latest in a long string of younger women he'd kept company with since my mother walked out on us seventeen years ago. He usually tired of most of them quickly, but after two months, Trude was still here. Still clinging to him like some clueless groupie.

"I told Trude to go on," Pop said. "She needed a night out."

"Every night's a night out for Trude," I said.

My father laughed. "That's what I get for marrying a woman so young, she thinks the Moody Blues is something she gets with menstrual cramps."

"You're not married yet, Pop."

He sighed. "I know. But I can't give her up. She thinks I look like a silver fox." His gaze shot past me to Eli. "Who's this? Your designated driver?"

"You didn't tell me your father was Les MacGill." Eli clasped my father's hand. "Good to see you again, Sir. You probably don't remember me, but—"

"Of course, I remember you, Eli. How's your mother doing?"

"Just fine, sir."

"I was sorry to hear about your grandmother's passing. I told Maggie it must have been a shock for the two of you to find her like that. When's the funeral?"

"There won't be a funeral," Eli said.

"Now, that surprises me," Pop said. "I was sure Connie would have planned something grand for herself. But I guess she thought she was going to live forever. Just like we all do."

Eli laughed. "You called my grandmother Connie?"

"Only because she hated it," Pop said.

"I would have driven home but Velma is having tire issues." I gave Eli a warning glance over my father's head. "I could have called Jesse to come get me, but I knew he'd be busy."

"My son Jesse owns a restaurant called Comfort and Joy," Pop said. "He's the executive chef there. Got a five-star review in the *Knoxville News Sentinel*."

"The place across from the old train station? I've been meaning to try it."

"Excellent food," I said. "Very comforting. Very

joyous."

"Jesse and Maggie have sunk every penny they have into that place." My dad's eyes misted over. "I thank God every day that my girl has a good job and a generous heart. Right now, she's the only thing keeping this family from going under."

"What did they put in that pain shot, Pop? Sodium pentothal? You really don't have to tell Eli every little single—"

"How much has she had to drink?" he asked Eli.

"Three tequila shots," Eli said.

Pop chuckled. "Bet she talked your ear off on the way over. One drink, and she's the funniest woman on the planet. Two, and she's your best friend for life. Three, and she'll get on a rant that'll make you wish you had a muzzle in your pocket."

"I am literally two feet away," I said. "I can hear you."

"What happened to you, sir?" Eli asked.

"I stepped back to put my foot on a scaffold, and it wasn't there. Broke my ankle and bruised two ribs. Last week I was on a ledge at Caroline's Bed and Breakfast painting crown molding, and today I can't go to the bathroom without sliding feet first into a pedestal sink. Fred thinks I forgot to lock the brake, but that's rubbish. I've been locking brakes on scaffolds for forty-three years. I wouldn't just forget to do it."

"Could someone have—"

"No one else was there. Just me and Fred and Pink Floyd."

"Pop likes to play soothing music while he works," I said.

"Hey, now," Pop said defensively. "Nothing more

30

soothing than progressive rock. Are you staying at Grayson House, Eli?"

"No, sir. Too many ghosts. Sir, I'd…I'd like to thank you for what you did for me all those years ago. You saved my life."

"Nonsense. I was just in the right place at the right time."

Eli pulled out his wallet and handed Pop his business card. "I'm at the Blue Ridge Motel, Room 102, for at least another week. If I can be of any assistance, please don't hesitate to call me. Or maybe we could just go for a beer sometime."

Pop grinned. "I do like beer. Give him one of my cards, Maggie, in case he needs a house painter. When you decide to get rid of Grayson House, son, a fresh coat of paint doesn't hurt the selling price. I hope you'll think of using Hit the Wall."

"Is that the name of your painting company?"

"It was Maggie's idea. She painted the logo on my work van."

After Eli left, Pop stretched out on the couch. "I didn't want to say anything in front of Eli, but I got a phone call while I was in the ER. You and I have been invited to attend the reading of Mrs. Grayson's will tomorrow morning. Her lawyer apologized for the short notice, but they're trying to get the estate settled as soon as possible."

"I bet she left you the new mower she bought," I said. "You've been mowing her yard for free for the last twenty years."

I hoped with all my heart that Mrs. Grayson had read my proposal before she died and been kind enough to make some kind of monetary provision for the Art

Factory. I'd talked it up for months, knowing the only way I could interest her in giving money to a children's art center was to convince her it would benefit her financially. I also suggested we might name it after her, which had seemed to work really well for the committee members building the new Constance Grayson Cancer Wing at the Wrenhaven Hospital.

"What do you suppose brought Eli back to Wrenhaven after all this time? Did he decide to visit Connie before she—well, we all knew how sick she was."

"He works for The Grayson Group. Mrs. Grayson brought him in as one of the financial consultants for Bainbridge."

"So she had her claws into the local elementary school too. It figures." Pop sipped the hot tea I'd made for him. "You know what else figures? That somebody in this town was sick and tired of her running their life and decided to take her out before her time was up."

"Take her out? You're talking like a gangster, Pop."

A chill skittered across my shoulders.

If Eli and my father's suspicions were true, and Mrs. Grayson hadn't died of natural causes, the person who had stolen the last weeks of her life might still be in Wrenhaven. They could be shopping for fresh corn at the farmer's market, picking up their kids from daycare, popping into Sam and Dan's Ice Cream Parlor for a peanut butter fro-yo with sprinkles.

They could be going about their business, living their everyday small-town life, flying directly under the radar.

Thinking they had gotten away with murder.

****

The next morning, Pop propped his broken ankle on the coffee table and winced.

"Promise you won't move around, Pop, at least until Trude gets here."

"Why do you keep calling me Pop? It makes me sound old."

"You are old."

"Then I might as well look old." He draped a crocheted throw over his legs.

"I thought Trude would be here by now." I tried to keep the annoyance out of my voice. "We have to be at the lawyer's office in an hour."

"She stayed out all night again." Pop sighed. "Don't say anything, but I think she's seeing someone else."

"You mean she's cheating on you?"

"Lately, I've caught her in a couple of lies. Just little ones. But you know how it is. Once you catch somebody lying to you, you never really believe them again."

The jangle of Trude's keys rattled against the front door.

"She's been coming in that way for two months," Pop said, "and she still can't figure out how to work the lock."

"I imagine she has other skills."

"Be nice, daughter." He shifted his leg. "I hope she doesn't start in on me again about moving up the wedding date. I told her I'm not marrying her unless she closes that party shop store she owns. It's on its last legs, and I can't take on that kind of debt. I don't know why she doesn't sell off her inventory and find a job working with computers. She a whiz at computers."

The door flew open and Trude's plump frame catapulted into the foyer, tumbling across my mother's favorite rug, her 42-D's bouncing like birthday balloons. She set the canvas bag she always carried on a chair and plopped down on the couch next to my father.

He groaned. "Watch the ribs, sweetheart."

She leaned up and kissed him. "Sorry I didn't call last night, but that last peach margarita did me in." She raked aqua fingernails through her long blonde curls. "I ended up crashing at Estelle's. I knew you wouldn't be here alone since your baby girl still lives in the attic." Trude scratched the gray scruff on his chin. "Tell her, Les," she whispered, just loud enough for me to hear. "Tell your daughter she needs to get a life."

"Not now, Trude," he said.

Trude turned to me. "You need to get a life, Frankie."

"Don't call her that," Pop said. "It's a disgusting nickname."

"I don't think you want to live upstairs after we're married." Trude snickered. "Les and I tend to be kinda loud. I doubt if you'd ever get any sleep."

"I don't get any now."

"Maggie has her own loft in the attic," Pop said. "With her own outside entrance. She's not really living inside the house."

Trude looked at me and did a double take. "Holy Cow! What happened to your hair?"

"She sure got it chopped off, didn't she?" Pop said.

Trude shook her head and laughed. "Honestly, Frankie, if you'd wanted the name of someone who knows how to cut hair, you could have just asked me."

Forget about the age difference. How could my father have fallen for a woman like Gertrude Claussen? He could have trolled every roadhouse between

Knoxville and Atlanta and found someone better. Someone with manners and a brain and a heart. Les MacGill was a good-looking, silver-haired fox. He was kind and sweet and funny. And single. And straight. There should have been hordes of women clamoring to take him off the market. How did he end up with an irritating, selfish party girl with the IQ of a dead plant?

I had never trusted Trude. Or her intentions toward my father.

"I got a call from that fancy lawyer last night," Pop said. "You know, the one who wears the pink striped shirts and the matching bow ties?"

"Percy DePaul?"

"Why would anyone name their kid Percy? You think his mother knew he'd end up looking like the tenor in a barbershop quartet?"

"Was it about the reading of Mrs. Grayson's will?" Trude said. "I heard it's this morning."

"Maggie and I have been invited." He checked his watch.

"Oh, Les." Trude snuggled into his shoulder. "I just knew she'd leave you something. Mama was sure of it too."

"I don't know why," Pop said. "All I did was cut her grass."

"You did more than cut her grass," I said. "You did her handyman work too."

"All I did was keep the paint on her house touched up and replace a few loose porch boards. I do it for all the older folks living on Victorian Row. Not many of them still around, though."

"Mama said Mrs. Grayson's grandkids wouldn't see a dime of that money when she died," Trude said, "and I bet she's right. Maybe she left it to you, sugar bear." She tugged playfully on Pop's ear. "What if she left you the house? Wouldn't that be *wonderful?* I've *always* wanted to live in Grayson House. And I'm glad the old witch is dead. She treated Mama awful—always yelling at her, threatening to fire her if she let her soup get cold. Mama said Mrs. Grayson kept a secret file hidden away somewhere with a list of all the things she'd found out about the people living in Wrenhaven."

"In case she needed to blackmail them?" Pop said.

"I guess." Trude smiled. "Hey, Mama's still got a key to the house. Do you want to go find the notebook and see if our names are written in it?"

"I'll pass," Pop said.

"How about you, Frankie?" Trude's blue eyes twinkled. "I'll bet there's some real juicy stuff about you in that book. Is that how Mrs. Grayson got you to do all that slave labor in her garden? Did she have something on you?"

"Don't make fun of Maggie working in the Grayson House garden," Pop said. "It's a showplace now. It looked like one of the jungles I waded through in Nam before she got hold of it." He smiled at me. "You and your mother always did have a green thumb. Of course, you kept yours in your mouth till you were seven."

"I'm gonna run upstairs and shower." Trude nibbled on Pop's neck. "You could come with me. We could wrap a plastic bag around your cast and take one together."

I sighed. Trude was right. I needed to move out before she married my father. I was no prude, but watching a twenty-something girl make out with my sixty-something father wasn't an activity I wanted to do before I'd had my morning coffee. I didn't care how much he looked like a silver fox.

"You think the Graysons will sell the house?" I asked Pop after Trude went upstairs.

"Of course, they'll sell. What else are they gonna do with that old monstrosity?"

I glanced at the clock on the mantle. "We probably need to get going. What time will Fred be at Caroline's to paint? As soon as we finish at the lawyer's office, I'll head on over there to help him."

Pop shifted in his seat. "Sorry, honey. I kinda forgot to tell you that when I swan-dived off that ledge, I pulled Fred down with me. He'll be fine as soon as his cracked collarbone heals."

I stared at him. "So that just leaves Bob Walters to paint?"

"Nope. I had to let Bob go."

"But you can hire him back, right?"

"He was drinking again, Maggie. I'd gotten complaints, and I had to fire him." Pain shot across his face, deepening the creases on his forehead. "I felt bad about it, seeing as how he still has his boy Travis to take care of, but I didn't have a choice. The painting is up to you now."

I suddenly felt so tired. Tired of taking care of everybody. Tired of shielding my father from financial worries that only seemed to get worse. Tired of feeling responsible that me and me alone had driven my mother out of our lives.

Filling the gap she had left hadn't been easy, but I wasn't asking for the moon. I just wanted enough money to make our lives less difficult. Money to fund my mother's beloved art center. Money to keep Pop's house painting business from going under. Money to repay Jesse and ensure that the restaurant he'd always dreamed of running was a success. Then, if all those wishes came true, I wanted to find a teaching job on the coast, sit by the ocean, and paint seascapes the rest of my life.

This probably would have been the smart time to tell Pop I had lost my job, but I didn't. I couldn't. Before I created another web of fine lines around his tired eyes and laid another worry on his back, I wanted to talk to Kath Davis, the director's assistant at the Art Factory. Maybe she knew something I didn't about saving the place and what my prospects were for a teaching job there.

Then I would tell him.

I grabbed my paint-splattered shoes and shoved them into a cloth tote along with my work overalls. "I was surprised to find out you knew Eli Grayson all those years ago, Pop. You never told me that."

"I had hemorrhoids when I was in the Army. I never told you that, either."

"So why does Eli owe you a debt of gratitude?"

"You'll have to ask Eli. It's his story to tell."

"Pop? Last night, were you serious when you said you wouldn't be surprised if Mrs. Grayson had been murdered?"

"I know you were becoming fond of the old girl, Maggie, but she wasn't a nice person. A lot of people in this town put their lives on hold waiting for her to die." He looked up. "Constance Grayson was a selfish woman who could be cruel and vicious if she didn't get her way. Ask Florence. Ask poor Mayor Nash. Ask Eli's mother. I never let Mrs. Grayson pay me for the work I did on her house because I didn't want to be obligated to her."

He unfolded the morning paper. "So no. I would not be surprised if Mrs. Grayson didn't leave this world without help. And when the truth comes out—and it will—I doubt if any of us will be surprised."

Chapter 4

Mayor Nash huffed and puffed up and down the sidewalk outside of Percy DePaul's law office like he'd sprinted the two blocks from City Hall. He spotted me pushing Pop toward him in a wheelchair and rushed over. "Maggie! Is it true? Are they really closing the Art Factory?"

"Where did you hear that?" Pop said.

"Kath said now that Mrs. Grayson is dead—"

"Kath Davis?" Pop shook his head. "I thought Dr. Gatz was in charge."

"No, he's just a figurehead," Mayor Nash said. "Someone Mrs. Grayson chose whose picture would look good on the brochures. Kath is his assistant, but she runs the place."

"I always wondered how Mrs. Grayson got that big hotshot obstetrician to come and work at a tiny hospital like Wrenhaven General," Pop said.

"How did she get anyone to do anything?" Mayor Nash said. "Mrs. Grayson promised me she would provide something for the Art Factory in her will. As you know, my daughter Holly goes there, and it's been life changing for her."

"That's great!" I said. "I wrote up a proposal and left it with Florence the afternoon Mrs. Grayson died. I have no idea if Mrs. Grayson even saw it. I tried to convince her the Art Factory was a worthy cause and needed her support, but I had no idea you'd already talked to her."

"I suggested she use it as a tax write-off." Mayor Nash's small brown eyes darted from Pop to me. "I hope I wasn't a fool to believe her. There was no love lost between the two of us, and I hated asking her, but I would do anything to help my daughter."

"Don't lose hope, Mayor," I said. "Even if Mrs. Grayson didn't provide for the Art Factory, I can't believe the town will let it close. There's a strong artists' community here in Wrenhaven. They've always had each other's back."

"They may not have a choice," Nash said. "I know your mother started the Art Factory, Maggie, but that was a long time ago. All the grants have dried up. These days, the cost of running a place like that is astronomical." He chuffed his thick neck into his shirt collar and sighed. "You understand why I'm so worried. I don't know what will happen to my little Holly if it closes. The Art Factory is her world. It's not easy being a single parent to a special needs child." He managed a quick smile. "But thanks to those art projects you keep inventing for her, she's finally starting to come out of her shell."

"I love volunteering there."

He nodded. "Say, you're an artist. We're looking for someone to paint a mural on the side of the courthouse. A picture of our beautiful mountain scenery or something to exhibit our Native American Cherokee connection. We have such a rich history here in Wrenhaven."

"I'm way ahead of you, Mayor. I read about it on the Art Guild's website and I've already turned in some sketches for consideration."

"Good, girl." He glanced at his phone. "Gotta run. Will you talk to Kath for me? See what you can find out?"

"Sure thing."

I didn't mention that I'd be finding out a lot more in just a few minutes.

When I learned the contents of Mrs. Grayson's will.

****

Percival DePaul's outer office was as frilly as a little girl's bedroom: ruffled curtains, a vase of fresh-cut lilies, crystal bowls filled with lollipops and bite-sized candy bars. I grabbed a few of the wrapped heart-shaped chocolates and shoved them into my jeans pocket. I hadn't bothered dressing up. I knew I would see Stephen there, which I'd been dreading more than my last root canal, and I didn't want to give him one more ounce of consideration than was necessary. The faded jeans he'd begged me to give to Goodwill and the sleeveless summer turtleneck and safari jacket I knew he loathed would do just fine.

I parked Pop's wheelchair beside the front desk and tried to ignore Eli and Steven sitting side by side in the waiting room. DePaul's longtime secretary, Delores, a plump cheerful woman with black Harry Potter glasses and a loose cluster of permed gray curls smiled at my father. "So nice to see you again, Les. I heard about your fall. I hope you're okay."

"Of course, you did," Pop said. "The whole friggin' town heard about it."

"You're getting too thin, Les. I'm going to have to bake you one of my famous butterscotch pies. Or I could bring you a salted caramel toffee blondie from Bear Claw Bakery. They are to *die* for." Pop winked and flashed her his best smile. The one where his gray eyes twinkled as they looked into hers. The one that caused most women of a certain age to take a delighted little breath before smiling back.

I pushed Pop's wheelchair to the opposite side of the room, avoiding the Grayson boys, and sat across from a twenty-something man wearing jeans and a denim work shirt and an older, attractive woman who looked very familiar. It took me a few minutes to remember where I'd seen her. She was one of the mothers who waited outside the Art Factory in the afternoon to pick up their kids.

I pretended to scroll through my phone while listening to Stephen's and Eli's deep voices whispering to each other.

"Don't bet on this turning out the way you want," Stephen said. "You know what happened when your father married your mother. One tiny act of rebellion and our grandmother cut him out of her life like a landscaper hacking off a diseased tree limb."

"Oh, that's good, Stephen," Eli said. "You should be a writer."

"How could you have left something this important to chance? You're the one who had medical power of attorney. Why didn't you pack up the old hag and stick her in a nursing home when she first got sick?"

"Because she wanted to live on her own. And she could do that with Florence's help."

"And you couldn't risk pissing her off and getting cut out of the will."

"No," Eli said. "I couldn't."

Florence Claussen pushed open the office door. Her petite, rail-thin frame, completely opposite of her daughter Trude's, disguised the fact that I'd seen her lift two twenty-five-pound bags of mulch at the same time without breaking a sweat. She pushed her graying hair back from her face, narrowed her brown eyes, and smoothed the front of her beige cotton skirt. If she'd been surprised to see me and my father there, she didn't show it. But Florence wouldn't. She had one of those sharp-featured faces that seem resigned to all the injustices in the world. The only two people I had ever seen make Florence laugh were Mayor Nash and the neighbor's eight-year-old son who snuck into the Grayson House yard last winter and peed his name in the snow.

"Y'all can go into the conference room now," Delores said. "Mr. DePaul is on his way."

The seven of us made our way down the narrow hallway single file. Eli and Stephen sat at the far end of the coffin-shaped table with the others in the middle. I moved a few of the upholstered leather chairs to accommodate my father's cumbersome wheelchair and sat beside him, keeping my gaze firmly on the far wall. I had avoided looking directly at Stephen and was grateful he hadn't made some kind of nasty crack about my unfortunate new haircut.

But the day was still young.

"I'm Irena Belka," the Art Factory mother said to me. "And this is Luke Pritchard."

Luke smiled at me warmly then ran his hand back through his dark auburn hair like Elvis. "I'm just here for moral support."

"Why are *you* here, Irena?" Stephen hissed. "You're not a Grayson."

"No, but my son Alex is. Kyle was his father, remember? And he is just as much of a Grayson as you

44

are," she said with the barest hint of an Eastern European accent. Her gaze shot past him to me. "Haven't I seen you at Grayson House working in the yard? That was you, wasn't it? Your hair is so…different."

Stephen snorted.

"Yes, I'm Maggie MacGill. And this is my father, Les. We're the Grayson House gardeners. He mows the lawn. I pull the weeds and set the mole traps."

This time Eli snorted.

"I also volunteer at the Art Factory," I said. "I know your son Alex."

I hadn't known Alex's last name, and it had never occurred to me that the sweet hearing impaired child at the Art Factory was Eli Grayson's nephew. Alex was probably around five or six, but verbal communication with him was tricky. Irena never stayed long when she collected the boy, or talked to any of the teachers about his progress. She always seemed to be in a hurry.

I studied her face: molded cheekbones, long thin nose, hypnotic, catlike eyes that could probably—and this was just a feeling—slice into an enemy's brain and force them to self-combust. She wore as much makeup as Trude and Mrs. Grayson combined, but her porcelain skin didn't need it. She was a beautiful woman. Just one I didn't think I wanted to cross.

Stephen knitted his brows together. "What are you doing here, Maggie? Is this the day sucking up to my grandmother by pruning her rosebushes finally pays off?"

"She did more than that," Eli said. "Have you seen the front yard?" His eyes met mine. "The garden at Grayson House is a work of art now. Florence says the whole town drives by to look at it."

"That yard is a disaster," Stephen said. "It looks like the clearance rack at a garden center." He glanced at me. "And the hedge needs trimming."

"I'll be sure to get right on that." Why had I never noticed how close together Stephen's eyes were? Or how his perfect Brad Pitt lips made me queasy when they flattened into a sneer? Why hadn't I realized how shallow and cruel he was?

"I'd like to trim his hedge," Pop mumbled under his breath.

The door opened and Percy DePaul swanned into the conference room. He set his briefcase on the table and pulled out a green folder. "May I start by saying how sorry I am for your loss. Mrs. Grayson was a client of mine for over thirty years, and she will be missed. The changes she made in her will three days before she passed were witnessed by my secretary, Delores Goldstein, and her attending physician, Dr. Herbert Moreland."

"Changes?" Stephen said. "What changes?"

DePaul adjusted his paisley bow tie. "It's all pretty straightforward. Mrs. Grayson's assets had long ago been placed in a revocable living trust."

"Why?" Eli said.

"There are many advantages to doing that," DePaul said. "It reduces state and federal estate taxes. It avoids probate, which can tie up an estate for years. And because it is revocable, it can be changed or dissolved at any time." He looked up and smiled. "Is everyone ready?"

"Just read it," Stephen said.

"Being of sound mind, memory, and understanding, I, Constance Clayton Grayson, bequeath my monetary

assets, my estate, and all my worldly goods to be dispersed in the manner in which I have stated in this, my last will and testament.

"To Florence Claussen, my housekeeper, I leave my unending appreciation for all she has done and my diamond and pearl choker which has been missing for six months. I'm sure she knows where to find it."

"I didn't steal anything from her," Florence said. "I swear, I didn't."

"To Leslie M. MacGill (Les), who has worked tirelessly for me without compensation for many years, I leave my Lincoln town car and the new riding lawn mower he refuses to use."

"Her house sits on a hill," Pop said. "I wasn't about to ride that durned thing on a hill."

"To Irena Belka, who I have only recently discovered was never legally married to my grandson Kyle, which in turn makes her son illegitimate and not a true part of the Grayson family, I leave nothing."

"Why, that old…witch!" Irena sputtered. "How did she find out Kyle and I weren't married? He's been dead for two years. Who told her? One of you told her."

"Shut up, Irena," Stephen said. "You've been hanging around grandmother's house for three weeks like a vulture waiting for her to croak. Did you really think one of us wouldn't get sick of seeing your face and let it slip that you and Kyle were never married?"

"This sure beats sitting home watching the game show network," Pop whispered.

"To my grandson, Eli Grayson, I leave the carved iris writing desk in my bedroom.

"To my grandson, Stephen Grayson, who never appreciates anything unless it has a designer label on it,

I leave my monogrammed walking stick by the front door."

"What about the company and the estate?" Stephen said. "Who gets the money?"

"And to Leslie M. MacGill (Maggie), who brought my beloved garden back to life, I leave Grayson House, its contents, and discounting all operating costs, the monetary assets from The Grayson Group for the next five years. Ms. MacGill has ten days to decide if she will accept this gift. If she refuses, or in the event of her untimely death, the revised testament will revert to the previous one, which is on file with Mr. DePaul. Whether or not Ms. MacGill accepts, I still want her to have my beloved books. I'm sure she will give them a good home."

All eyes turned to me.

And not all of them were friendly.

Pop whistled through his teeth. "Well, I'll be damned."

"Ditto," I whispered.

I didn't dare look at Eli. Or Stephen. Or anyone. I felt as if I'd been hit by a stun gun.

If what I'd heard was true—and from the horrified expressions on the six faces staring back at me, I had to believe it was—I had been handed Mrs. Grayson's personal estate forever and the bulk of The Grayson Group's profits for the next five years.

Five years.

Which, with a bit of luck and some first-rate financial advice, should be plenty of time to wipe out the MacGill family's monetary worries forever.

"Oh, no," Stephen said. "Not happening. I spoke with my grandmother two weeks ago about her will, and this is not what her wishes were."

"I explained all that," DePaul said. "Mrs. Grayson revised her will three days before she died, which was her prerogative. The only correction my secretary made this morning was to add names in parentheses beside the MacGill family members' initials for clarification."

"I don't care what her prerogative was," Stephen shouted. "This is not what she intended. We're talking millions of dollars here. This is outrageous!"

DePaul slid the documents back into the folder. "I've seen this kind of thing before, Mr. Grayson. Sometimes, when a person realizes the end of their life is imminent, they begin to see things quite differently."

"That's a load of crap!" Stephen slammed his fist on the table. "If my grandmother rewrote her will three days before she died, she was either so high on pain pills, she didn't know what she was doing, or she was coerced. Why did she leave it to Maggie? Why does Maggie get it all?" He turned to me. "Want to tell us how you did it? Just how in the hell did you convince my grandmother to cut us all out of the will and leave everything to you?"

"I'd like to know that too," Irena said. "Who are you to come in here and turn our lives upside down like this? Eli and Stephen and Kyle took that woman's verbal abuse for years. They bent over backward to make her happy. Then *you* show up out of the blue, and—"

"Not exactly out of the blue," Pop said.

"Calm down, Irena," Eli said. "Just tell me, Maggie. Did you have any idea this was going to happen?"

"No," I said. "Absolutely not."

Eli's eyes met mine. "Then that's good enough for me." He turned to Florence. "You were with my grandmother every day. Did you know about this?"

Florence shook her head. "I knew she'd changed her will, but I thought—"

"Enlighten us, Maggie," Stephen sneered. "When did you find out you were going to lose your teacher's salary? Did you find out your job had been cut before or after my grandmother passed away?"

"What are you insinuating?" Pop said. "That my girl had something to do with Mrs. Grayson's death? I swear, if I wasn't in this wheelchair, I'd—"

"Please, everyone!" DePaul said. *"Please."* He straightened his bow tie and handed me a small envelope. "Here is the key to Grayson House. If you decide to sell it, give me a call. I may know an interested buyer."

"So that's it?" Stephen said. "We're just supposed to say, 'Congrats, Leslie Margaret MacGill,' and go our merry way?" He gripped the edge of the table. "I want to know what our options are. Does anyone know the results of the autopsy? Grandmother's brain must have been ravaged with dementia. No one in their right mind calls a lawyer three days before they die and changes their will to leave everything to the girl who deadheads the damned daisies."

"Petunias," I corrected.

"Why does Maggie get everything in the house?" Stephen said. "Grandmother collected priceless historical antiques. Maggie wouldn't know a Duncan Phyfe drop leaf table from an IKEA TV stand."

"Now, hold on a minute, buster," I said. "It took me three hours to put together my IKEA TV stand, and I most certainly *would* know the difference."

"The things in that house are priceless," Stephen wailed. "They should be in a museum. You don't deserve them."

"Can we contest the will?" Irena said.

"That is your right, of course," DePaul said. "But it would be a long, costly, and rather futile process. A person's last will and testament is one of the most iron-clad documents in contract law. The changes in Mrs. Grayson's will are legal and binding. Dr. Moreland examined her mental state, and I can assure you she was completely cognizant. If you wish to contest her will, I'll be glad to suggest other avenues of legal representation; I cannot be involved."

"I want to see the previous will," Eli said.

"I'll get it for you," DePaul said. "It was updated after your brother Kyle passed away."

"And *you.*" Stephen pointed his finger at me again. "I thought I knew you."

DePaul scooped up the sheaf of papers and quickly excused himself.

Stephen stared at me with contempt. "It makes me sad you used me like this, but you're not going to get away with it. I'm not sure how our family is going to stop you from stealing what's rightfully ours, but we will."

"That sounds like a threat, Stephen," I said.

"Enough," Eli said. "Back off, cousin."

"Time to go, Maggie." Pop flipped the brakes on his wheelchair and pushed it away from the table. "It's getting a little claustrophobic in here."

"When can I drop by the house to get the desk and walking stick Grandmother left us?" Eli said.

I turned away from him. "You know where the key's hidden. Go whenever you like."

"You okay, honey?" Pop said when we were safely rolling down the hallway toward the front door. "Stephen said some pretty nasty things to you back there."

"I'm okay, Pop. And I'm sorry I didn't tell you I lost my job."

"Oh, honey, I've known about that since six this morning when Marianne Spires sent out a group text. The digital age sure has sped up the Wrenhaven Grapevine." He smiled up at me. "And Maggie? I don't care what those idiots back there said, Mrs. Grayson left you her house and money for a reason."

"I know she did, Pop. And I think that reason is spite."

****

I drove down Victorian Row and stopped in front of Grayson House.

I parked Velma, who had somehow magically been cleaned and re-tired overnight. I was pretty sure I had Eli to thank for that, and I was grateful. But it still annoyed me because, like my father, I didn't like to be beholden to anybody.

Grayson House loomed in front of me. The façade had always reminded me of an upside down face. The arched attic window resembled a mouth. The two gables jutting out from the slanted roof looked like eyes beneath a pair of heavy, frowning brows. The gray shingles and the darker gray trim had been painted by my father two autumns ago on a ladder so high, the thought of even climbing halfway up made me feel woozy.

I stood on the porch and gazed down at the Grayson garden. Mrs. Grayson had loved the way I had rescued it from chickweed and poison ivy. The perennials I had planted beside the wrought iron fence were thriving— purple coneflowers, black-eyed Susans, Russian sage, and Shasta daisies, all growing up and over each other in wild abandon. I hadn't had a plan, which was totally unlike me, but the messiness of it seemed to suit the staid house towering in the background. The riot of color and textures softened the old Victorian and made it look like someone other than the Addams family had taken up residence there.

I unlocked the front door and tried to ignore the uneasy feeling that had begun to niggle at my conscience. I hadn't asked for this windfall. And I didn't deserve it.

I was sure by now most of the tongues in Wrenhaven were wagging about the inheritance I'd just received. And I had to admit, it looked a little suspicious. But I hadn't spent my Saturday mornings knee-deep in compost and sheep manure hoping I might be named in Mrs. Grayson's will. All I had wanted was time to get to know the woman a little. Find out what it would take to convince her to make a donation to the art center my mother had started, which, besides a silver ring, a hand braided rug, and a few photographs, was the only thing I had left of her.

The morning had felt like a miracle. Mrs. Grayson hadn't mentioned the Art Factory in her will, but she hadn't needed to. If I sold Grayson House—and Mr. DePaul said he might have a buyer—I would have enough money to save my beloved art center and keep Jesse's restaurant and Pop's house painting business afloat for years. I might even have enough left over to rent a little cottage at the beach where I could finally sit down and breathe a sigh of relief.

I glanced up at the rectangle window, half-expecting to see Mrs. Grayson standing there in her pink flowered kimono, nodding if she liked something, waving her thin birdlike hands in the air if she didn't. The woman had been a mass of contradictions. She'd given generously to charities, then threatened her neighbors with lawsuits if they didn't keep their hedges trimmed. She'd subsidized the local food bank, then bought all the low-income houses down by the river for a song, displacing families who had lived there for generations to build a park in her name. She'd promised Mayor Nash she would take care of the Art Factory, then left all her money to me.

I stepped into the foyer.

The scent of old books and dead flowers floated in the air. The soft *tick-tick* of the grandfather clock echoed from the corner. A spray of dust motes hovered over the pedestal table, glittering in a wedge-shaped shaft of light. Every available surface—and there were plenty of them—was covered with curios and bric-a-brac. Silver candlesticks, cut glass candy dishes, fringed silk coverlets, all coated with the same fine film of white gray dirt. I didn't know what Florence Claussen did at Grayson House, but it wasn't dusting.

Everywhere I looked, there were bookshelves tucked away holding gardening books, bestsellers, mysteries, the classics. And the clocks. They hung on the walls, sat on mantelpieces, stood abandoned in cobwebbed corners with their huge, tarnished pendulums motionless and still. This house had belonged to a hoarder who had spent her life collecting the most exquisite things, yet never found the courage to let go of any of them. Priceless treasures that could have done so much good for other people instead of staying buried in the clutches of a lonely old woman who defined herself by the things she owned.

I couldn't keep it, of course. I couldn't keep any of it.

Or could I?

Stephen had been right when he said I didn't deserve it. And it would be soul-suckingly dishonest to pretend that I did. My name wasn't Grayson. It wasn't my money. But Mrs. Grayson had given it to me, knowing, I'm sure, that she was setting me down in the middle of a firestorm. But why? I wanted to know why.

I ended my house tour in Mrs. Grayson's bedroom, a room she rarely left except in the afternoon when she liked to sit on the garden terrace and have her tea. I hoped I might find some answers there. I also hoped seeing the place where she died would help shake the memory out of my head once and for all. That poor woman. With her makeup still intact and her hair neatly combed, tucked into her four-poster bed like a child who's drifted off to sleep. Only she hadn't been a child. And she hadn't been asleep.

I took a deep breath and went inside. The bed had been stripped and the vases of fresh flowers had been emptied. The air felt thick and still.

I ran my hand across the top of the desk Eli had inherited. Mrs. Grayson had called it the carved iris desk, and rightly so. It sat five feet wide and almost as high, fashioned out of black wood and intricately carved with life-size irises to appear as if they were part of the desk. I fought the urge to open its drawers, although I longed to look inside. But Mrs. Grayson had left it to Eli, not me.

The marble-topped bedside table held a crystal water decanter and some hardback books. Beside a round magnifying mirror, jars of high-end face creams were spread across the dressing table like a buffet. I had never seen Mrs. Grayson without makeup, and judging from the number of eyeshadow compacts and rouge pots scattered about, even in her last days, she had managed to look groomed and gilded to the max. I had to give the old girl props for that.

On the pink velvet settee, a little white throw pillow caught my eye. I picked it up and ran my hand over the silk embroidery: sprigs of lily-of-the-valley intertwined with tiny blue forget-me-nots. My mother had owned one almost identical to it. She'd called it her "mad money" pillow, and had tucked folded dollar bills into a little pocket sewn into the back of the sham.

I turned the pillow over.

Streaks of flesh-colored makeup stained the underside of the white cloth. Two rings smudged with blotches of blue and brown stared back at me like the eye sockets of a skull. A smear of crimson formed a jagged O, as if someone's mouth had been silenced mid-scream.

I stared at it in horror. Cold slashed across the back of my neck.

The door creaked. My head shot up.

Florence Claussen stood in the doorway staring at me. Her thin mouth, usually crimped into a tight scowl, hung open. "Did you—" Her eyes, so dark I couldn't tell where the pupil ended and the iris began, stared at me accusingly. "You killed her, didn't you?"

"No, I—"

"You smothered her with that pillow, then you came back to destroy the evidence."

"Florence, no. You can't believe I would do a thing like—"

"You killed her!" she screamed. *"You killed Mrs. Grayson!"*

The pillow slid from my hands to the floor. It landed

on the tufted bench in front of Mrs. Grayson's vanity, the smeared face staring up at me like a ghost.

I looked up, but Florence had bolted.

Her sensible shoes clacked against the hardwood floor as she ran down the staircase. Her hoarse, high-pitched shrieks echoed through the foyer like the Dark Ride at a carnival.

Chapter 5

"So Eli was right. Mrs. Grayson *was* murdered."

"Sure looks like it." Sheriff Conley shook his head. "Good thing the Graysons already asked for an autopsy, otherwise I'd have to request one. I've never had to pull anybody out of the morgue, and I sure as heck don't want to start now." He picked up his coffee cup and smelled the contents, "This is going to be a little tricky, though." He set the cup back down and looked at me. "Seeing as how Mrs. Grayson left everything to you."

"Not everything."

"And Florence saw you holding the pillow." He glanced at the deputy on the other side of the glass office door and lowered his voice. "I talked to her, Maggie. She's convinced you're a murderer."

"What motive does she think I have? Even if I expected Mrs. Grayson to leave me something in her will, which I didn't, why would I kill her? Everyone knew she was in fragile health. Her days were numbered."

"Maybe you needed the money sooner rather than later. Trude told Florence your family is having a hard time right now. I know you lost your job. Now don't look at me like that. I'm just trying to cover the bases."

"By considering me a suspect?"

"A person of interest."

I stared at the smiling faces of Conley's wife and

kids captured in a black frame on a table shoved against the wall. "It's true my family's finances aren't exactly booming right now. Pop won't be able to work for a while since his accident, and Jesse's restaurant has taken more capital to get started than we hoped. And yes, I just lost my teaching job at Bainbridge. But I'll find another job soon, and—" My eyes filled with unexpected tears. "Sheriff Conley, I swear, I never—*never* could have hurt Mrs. Grayson. Not for any reason. Not in a million years."

"Then we need to find out who did. The medical examiner determined her time of death between 8 and 10 p.m. Eli said he talked to her on the phone around 7:45. So, just for the record, I need to ask—"

"If I have an alibi for the night she died?"

"Yes. Sorry, Maggie."

I tried to think. "I was working at Jesse's restaurant from around six until eleven. He's short-staffed, and I ran orders for a while. But it wasn't very busy. Then I wrote the specials for the next day on the standing chalkboard at the entrance."

"And you were there the whole time? Never left the place or ducked out for some air?"

"I did run a box of takeout home to Pop. But that was around seven thirty." I stared at him, willing him to believe me. "But I came right back."

He took out a little notebook and wrote something down.

"That night, I couldn't sleep. So I painted for a while then went for a run about 12:30 a.m. When I got to Grayson House, the lights were on. Why were all the lights on?"

"There's a panic button on the wall beside Mrs.

Grayson's bed. It rings the station and automatically switches on every light in her house."

"I was only alone on the porch for a few minutes before Eli showed up. Did one of your deputies drive out to check on her and forget to disable the alarm?"

"No one from the station drove out the night she died. Only two deputies were on duty, and when the alarm rang, they thought Mrs. Grayson was crying wolf again. She'd started ringing that durn button three or four times a week. We'd stop what we were doing, hustle out to Grayson House, and she'd say she just wanted to make sure it was working. At that point, we stopped making it a priority." He leaned his elbows on the desk. "This sure changes things, though. Eli told me he suspected his grandmother didn't die of natural causes, and I didn't take him seriously. He's on his way down here now. I'm gonna talk to him again."

"If Mrs. Grayson was smothered with a pillow, it will show up in the autopsy, right?"

"It should. I called the county coroner and asked him to check for signs she'd been asphyxiated in case he wasn't looking for it. We're just waiting for the forensic expert to get here from Knoxville to examine the pillow." Sheriff Conley grinned. "Kind of exciting, though, huh? Nothing like this ever happens in Wrenhaven." He lowered his voice again. "Don't quote me, but that woman was a pain in everyone's backside. She ran this town—into the ground, some would say—and I haven't talked to one person who isn't relieved she's gone. People around here haven't been this happy about somebody dying since Bud Jones was caught rustling the Kesterson's cattle and fell into the fishpond and drowned. No, sir. Mrs. Grayson's passing is the best thing that's happened to Wrenhaven in a long time. Nobody will miss her."

"What will this do to the disbursement of her estate?"

"I'm sure a hold will be put on it until the investigation is over, but you'd have to talk to her lawyer about that. Who's she got, DePaul?"

"Yes."

"He's a good man." Conley clucked his tongue. "Can't say I'm crazy about some of his ties, though. Especially that flowered one. Looks like he's batting for the other side."

"Who had access to Grayson House besides Florence? I went through it today, and there were no signs of forced entry. I know Stephen has a key. Florence and her daughter Trude have one. And there was one hidden in the porch planter. I wonder how many people besides Eli knew it was there."

"We'll check all that out, honey. Don't you worry about it."

"But—"

"No buts, Maggie. Once I talk to Eli Grayson, we'll get it all sorted."

A deputy tapped on the office door. "You're gonna love this, Sheriff." He handed Conley a piece of paper and laughed. "This is gonna make your day."

Conley scanned the printout. "Damn. It Looks like Mrs. Grayson died of natural causes after all."

My eyebrows shot up. "Are you sure?"

"It says if suffocation has taken place, the eyes of the deceased will be bloodshot, and hers were not. Any kind of asphyxiation—Man, that word is hard to say—shows pinpoint hemorrhages in the skin and cyanosis of the face—Why can't they just say it *turned blue?*—bruising around the lips or nose, and a dark red protruding tongue." He looked up. "Sounds nasty, doesn't it? But none of those things were visible on Mrs. Grayson, and the toxicology report states that the only drugs in her system were the ones she'd been prescribed—so no overdose. My guess is someone tried to smother Mrs. Grayson after she was already dead."

"Seriously?"

"They may have thought she was asleep. It's actually pretty hard to smother a person unless the victim is old or in poor health, which she was both. Normally, it takes from three to five minutes, but a woman her age would have gone into cardiac arrest almost immediately."

"She had enough strength to push the panic button."

"Or someone did. By mistake, maybe. If they didn't know it was there, they could have backed into it. Or—" Sheriff Conley slid the paper into a folder then leveled his gaze at me. "Or she looked up, saw the pillow coming toward her face, had a heart attack, and died on the spot."

"That would still be murder."

"Well, technically, attempted murder."

"Is that why the Graysons requested an autopsy? To clear their name?"

"You think Eli and Stephen are suspects? That they were in this thing together?"

"I don't know," I said. "But we need to find out who was at Mrs. Grayson's house the day she died. Everyone knew she stayed alone in the house at night after Florence went home. If her murder was premeditated, and the killer didn't have a key, they would have had to steal one beforehand or figure out some other way to get inside. I know Florence is a little wary of me—"

"To put it mildly."

"But I'd like to ask her—"

"No, Maggie. I don't want you talking to anybody about this case, understand? Not now. Not ever." His expression softened. "Please, honey. You and Les and Jesse are like family to me. So when I tell you to stay out of a murder investigation and let me handle it, I'm saying it for your own good, understand?" I nodded. "Promise you'll stay out of it."

"If we're finished, I need to go. That bed and breakfast isn't going to paint itself." I looked into Sheriff Conley's tired brown eyes and smiled. We both knew I wouldn't make a promise I didn't intend to keep.

****

After spending a sleepless night trying to come up with some kind of strategy to clear my name and not succeeding, I loaded Pop's work van with supplies from the storage shed. I was proud of the logo I'd painted on it—huge paint splatters in primary colors with *Hit the Wall* and our phone number and website lettered beneath it in black.

I still felt torn about accepting the inheritance that had suddenly dropped into my lap, but how could I refuse it? I was out of work with, face it, very few prospects on the horizon until my name was cleared in the murder investigation. I had to think of my family. I didn't have to be greedy and keep all the money. Just enough to get us through this rough patch. I could share some of it with the Graysons and give some to charity. A charity like the Art Factory.

I fastened my seatbelt, switched the radio station from my father's favorite golden oldies channel to something more contemporary, and glanced in the rearview mirror. Tufts of hair stood up from my scalp like I'd slept in a wind tunnel. It was a drastic change, but I had to admit that this funky new look was starting to grow on me. Literally.

The fog rolling in off the river had encased the streets in a thick layer of murk and mist. It would burn off in an hour or so, leaving the little valley town steeped in humidity. But right now, coasting down Chestnut Street toward the center of town felt like I was gliding through a dream.

I had lived in Wrenhaven all my life, and I loved the quirky little place. It was a hybrid community: a strange mixture of artisans and country farmers. Artsy uptown sophistication and downhome comfort. Chardonnay and moonshine. Red and blue split right down the middle. And all of it surrounded by some of the most beautiful mountains on the Tennessee-North Carolina border.

I passed the Blue Ridge Motel where Eli was staying and wondered how the conversation had gone between him and Sheriff Conley. I would have loved to have seen his face when Conley told him I'd found the smother pillow. The Smother Pillow. What a strange thing to call a little ruffled pillow. It sounded like a 60's rock band.

Had Florence told Stephen she thought I was a killer? Probably. It would have validated his belief that I was guilty of stealing his inheritance. But then, Stephen had a tendency to believe the worst about people. I wondered if he had always been that mistrustful.

I scarcely remembered the three Grayson grandkids the summer they came to visit. I'd ridden my bike up and down Victorian Row every day but hadn't laid eyes on any of them. No basketball goal sat at the end of the driveway. No stray soccer balls lay in the yard. Once, I thought I saw a little boy gazing out the attic window, but when I slowed my bike and turned around, he was gone. Some family emergency had forced them to stay with their grandmother through most of the school year, but I'd never even seen seventeen-year-old Eli until we met in the fall at Wrenhaven High.

The fog on Chestnut Street had begun to clear. Wisps of white mist floated between the crape myrtle trees like ghosts drifting home after a long night. I took the sharp turn past the Civil War cemetery a little too fast and pressed my foot on the brake. It felt like I'd stepped on a marshmallow.

The old van was more unwieldy than I remembered. The two-mile stretch down the hill leading to the train station seemed endless. The metal ladders fastened to the top rattled, warning me to slow down. I knew I needed to cut my speed—and fast—so I pushed my right foot hard against the brake pedal. It went to the floor.

"What the—"

Reality hit me like ice water.

There were no brakes. None. Zip. Nada. Zilch.

My heart slammed against my ribs. Adrenaline shot through my veins. I pressed the car horn on the steering wheel with the palm of my hand, then leaned into it hard, blasting it nonstop like a tornado siren. My heartbeat pounded in my throat while the rickety van sped untethered down the hill, banging and swerving like it was possessed.

Objects rushed by in a blur—green and white and black, swirling around the edges of my peripheral vision like glass in a kaleidoscope. I heard people yelling. Felt the wind against my face. I needed help. And I needed it now.

I couldn't let go of the steering wheel long enough to fish my phone out of my purse. And I couldn't take my eyes off the road to glance at the speedometer. I had no idea how fast I was going. Or how many obscenities and prayers were flying out of my mouth.

My father's Hit the Wall van was a runaway train screaming through the night. Barreling down the tracks toward the middle of town.

With zero chance of stopping.

****

The van tore past the shops on Hawthorn Street then ripped through the intersection at Chestnut and Main.

It sped through the hastily cleared path formed by three cars, two trucks, and a yellow crotch rocket motorcycle waiting at the red light. Two men standing on the crosswalk curb scrambled to get out of its way. Someone was screaming, *"Oh, God,"* over and over again, and it took a few seconds to realize it was me.

Cars and trees and storefronts whizzed by as I flew beneath the traffic light. I tried to force the key out of the ignition, but it wouldn't budge. I yanked at the emergency brake, but it only made a high-pitched grinding sound. I missed the mailbox at the corner of Cornwall Avenue by inches. A car horn sounded behind me.

I glanced in the rearview mirror. A white SUV had turned on its flashers and was hot on my trail. I hit a giant pothole and felt the belly of the van scrape against the concrete. It wobbled to the left then slowed a little, but there was still another long downhill section of highway to survive before I made it to the bottom of the foothills.

Three choices presented themselves simultaneously:

The road out of town, the road up Blue Wolf Mountain, and the front window of Sam and Dan's Ice Cream Parlor, still draped in red, white, and blue bunting from the Fourth of July.

I chose the road out of town.

Going up Blue Wolf Mountain would have cut my speed, but I never would have made the first switchback without flying off into the gorge. Route 16 was a straight shot slightly downwards across four miles of farmland where Jesse and his high school friends had held their Saturday night drag races. If I could keep the van steady long enough to find a field to pull off in, it might stop on its own without flipping over.

The SUV behind me flashed its headlights, signaling it was trying to catch up. For one fleeting second, before the panic burning a hole in my chest took over, I was comforted by the fact that someone had recognized my plight and was trying to help me.

One by one, the horse and tobacco farms on Route 16 flew by while the van kept up a steady, relentless downhill speed. All I could do was hang on.

Finally, only one farm was left—the Kesterson's. The road curved dramatically to the right a few hundred feet past their property. If I couldn't stop the van before I reached it, I was toast. This was my last and only chance. The car behind me knew it too because the driver blew his horn to warn me. Pulling off and not getting myself killed, whether I ran through a fence or not, was all I could hope for.

I swerved to the right.

My left wheels rose from the pavement. The van careened off the road, narrowly missing the brick archway spanning the entrance to Roone Kesterson's dairy farm. It crunched across the gravel driveway and sailed past a dented mailbox. Then plowed front first through a waist-high barbed wire fence.

I held on to the steering wheel with both hands.

My father's van, which I feared would never be the same, bounced jauntily over the rutted field dragging a trail of wooden fence posts and barbed wire behind it like a cathedral-length wedding veil. In the distance, a flash of green glinted in the sunlight. I veered to the right, away from the Kesterson's pond, and slammed into a fresh stack of round hay bales. My head lurched back, banging into the headrest. The van shuddered to a stop.

I sat for a moment, jolted into silence. It felt like I was still moving through the tall grass even though the huge vehicle beneath me had heaved its last breath. I unlatched the door and slid out. The pungent odor of damp hay ripped through my sinuses.

"Hey!"

I looked up.

Thrashing through the tall weeds beside the pond, a man stumbled and hopped over the hard clumps of dirt trying to get to me. "Hey!" he cried again. "Are you okay?"

I opened my mouth, but nothing came out. I gulped in mouthfuls of air like a swimmer who's been underwater for too long. I swayed to the side and held out my hands. They were shaking so hard, it took two tries for him to grab them in midair.

"Hey, it's okay," he said gently. "You're okay."

It was only then that I realized I'd met him before. At the reading of Mrs. Grayson's will. He was the man who'd come with Irena Belka. What was his name? Luke something?

He slid his arms around my waist and pulled me to him. I held on to him as if he were the last life preserver on the *Lusitania*. I hadn't taken much notice of him at DePaul's office, but now I gave him my full attention. He was younger than me, probably in his early twenties, with dark blue eyes, a short thatch of copper-colored hair, and that white bloodless skin every redhead I'd ever met despised.

"Were you following me in the white car?" I croaked into his collarbone.

"Yeah," he said. "I'd just driven up to the intersection when I heard your horn."

"My brakes went out."

He laughed. "Ya think?"

The sun shone down on us, turning the stacks of matted brown hay into pillars of gold. Dust motes floated in the air like glitter. The whole thing felt surreal and romantic, like a scene from a Hallmark movie without the fake snow and the gay leading man.

I pulled back and tried to smile. "Thanks for rescuing me."

"Are you kidding? You rescued yourself." He grinned, showing some very nice teeth between his auburn mustache and neatly trimmed beard. "That was some driving you did back there."

"I tried to call 911, but my phone fell between the seats."

"That's okay. I called them when we passed the turnoff to Blue Wolf." He held out his hand. "We never formally met at the lawyer's office. I know you're Maggie MacGill. My name is Luke Prichard."

I clasped his calloused fingers in mine, grateful for the warmth they were generating around my cold ones.

"Do you live near here? I thought you and Irena were from out of town." I felt like I was two margaritas in and not making much sense.

"I'm from Wrenhaven," he said. "Irena and I met three weeks ago when she came here to introduce her son to Mrs. Grayson."

"You're local?"

"Yeah, but you probably wouldn't know me. Our family's house was at the bottom of Redbud Hill behind the train station. Where the new park is now."

"Constance Grayson Park. They tore down all those houses to build it, didn't they?"

"They sure did." He held my hand. "Come sit on this haybale. You're trembling."

The screen door banged open against the Kesterson's white clapboard house, and the Kesterson family spilled out.

"Maggie MacGill? Is that you?" Roone Kesterson ran down the front steps and sprinted across the field, followed by his three grandchildren, two barking black labs, and a small gray-haired woman in a long, calico dress.

"Hey, Roone," I said shakily. "Sorry about the fence."

"My Lord, Maggie!" Roone's wife hiked up her skirt as she hopped over a cow pile. "We saw the whole thing from the kitchen window. I was scraping leftover gravy into a bowl when I heard the car horns. Wasn't I, Roone?"

"Scraping gravy," Roone said.

The two big dogs circled Luke, wagging their tails, nosing his crotch.

"I didn't know what to think," Roone's wife said.

"We couldn't imagine what the ruckus was, could we, Roone?"

"Couldn't imagine." Roone shoved his hands deep into the pockets of his overalls.

"Why, you're shaking like a maple leaf." Roone's wife, whose name I couldn't seem to remember, patted my shoulder.

"I'm fine."

"She's not fine," Luke said. "She needs to sit down. The sheriff is on his way."

Roone's wife squinted at Luke. "Why, I know you. You're Annie Prichard's boy." She couldn't have looked more surprised if he'd been an alien who'd beamed down from the mothership and crash-landed in her backyard.

"Yes, ma'am," Luke said. "I'm Annie's boy."

"I was so sorry to hear about your mother dying last week, Luke. She was a good woman. A God-fearing woman. The Lord must have wanted her home real bad to bring the cancer to her twice like that. My prayers are with your family."

"Yes, ma'am," Luke said. "Thank you."

I let Roone's wife propel me across the field wrapped in the safe cocoon of her rowdy family. She chattered about Roone and the kids and the apple butter she was going to make for the Wrenhaven Fall Festival, and how grown up Luke Prichard looked all of a sudden. But I didn't care. The drone of her voice was like white noise. It gave me time to calm down. Time to stop saying the words *untimely death* over and over in my head.

I turned to wave to Luke, but his white SUV had already pulled out onto the highway and was making its way up Route 16 toward town. Had I even thanked him? I wasn't sure. When I got home, I needed to find him and tell him how grateful I was.

But for now, as the last of the adrenaline buzzed through my limbs, all I could do was stand on the Kesterson's porch and watch him drive away. While the sound of a siren echoed in the distance.

Chapter 6

I stood in the takeout line at Mac's Diner watching rivulets of rain drizzle down the cracked windowpane, thankful the skies had waited to open until after I'd ripped through the middle of Wrenhaven like Cruella De Vil on steroids.

After one of Sheriff Conley's deputies had driven me home and helped transfer the painting supplies to my father's old Honda Civic, I realized I was starving. All I wanted was one of Mac's cheddar sausage biscuits, which had long been my tranquilizer of choice.

I pulled my red cardigan closer around my shoulders and gave in to the mouthwatering smells in the tiny restaurant—griddle pancakes with warm maple syrup, crispy hash browns, buttermilk biscuits drenched in sawmill gravy. Mac's Diner served breakfast all day, and the place was always full. Mostly regulars who'd been coming there for years and sat in the same shabby booths and ordered the same things off the menu every day. What Jesse wouldn't give for a crowd like that at Comfort and Joy.

The whispers and sideways glances directed at me as I'd walked into the diner felt a little unnerving. But it didn't surprise me. By now, everyone sharing and forwarding texts on the Wrenhaven grapevine knew I had come into a considerable amount of money, undeservedly so, and had been accused by Florence

Claussen of taking out my benefactor with a twelve-inch square throw pillow. I couldn't blame them for believing it. People hid who they were all the time. Why shouldn't the elementary school art teacher who lived down the road be any different?

Whoever had slipped into Grayson House, found Mrs. Grayson asleep in her bed, then attempted to smother the life out of her, could be sitting in this room right now eating a mushroom omelet with a side order of cheese grits. Why had it been so important to kill an old woman who didn't have long to live? Had the would-be killer known Mrs. Grayson had changed her will? Or had they assumed the old one was still valid?

I needed to find out who would benefit most from Mrs. Grayson's death in the original will. And why the brakes on my father's van had suddenly failed.

Dr. Harold Gatz walked up to me, flashing his million-dollar smile. "Hey, Maggie." His blue scrubs were the same color as his eyes, his Dudley Do-right chin was clean-shaven, and his teeth looked like the "after" photos you see on a dentist's wall while you're waiting for the lidocaine to kick in. "I've missed you, Maggie. Have dinner with me."

"No."

"Then marry me."

"No."

"Then sleep with me."

"Not a chance," I said.

"Why not? We're both tall and good-looking. What more could anyone want?"

"Brains and a personality might be nice. One or the other."

"You always make me laugh, Maggie."

It's not that I found the prospect of having some adult fun with Dr. Harold off-putting. It's just that I didn't have the energy for another rejection. But maybe I wasn't giving Dr. Harold enough credit. He was a respected OB-GYN. Over the years, he'd seen hundreds of women's chests in all their beautiful flawed glory. I hoped he wouldn't take one horrified look at my heart surgery scar, like one of my more memorable dates had, and ask me to put my shirt back on.

"I heard you found Mrs. G's dead body," Harold said. "That must have been exciting."

"Not even close."

"I can't believe she's finally gone. That woman's death is going to be a game-changer."

"You chair the Board of Directors at the Art Factory. Any word on the situation there? Is it as dire as Mayor Nash believes?"

"Doesn't look good, Maggie. But now that the Wicked Witch of the Northeast is gone, I'm pulling out. I've done my time in Wrenhaven."

"I've always wondered how Mrs. Grayson got a big fancy obstetrician like yourself to come here in the first place."

"How did she get anyone to do anything?"

"That's what I'm asking."

"Oh, she could be very persuasive." There was that smile again. The one that never quite reached his eyes.

My gaze shot to the door. "Florence Claussen just walked in. I wonder what she's going to do now that Mrs. Grayson is dead?"

"Dance on her grave?"

Florence glared at me for a long, excruciating moment then turned and walked to one of the booths in the back.

"That woman gives me the creeps," Harold said. "I think it's the way she looks at me. Like she knows the day I'm going to die. "

"Maybe she does."

"I heard Mrs. Grayson made her take potshots with a BB gun at anyone who trespassed on the Grayson property—children, squirrels, the water meter man."

"Two cheddar biscuits with sausage." Mac handed me a brown paper bag. "How's Jesse doing with Comfort and Joy? I hear his food's really something. I have no idea what savory rugelach is, but I can't wait to try it."

"That's sweet, Mac. I'll tell him."

"And sorry to hear about the brakes going out on your van this morning. Sure hope you're all right."

"I'm fine, Mac, thanks."

So it was official. Everyone in town knew what had happened to pop's van except Pop.

I walked outside. Before I spent another day rolling Honeysuckle Beige paint onto the walls of Caroline's Bed and Breakfast, I needed to talk to Kath at the Art Factory. She loved the place as much as I did, and I wanted to reassure her that I planned to do everything in my power to keep it open.

The idea I'd had about the inheritance money was beginning to take hold. Once Mrs. Grayson's murder was solved and my name was cleared, I could use some of the Grayson money to save the Art Factory. Nothing too extravagant or outrageous. Just enough funds to refurbish the old leaky building, buy some much-needed supplies, and hire one or two qualified full-time arts and crafts teachers—like me. Surely, the Grayson family would be on board with that.

I checked the time on my phone. If I hurried, I might be able to arrive at the Art Factory before the parents collected their kids from their morning classes. I wanted to chat with Irena Belka when she picked up Alex. Stephen had accused her of hanging around Grayson House like a vulture, and if that were true, she might be able to tell me who had visited on the day Mrs. Grayson died. Florence wouldn't divulge that kind of information. Especially to me. But if Irena had hated Mrs. Grayson as much as everyone else, she might be inclined to talk.

****

By the time I pulled into the Art Factory parking lot, the rain had stopped.

The breeze shuttling down Blue Wolf Mountain smelled fresh and new against my face. Raindrops glistened on the red petunias hanging in a basket beside the entryway. Put there by Kath, I guessed, to impress Dr. Harold. He only visited his office at the Factory twice a week, but Kath guarded him like a Rottweiler in heat.

I pushed open the front door and stepped into the skylighted atrium. The textile art piece of a mountain sunrise that my mother had woven out of scraps of silk hung on the far wall. I always felt a pang when I looked at it. It made me feel guilty. And more determined than ever to keep the art center going that she had created. Was I hoping she'd come back one day to check on its progress? Did I think she had gotten over her own guilt—and she must still feel some—at leaving her seventeen-year-old daughter to face a second heart surgery without her mother because the whole hospital/sickness thing was just too depressing to slog through again?

Kath was away from her desk so I drifted down the hall toward the activity room, stopping to check out some of the kids' artwork exhibited on the giant bulletin board. A familiar voice stopped me cold. I ducked into the shadows. Eli Grayson sat balanced on a bright blue two-foot-high children's chair with his arm draped around his nephew, Alex.

I stood watching them from the doorway. In the shimmering square of sunlight, with their heads bent over a Superheroes coloring book, Alex's straight blond hair was a sharp contrast to Eli's unruly brown waves. Eli laughed suddenly, a big, boisterous laugh that filled the room and spilled over into the atrium. Alex glanced up and spotted me.

"Muggie!"

Alex's sneakers slapped against the tile floor as he ran to me. I knelt and opened my arms. "Muggie!" His nasally little voice bounced off the walls. I hugged him hard, then pulled back and signed, "Hello. Happy to see you."

"Happy to see you," Alex signed.

"I like your smile," I signed.

"I like *your* smile," he signed back.

I took his hand and walked him back to Eli.

"You didn't know this was my brother Kyle's son, did you?"

"Not until today at the lawyer's office. We just use first names in class, and Stephen never mentioned having a nephew."

"He never mentioned having a girlfriend, either." Eli grinned, and I felt a slow rush of blood creep up my neck. "I can't believe you taught him to say your name. Or *anything.*" His eyes misted over. "I think this is the first time I've ever heard him say a real word."

"Seriously?"

"The kid never speaks. Won't even try to make a sound. And you've got him talking."

Alex pulled a fun-size packet of chocolate candies out of his pocket and ripped it open.

"He eats those all day," Eli said. "That much candy can't be good for him." He held out some colored markers to Alex. "At least you know American Sign Language."

"Only the alphabet and a handful of words and phrases."

"I've taught myself the deaf alphabet by watching YouTube videos," he said. "I'm trying to use it with Alex, and so far, he's been pretty receptive."

"Is he homeschooled?"

Eli blew out a frustrated sigh. "Irena isn't interested in teaching him anything. She says he'll learn all that at school. He's old enough to start kindergarten this fall, but he's not ready."

"Has she considered sending him to a special school? The Tennessee School for the Deaf is right down the road in Knoxville. It has an excellent reputation."

"Now that Grandmother's will has been read, Irena won't hang around. She only came here to try to get her grubby hands on as much of the Grayson money as she could. I've offered to get Alex enrolled in a program somewhere, but she doesn't seem to be open to that idea." He crossed his arms. "Or any of my ideas."

"Taking care of a child who was born deaf can't be easy."

"Alex was born hearing."

"Oh. I just assumed…what happened?"

"When he was two—" Eli faltered. "He got sick, and it damaged his hearing. He used to have a tiny bit left in his right ear, but I'm not even sure he has that now."

"Most public schools are required to provide an interpreter for a deaf child. But if he can't communicate, it will be hard. Has he ever been evaluated for implants?"

"I doubt it. But as long as Irena is calling the shots, my hands are tied. Without Kyle here…" His voice trailed off. "I want to do what's best for the boy, but Irena resents my help. I'm thinking of petitioning the court for permanent guardianship." He glanced toward the doorway. "She's here. I shouldn't have said her name. It's like saying Beetlejuice three times."

Irena and Luke walked into the activity room hand in hand, then stopped abruptly when Irena spotted Eli. "What are you doing here?"

"I came to see how Alex was doing. I'm his uncle, remember?"

"Oh, yes," she said. "That is not something I can forget."

Luke let go of Irena's hand and smiled at me. "Nice to see you again under calmer circumstances. I see you survived your ordeal."

"Thanks to you." I laughed. "My knight in a shining white SUV." It was nice meeting him again in a more normal situation instead of wheeling downhill through a fog of fear and adrenaline. "I'm one of Alex's teachers here at the center." Alex stood next to Irena. I touched his shoulder to get his attention then signed the word "teacher" and pointed to myself.

Luke slid his arm around Irena's waist. "That's great. We only want the best for this little guy, don't we, baby?"

"Of course, we do," Irena said.

"I really appreciate your help this morning," I said

to Luke. "Just knowing you were behind me kept me from totally freaking out."

Irena's amber eyes darted from Luke to me then back again. "What is this? Why were you behind this MacGill woman?"

"My brakes went out on the highway this morning," I said. "Luke followed me in his car until I could stop. He's a hero. He called 911." I gave her my most sincere smile.

Irena's gaze swept from my short spiky hair to my paint-stained Nikes in record time, spending a few extra seconds on the chest I had inherited from my Aunt Charlene, who had put herself through nursing school by working as a stripper for The Great Alaskan Bush Company in Anchorage. At first glance, my chest could be impressive. Until you saw my scar.

"I wish you guys could have seen her steer that rickety old van through the downtown intersection with no brakes." Luke laughed. "It was *awesome*."

"You really didn't have any brakes?" Eli said.

"No."

Irena turned to Luke. "Take Alex to the car. I need to use the little girl's room."

"Sure, baby." Luke touched Alex's shoulder. "Come on, buddy. Time to go."

Irena crossed the atrium and ducked into the back corridor marked Restrooms.

"Gee," I said, "I think I need to go too. I probably shouldn't have drunk that caramel cappuccino from the Coffee Nook so fast." I hadn't actually finished it—it was still sitting in Velma's cup holder—but I needed an excuse to follow Irena into the bathroom.

I waited outside the door for a good two minutes,

just to give her time to take care of business, then I waltzed in. No use pretending I had to use the facilities; she'd know soon enough I was just there to talk to her. I stood in front of the sink and gazed at my reflection in the lighted mirror. Man, my hair was short. How fast did hair grow? A half an inch a month? I fluffed it with my fingers.

The toilet flushed and the stall door opened. I don't think Irena had heard me come in because she jumped when she saw me.

"Hey." I glanced at her in the mirror. "I'm having second thoughts about my new haircut. Yours looks great, by the way. I've always wished I had the guts to go blonde."

She sighed and turned the water on in the sink beside mine. There were only two sinks. If she wanted to wash her hands, she was out of options.

"I know this is slightly awkward," I said. "Since we met at the lawyer's office."

No answer.

"Okay, a *lot* awkward. But I want you to know I was just as surprised as you when I heard the contents of Mrs. Grayson's will."

She yanked a paper towel out of the dispenser and glared at me. "I doubt that."

"I'm still trying to figure out why she left the estate to me. And whether or not I'm going to keep it. I want to do the right thing. I'm just not sure what that is."

Irena's perfectly shaped brows raised a quarter inch.

I plowed on. "Stephen said you were at Grayson House quite a bit during Mrs. Grayson's last days. Being an outsider must have given you extraordinary insight. Observing all the comings and goings from the sidelines, listening to conversations, getting a feel for the vibe there. Kind of like being a fly on the wall. Only with better hair."

The corner of her mouth twitched.

"It must have been like Grand Central over there. People in and out all day—her doctor, her lawyer, Mr. DePaul's secretary, Florence bustling around trying to control the chaos."

"When she wasn't cozying up to Mayor Nash," Irena scoffed. "That woman thought she owned the place. And that daughter of hers—Trude—always sneaking in and out the side door like a burglar. Always carrying that big canvas bag like she was going to the beach."

"Who else did you see there?"

Wrong question. Way too direct. Irena shot me a suspicious frown, wadded up her paper towel, and tossed it in the trash.

"I didn't really notice anyone else." She smiled. "Like you said, I was a little fly on the wall. A very tired, very bored fly. Which is how I am feeling right now."

She pushed the door open and walked out, and I had no choice but to follow her.

Eli was waiting in the atrium alone. "I have a question for you, Irena. Why am I just now finding out you and Alex have been in Wrenhaven for the past three weeks? If you want me to keep sending my nephew money every month, then you're gonna have to let me know where he is. Where are you staying?" No answer. "Where, Irena?"

The steel in his voice made her tiger eyes blink. "I'm renting a room above the hardware store."

"Giles Hardware?"

Irena's lips curled into a smile. "Mr. Giles has been very nice to me."

"I'll bet he has," Eli said. "As much money as I deposit into your account, a room over a hardware store is the best you can do?"

"What a snob you are," Irena said. "You sound just like Stephen. You Graysons are always so condescending."

"*Condescending?*" he said. "Someone's been reading the thesaurus online again." He laughed harshly. "You got lucky in Kitty Hawk when you discovered the guy helping you clean shrimp in the Black Pelican's kitchen stood to inherit one-third of The Grayson Group's holdings. Is that when you decided to let him knock you up?"

"I came to the Outer Banks because my family in Krakow was so poor we couldn't afford food," Irena said. "I had never heard of The Grayson Group when I met Kyle. But none of that matters now, does it?" Irena looked at me. If I'd been a scrap of paper on the sidewalk, I would have burst into flames. "It doesn't matter because Mrs. Grayson left everything to this…this *teacher!*" She turned on her heel and left.

Eli and I watched Irena climb into the front seat of Luke's car. He took a deep, steadying breath. "Sorry about that."

"Families aren't perfect," I said. "You should see mine."

He laughed gently. "Seeing you and Irena together was like glimpsing heaven and hell in the same nightmare. And believe me, I know a thing or two about nightmares."

Sheriff Conley rounded the corner. "Hey, Maggie. I

was hoping I'd catch you here. I need to talk to you. Privately. I've got news about the van."

"No need for privacy," I said. "Everyone in Wrenhaven already knows about it."

"Except me," Eli said.

Conley crossed his beefy arms over his chest. "Honey, it's not good. The brakes going out on your daddy's van was no accident. All four lines were cut intentionally."

"Are you sure about this?" Eli said.

Conley nodded. "There were tool marks and smooth edges on the outside of the tubes. I saw them myself."

"Whoever did this had to be someone who knew a lot about cars, right?" I said.

"Not necessarily," Eli said. "Brake lines aren't that hard to cut. Not if you have a strong pair of clippers or some Channellock pliers."

I stared at him. "And you know this because…"

"I've worked on cars," Eli said. "It's no big mystery."

"The emergency brake cable was cut too," Sheriff Conley said. "That's why the car wouldn't slow down when you pulled the emergency brake lever."

"The Hit the Wall logo is all over that van," I said. "Everyone knows it belongs to my father."

I let that sink in.

"You're going to investigate this, right?" I said. "Dust for fingerprints? Question the neighbors? Find out if someone saw something?"

"Yes, Maggie," Conley said.

"I don't understand why this happened," I said. "My father is the most benign person on the planet. He volunteers at a soup kitchen. He mows old ladies' lawns for free. He gives out full-size candy bars on Halloween. The most radical thing he does is listen to hard rock while he's skim-coating plaster. Why would anyone want to hurt him?" I stopped. "Wait a minute. Monday night, when I talked to Pop on the phone at Fat Daddy's, he said he heard a scratching sound outside the window. Could someone have been cutting the van brakes then? He always keeps it in the driveway."

"Maybe," the sheriff said. "But really, I wouldn't worry about it too much, Maggie. I'm sure it was only a prank. It's summer. Kids are out late. They get bored and prank people."

"I disagree," Eli said. "A prank is writing curse words on the windshield with shoe polish. A prank is dropping a golf ball in the gas tank. This is way more than a prank, Sheriff, and I strongly recommend you take it seriously."

My head was reeling. Why would someone want to hurt Les MacGill? He was beloved in Wrenhaven. Respected. He didn't have any enemies.

"Did you tell him what happened to your car?" Eli said. "Someone dumped some pretty vile garbage on Maggie's car and slashed its tire."

"I don't like this," Conley said. "Any enemies of yours I should know about, Maggie?"

"I teach art, not algebra."

Conley sighed. "Okay, I'll ask around. Put the word out. If somebody has it in for you and Les, someone in town will have gotten wind of it."

After the sheriff had left, I said, "Maybe that prank that wasn't a prank was meant for me. Everyone knows I paint for Hit the Wall in the summer. Since Pop got hurt, I suit up in my paint splattered overalls every day and drive the van. People see me come and go. I wave to them. They wave back. Sending the van into a ditch—or worse—could have been meant for me."

"Maybe," he said.

"Here's another theory you might find interesting: Maybe someone who stood to inherit a large chunk of your grandmother's estate wasn't too happy she left it to me instead. Crashing my father's van with me driving would solve that problem, don't you think?"

A bicycle careened around the corner, knocking me off balance. It flew past the Art Factory front steps, raced around a barrel of geraniums, then back out into the street. The teenage boy riding it glanced briefly over his shoulder before speeding off.

Eli caught me before I toppled against the fire hydrant. He was stronger than I'd given him credit for, and as he held me airborne, with my hands still flailing and my back arched like I was ready to limbo, I was never so glad he was there.

"Are you okay?" he said. "That bike came out of nowhere."

"I'm fine. But I am *not* buying a lottery ticket today."

"Who was that kid? He's gonna kill somebody being that reckless."

"Travis Walters," I said. "His father is Bob Walters. He worked as a painter for Hit the Wall until Pop fired him for drinking on the job."

"So that kid wasn't reckless; he was angry."

"Looks that way."

"And are you going to mention this to your father?"

"Pop's been through a lot the last few days. I don't want to worry him."

"Your father broke his ankle, not his brain. If someone cut the brake lines on my car and tried to run my daughter down with a bike, I'd sure as hell want to know about it."

"This is my call, Eli."

"Okay, but you're wrong." The light caught his clear gray-green eyes. "Just don't wait too long to tell Les about the van and Velma. He should hear it from you, not from some well-meaning neighbor. And maybe your dad *was* the target. Could he be hiding something?"

"Like what? A wife and three kids in Albuquerque? A terrorist cell in the basement? He doesn't have a secret life. He doesn't have time for one. I know him, Eli."

"I'm sure you do, but people aren't always who we think they are. Especially the ones we're closest to. Everybody has secrets."

I tossed my purse on the front seat of my car.

"Tell your father about the brakes. If he's in some kind of danger, he needs to know."

"I will."

"Today, Maggie." He squinted into the sun as if he half-expected to see a seagull winging its way across the horizon.

He was right about telling Pop, but he didn't understand how fiercely protective I was. After my mother left, I had made it my mission to shield my father and brother from as many unpleasant things in life as I could. It was the least I could do since I was the reason she walked out. I'd taught myself to put on a brave front and I waited for the day Pop would look at me and not see a frail little girl whose lips were always turning blue because she'd been born with a hole in her heart. I was the peacemaker, the caretaker, the problem solver. I was the silent stagehand moving props in the dark, setting up the next scene before the lights came up.

Before I saddled Pop with another problem, I needed concrete, indisputable proof that someone was out to deliberately hurt him. Or me.

And that wasn't going to be easy.

Chapter 7

I propped my feet on the deck railing and reached for my glass of white zin. Two in the morning, and I was still awake. A three-quarter moon shone down through the only elm tree in my father's backyard that had escaped Dutch elm disease. I raised my glass to it. It was a survivor. Like me.

Suspects.

That's all I could think about.

Irena was at the top of my list. Not because I had any real evidence to prove she had a motive other than securing her son's inheritance, but because I didn't like her. I didn't like Florence much either. But I felt sorry for her. She seemed like an overworked, unappreciated employee with no other job prospects. Trude had implied that Mrs. Grayson made it a practice to gather information on some of the Wrenhaven citizens, then blackmailed them to get what she wanted. Did that include the faithful housekeeper she'd employed for years?

Irena had been in Wrenhaven for three weeks, which meant that when she first arrived, the previous version of Mrs. Grayson's will would have still been valid. Were Irena and Alex named as beneficiaries in that version? And was Irena aware of that?

Eli had asked DePaul to get him a copy of the original will, so by now, Eli might know what the terms were. Or maybe he had always known. I needed to find out from him exactly who benefited and who was aware of the contents. Stephen had been pretty confident he'd been one of the beneficiaries. But had Florence and Irena been just as confident?

I gazed past our low rolling lawn to the neighbor's backyard. I would miss hanging out on this deck late at night when I couldn't sleep. But an apartment of my own would afford me more privacy. If my father ignored all the huge red flags whipping around Trude and married her, hiding in the attic like Mr. Rochester's first wife might not be so much fun once the newlyweds started living together. It was probably time to move out anyway. Past time. Whether Pop married Trude or not.

Who was I kidding? Until my name was cleared and the Grayson inheritance came through, all of this didn't matter one whit. I had used up all my savings helping Jesse open Comfort and Joy. Which I didn't regret for one minute. But it had left me low in funds. And what school would hire a teacher who was a person of interest in a murder investigation?

"Frankie," someone whispered.

I jerked my head around. "Who's there?"

At the bottom of the staircase, man in a white jacket crouched in the shadows. My heart picked up speed.

I was one second away from grabbing the closest terra cotta flowerpot and flinging it at him when my brother Jesse stood up, laughing. He swung around the banister and took the rest of the steps two at a time. "I had a feeling you'd still be up."

"I'm always up. Are you just now getting off work?"

"Yeah." He pulled off the red bandana tied around his head and stuffed it in his back pocket. The soft glow of the indoor lamp made the dark hollows under his eyes seem even more pronounced. "Mags, we need to talk."

"Then let me get you a beer."

"Just water," he said.

I went into my tiny kitchen and poured him some filtered water from the fridge. I glanced at him through the window, sitting in my old wicker chair, elbows on his knees, leaning over like he had the weight of the world on his shoulders.

I'd always felt as if I were the oldest sibling, even though I was a year younger than Jesse. We had the same wiry build and the same quick temper. But Jesse, who had inherited our father's long narrow face and gray eyes, could turn on an endless reserve of charm to get what he wanted. While I, who didn't consider my charms exciting enough to bother with, was the dark-haired, exotic mirror image of my mother.

"Here." I handed him the water.

He looked at me and laughed. "So I guess the big question is: Who stole your hair? Pop said you got it cut, but you got it deleted."

"I might ask you the same thing."

"I shave my head because I'm leaning over boiling water all day."

"And I donated mine to Locks of Love because I was tired of looking like a sister wife." I sipped my wine. "You look tired, Jesse. When's the last time you slept more than four hours?"

"I didn't come over here for a lecture." He smiled, but his eyes betrayed him.

"If you don't start delegating responsibility at the restaurant, you're going to crash and burn. One open-faced Irish stew sandwich at a time."

I figured he'd stopped by because he'd heard about the brakes going out on Pop's van, but he didn't mention it. I knew I should tell him. But after seeing his worn-out face, I couldn't bring myself to do it.

Jesse had always been my rock. The guy who had seen me through everything from bad breakups to food poisoning to open-heart surgery. He had let me cry on his shoulder the day our mother left. He gave up his dream of going to culinary school and used his college fund to pay my medical bills. I knew my brother could never have made Comfort and Joy happen without my help, but I owed him. I would always owe him.

"So, thanks to your ex and Florence Claussen, half the town thinks you killed Mrs. Grayson for her money." He laughed. "Don't look so surprised. I do hear some things chained to that six-burner stove. I just wish you'd confided in me."

"Yep. I'm the talk of the town. And not in a good way."

"You need to see this." He pulled out his phone and brought up a screen.

I looked at it and almost choked on my wine. A grainy photo of me, culled from the Bainbridge Elementary Yearbook faculty page, was prominently displayed with the caption *Local Teacher Inherits Fortune. But Did She Kill to Get It?* I scrolled through the comment page in horror. People I'd never heard of had weighed in on whether or not I had forced Mrs. Grayson to change her will then smothered her in her sleep. The post went on to say that my older brother owns the restaurant Comfort and Joy down by the old train station.

"Now I know why business has suddenly picked

up," Jesse said. "When I first saw this, I thought it was a joke. Was Mrs. Grayson really smothered? She was ancient. I thought her heart just stopped."

"It did stop. The sheriff thinks the killer literally scared her to death while holding a pillow above her face."

"I'm glad you aren't seeing Stephen anymore. Word on the street is he's in debt up to his eyeballs. Might even get that cool car of his repossessed."

I laughed. "And wouldn't that just be a shame."

"You don't think Stephen smothered her, do you? I always thought he was kind of shady beneath that rich boy exterior."

"Technically, no one did. She died before the pillow ever touched her face." I set my glass on the table. "There's something I need to tell you."

"I already know you lost your job. Principal Whitson ate lunch at the restaurant yesterday and told me how sorry he was."

"Sucks, doesn't it?"

"Well…no. I mean, for most people it would suck. But not for the girl who inherited the Grayson estate and five years of profits from The Grayson Group. Not for that girl." He unhooked the neck of his white chef coat and folded the flap back. "If you sell that big house and all the crap inside it, you'll be rolling in dough."

"Rolling in dough? What is that, chef humor?"

"Pop is so happy. I talked to him after you got back from the lawyer's office, and he sounded like he'd won the lottery."

"Jesse, I—"

"Because you *are* going to accept the inheritance, aren't you?" He was always more perceptive than I gave him credit for. "Please tell me you're going to take it."

"Maybe. Some of it. At least enough to help us out financially and save the Art Factory."

"Why the hell do we always have to worry about the Art Factory? Screw the Art Factory. Our mother cared more for that place than she ever did for either one of us." He ran his hand across his bald head. "I don't know why you're so damned worried about keeping it going. I would have let it run itself into the ground years ago." He stopped, and his face softened. "Please don't throw this chance away, Mags. Please accept this amazing gift Mrs. Grayson gave you and take the inheritance."

I got up and walked to the railing. Wispy white-gray clouds trailed across the moonlit sky, piling up like little pillows at the edge of the universe. A soft ring of light had wrapped itself around the moon. It would probably rain again tomorrow.

I smiled at my brother. "Don't worry, Jesse. Whatever happens, it'll all work out. I promise."

"After I took Pop his lunch today, I drove by Grayson House and saw Mayor Nash coming out the side door. He locked it behind him and put the key in his pocket. Then he glanced around to see if anyone had seen him. Looked kind of suspicious to me."

"I think he met with Mrs. Grayson a lot after hours. She must have given him a key."

"Just thought you should know. Since the house belongs to you now."

After Jesse left, I went inside my little attic apartment and closed the door. Jesse knew me so well. He knew I would struggle trying to justify taking money I didn't deserve. No matter who had given it to me. If I only kept enough to subsidize the Art Factory and see our family through this bad patch, we'd be all right.

There were other ways of making money. I could try harder to drum up more business for Hit the Wall. Advertise on social media. Get the word out. I could paint more dog portraits. Orders from the Internet business I'd started before Christmas were still trickling in. I was pretty sick of painting spoiled golden retrievers, but it was an easy way to get cash.

I glanced around. Everything I loved most in the world, besides my family and the Basset hound next door, was in that room: A basket of seashells I'd bought at a flea market, a framed photo of my old springer spaniel Katie in a frame, hundreds of cherished books I couldn't bear to part with, a bin overflowing with the seascapes I'd painted. I wondered if the things in Mrs. Grayson's house had given her as much joy.

I moved to my easel beneath the skylight. Sleep wasn't going to come anytime soon, so I might as well finish the French bulldog's portrait I'd started. What was his name, Winston? I squeezed a glob of paint onto my palette and tried to form a list of the people whose lives would benefit the most once Mrs. Grayson was gone. I always kept a couple of lists running in my head; it helped me stay organized. Which made me think of another list. The one that Trude said Mrs. Grayson kept.

Was that what Mayor Nash had been doing at Grayson House? Searching for a list of names and blackmail-worthy deeds that Mrs. Grayson kept hidden? If Mayor Nash's name was on that list, wouldn't that be a rock-solid motive for murder?

I needed to find that list.

And luckily, thanks to Mrs. Grayson's lawyer, I had a Grayson House key of my own.

Chapter 8

I parked Velma at the end of the driveway behind Grayson House where she couldn't be seen from the street. Neither Sheriff Conley nor Attorney DePaul had informed me that I no longer had a legal right to go inside, but I didn't want to broadcast the fact to the rest of the neighborhood that I was spending time there alone. I didn't feel completely within my rights snooping, but I was sure the blackmail list Trude had mentioned was hidden in the iris desk Mrs. Grayson left Eli. And I was determined to find it before he took it away.

My brother had seen Mayor Nash sneaking out of Grayson House the previous afternoon. Was Nash's name on that blackmail list? Had he gone to Grayson House to search for it? If Mrs. Grayson was blackmailing the mayor, that could explain a lot. Like why he always championed her suggestions for the town and bent over backwards time and time again to make sure her demands were realized. The residents of Wrenhaven joked that Nash was nothing more than a sniveling yes-man the richest woman in town kept tucked in her back pocket. I hoped that wasn't true—I liked Nash—but he had been instrumental in helping swing the aldermen's vote to build the park she'd wanted. Including tearing down a beloved old neighborhood to make room for it. Everyone I talked to had been against it. And yet, Mayor Nash had made sure Constance Grayson Park became a reality.

I let myself in the side door, looking cautiously to the left and right. The houses on Victorian Row were quiet today. Besides the soft bird chirps above me in the trees, the hum of a distant lawn mower and the soft clink of metal wind chimes were the only sounds I heard.

I locked the door behind me and stood in the airless foyer. The sheer size of the house still amazed me. What a wonderful school this would make. Light filling every odd-shaped nook and cranny. Children's laughter bouncing off the high walls. I had just started up the long staircase when the ringer on my phone blasted the first four notes of Beethoven's Fifth. I fished it out of my back pocket and stared at Eli's name on the screen. I had added his number to my contact list in the hopes he would decide to let Pop paint Grayson House before they put it on the market. Of course, all that had changed now.

"Maggie?" His deep voice cracked. "Can you come here? Please? Now?"

"Come where? Are you all right?"

"I'm at Grayson House," he said hoarsely. "In the attic." He wheezed and coughed. "Help me, Maggie. I don't think I can breathe."

"You're here? In Grayson House? I just walked in. Where's the attic?"

"Second floor. The door in the middle of the hallway. Across from the tiny bedroom with the slanted roof."

I ran up the stairs and opened the attic door. *"Eli!"* I yelled into the stairwell.

No answer.

"Eli!" I started up the narrow steps, so steep I had to pull myself up by the banister rail. The heat from the

room pushed against me. The attic ran the length of the back wing with a high-pitched ceiling and a rough-hewn hardwood floor. It was empty except for a small wooden table and chair, a sharp contrast to the rest of the cluttered house. On the ceiling, where the slanted sides met, a dimly lit bulb dangled from a cord. A few shards of sunshine braved their way through a pair of dirt-streaked arched windows on the far wall.

"Eli, where are you?" I shouted.

His gravelly voice seemed to come from thin air. "There's a four-foot door behind the chimney. I'm on the other side of it."

I strained my eyes in the shadowy light until I found a tiny slanted door hidden beneath the eaves. I ran to it, flipped the latch, and swung it open.

Eli fell out on the floor.

"Oh, my God," I cried. "Are you okay?"

"I'm fine." He scrambled to his feet and wiped his forehead with the back of his wrist. "I accidentally locked myself in." His blue oxford shirt lay open at the neck. Splotches of brown dirt dotted the knees and cuffs of his khakis. He pressed his back against the brick wall then bent over with his hands on his knees, panting like he'd finished a 5K run.

"I may or may not be slightly claustrophobic," he rasped.

"Then why did you crawl into a room the size of a postage stamp?"

He forced a laugh. "Good question."

"How long have you been in there?"

"I don't know. A few minutes. A couple of hours."

"I just got here. I didn't see your car."

"I parked around the corner on the street. I didn't

want the neighbors to—" He pulled in a ragged breath.

"Do you need to sit down? Your face is that funny gray color people turn right before they check out."

"Check out of what?"

"That big hotel called Life."

He held both hands against his chest. "I just need to breathe for a minute."

The blood had returned to his face, but he looked shaken. Like a warrior who'd spent the last two hours slaying demons, and couldn't remember why.

"What's in the little room?" I asked.

"That little room and I are old friends. This is where the Grayson boys spent timeout when we'd been bad. Yeah, I know. It's grim." He looked up. "Staying in this house was like spending summer vacation in the Fifth Circle of hell."

"If it was so bad, why didn't your mother come and take you home?"

"At first we stayed—I was determined to stay— because I knew she was afraid we'd lose our inheritance." He laughed. "Which happened anyway."

"But why—"

"Then my mother had an accident and ended up in a wheelchair and we *couldn't* go home. Not until she healed, anyway."

"She didn't fall off a scaffold, did she?" I teased.

"No, she went to a Grateful Dead concert, smoked too much weed, and took a flying leap off one of the lighting platforms into the crowd. She injured her spine and was in therapy for months, which is why we had to stay at Grayson House. One night, in the spring, while Grandmother was locking Stephen and Kyle in their rooms, I decided I couldn't take it anymore. I knew I had to save them, so I escaped out the attic window. If your father hadn't found me on the roof and tracked down my mother, I don't know what would have happened. I'll always be grateful to him for that. No pun intended."

"Which brings us back to the claustrophobic present," I said. "Why did you go into the attic room?"

"Because there are ghosts in this house I need to put to rest. I wanted to find out if a piece of paper I had hidden behind a loose brick when I was seventeen was still there. I wasn't sure it was real. I thought I might have dreamed it."

"And did you? Dream it, I mean?"

"No, it was real."

He pulled a crinkly strip of yellowed paper out of his pocket and handed it to me. On it, a short list of names had been scrawled in pencil, smeared and faded with age. *Miss Starnes, Dr. Moreland, Mayor Nash, Reverend Lyon, Florence Claussen.*

"Is this a hit list?"

Eli laughed. "No, it's a list I made to remind myself who I could trust. And who I couldn't. These are the people I begged to help me find my way home. These are the people who didn't believe me when I told them our grandmother was mentally abusing us. Florence knew; she was there when it happened. Your father was the only person brave enough to stand up to her and try to help me."

"Trude said your grandmother kept a list, supposedly in the desk you inherited. A list that would keep the people of Wrenhaven in line—names, dates, deep dark secrets that could ruin a person's life if they came to light. I wonder how many residents only stayed in Wrenhaven because the woman who ran the town knew something about them they didn't want to be discovered?"

"Do you think that was the killer's motive? To stop her from exposing a secret?"

"I don't know," I said. "But that's why I'm here. To look for that list."

"I wonder if Stephen knows where it is. He was here every other day, and he hated every minute." Eli looked around. "There was always so much hate in this house."

"I thought the terrible stories I heard about Mrs. Grayson had been exaggerated. Even now, it's hard for me to believe that a woman who would stoop to blackmailing her neighbors was the same woman who drank ginger tea with me and talked about Jane Austen."

"I think she was different with you."

"Or maybe part of her was starting to mellow at the end of her life and she'd come to regret some of the things she'd done. It might have made her a little more generous."

"Says the girl who inherited her estate."

"Fair enough."

"I don't think people ever change. They just get craftier at hiding who they really are." Eli straightened up. "Thanks for rescuing me," he said huskily.

"No problem."

"Sorry I turned into a complete wuss when the attic door wouldn't open."

"I've thought of you as many things, Eli Grayson, but wuss was not one of them."

He grinned at me then. Full force. Knocking me a just little off-kilter.

"Can we go downstairs?" he said. "I can't breathe up here."

"You need to learn to relax. When the world tries to suck the air out of my lungs, I go for a run. What do you do?"

"I take my father's old fishing boat out past Oregon Inlet, crank up the B-52s, and sail into the wind." He laughed. "Works every time." He waited for me at the stairs. "Now, let's go find that list."

I followed him down the dimly lit hall to Mrs. Grayson's sitting room. "Before we look through the iris desk, I want to check something." He passed the built-in bookcases on either side of the brick fireplace and stood scanning the shelves on the far wall. "Walking through the house earlier, I noticed a few of her possessions are missing. I know it's been a long time since I've been here, but some of the things she owned are etched into my memory. And, according to Stephen, she never got rid of any of it."

"Like what?"

"A bronze unicorn head sat on the mantle. I tried to move it once, but I could barely lift it." He pointed to the lower shelves. "This is where my grandfather displayed his Civil War collection. Stephen said he thought some of the pieces had disappeared, and he's right." Eli opened the cabinet doors and rifled through the drawers. "There was a bullet with mangled teeth prints found near a field hospital in Antietam that used to freak me out. And a gold mourning brooch made out of woven human hair, which was even creepier than the bullet. There were Civil War belt buckles and swords and hats, and an ivory letter opener that belonged to Thomas Jefferson. I don't see any of it here."

"Maybe Florence put it somewhere for safekeeping."

"Maybe."

"Do you think Mrs. Grayson noticed her things were disappearing?"

"Her eyesight wasn't the best, but I can't imagine she didn't notice. You've talked to her. Her mind was sharp. She had deteriorated physically, but she was far from clueless."

He opened the door to his grandmother's bedroom, and I had a flash of the night we'd stood outside waiting to go in before finding her dead.

Eli walked to the iris desk and slid open its drawers. Together we sifted through the contents. The smaller ones contained everything from safety pins and binder clips to out-of-date credit cards. The larger ones held stamps and stationery and pens. She'd kept a few mementos: a couple of birthday cards from a local church, an invitation to a christening, stacks of calling cards with Bible verses written on them, a recent photo of her standing in front of the entrance to the new Constance Grayson Park.

But no notebook.

And no list.

I put my elbows on the smooth black desk and sighed. That list had to be in the house somewhere. I was sure of it.

"Okay, we need help." I pulled out my phone and Googled *Finding secret compartments in antique furniture.* Three YouTube videos later, we set to work. Because my hands were smaller, Eli held my phone while I ran my fingers over every part of the desk: the carved iris blossoms across the back, the long wooden stems, the flat recessed alcoves holding the drawers. I gently pressed down on each flower as they skimmed the smooth wood. I pushed against the six-inch strip of wood above the center petal and felt it shift. "Bingo," I whispered.

Holding on with my fingers and thumbs, I pulled the strip of wood toward me, sliding the hidden rectangular box out of the back of the desk. I held my breath and looked inside. It held only one thing: a small brown leather address book.

As we looked through the tiny pages, familiar names jumped out at me—Doc Moreland, Mayor Nash, Principal Whitson, Dr. Harold Gatz, Dan Hobbs.

"Dan Hobbs?" I said. "Aren't he and his partner Sam the owners of Sam and Dan's Ice Cream Parlor? Did she seriously blackmail someone to sell ice cream in Wrenhaven?"

"Maybe she wanted to eat free strawberry swirl waffle cones with sprinkles for the rest of her life." Eli looked through the book. "This is just a book with phone numbers written in it. There's no incriminating information. Are you sure Trude knew what she was talking about?"

"I think so. She was bragging about it. And if she's right, there have to be notes hidden somewhere containing the evidence Mrs. Grayson gathered."

"Grandmother didn't own a computer—not many people of her generation did—so she must have written down the information and kept it close by for easy accessibility. But where?" He glanced around. "Someplace safe and sound, I'll bet. Away from the prying eyes and ears of Florence Claussen."

I glanced up. "I'd heard complaints about Mrs. Grayson from the people who lived here for years, but I'd always given her the benefit of the doubt. Some days, she seemed so fragile. It's hard to believe that someone who loved flowers and books as much as she did could have had such a cruel side."

"You don't know the half of it." Eli ran his hand back through his hair. "Come on. You hang onto that book while we search the rest of the house."

I slid the address book into my jeans pocket.

****

"It's not here," Eli said.

For two hours, we'd opened every drawer, searched every closet and cabinet, and looked under every bed. We'd lifted box after box, scoured the shelves, even turned over vases on the dusty mantlepiece. And nothing.

If there was a blackmail list hidden in Grayson House, neither Eli nor I could find it.

We started down the main staircase.

The last fragments of afternoon light streamed through the mullioned windows on either side of the door, bathing the foyer in amber.

"I want you to know I'm okay with Grandmother leaving you Grayson House. I despise this place." He grinned. "But handing over five years of The Grayson Group money? Maybe not so much."

"Well, at least you're honest." I pointed to the brass umbrella stand beside the front door. "Is that the walking stick your grandmother left Stephen?" I picked up the smooth piece of wood and lightly touched the carved letters. "These initials aren't hers."

"I've never looked at it closely. It's the stick she always threatened us with."

"You're going to think I'm crazy, but the monogram inside this carved circle looks just like the signature on Toulouse Lautrec's paintings."

"The crippled French artist who painted the dancers at the Moulin Rouge?"

"He was a 19th-century Post-Impressionist. He fractured his legs as a child and they stopped growing, so he always used a cane. Usually one with liquor hidden inside it. He was an alcoholic."

"A tippling cane, isn't that what they're called?"

"Absinthe was his drink of choice."

Eli laughed. "And absinthe makes the heart grow fonder."

"It ended up killing him." I twisted the silver handle and unscrewed the cap. "Did your grandmother keep brandy in here?"

"I doubt it. But if this cane belonged to Toulouse-Lautrec, it would be worth a lot."

"That's for sure. I don't know what the iris desk is worth, but this isn't exactly cutting you guys out of the will, is it?"

"No," he said quietly. "But Grandmother has been very sly about it. If you hadn't spotted the carved initials on this cane, I don't think any of us would have noticed they weren't hers." He glanced around the foyer and sighed. "This was not a house for children. I learned how to hate in this house. And how to lie. I taught myself to be more devious than anyone could imagine to survive. I could have been a Ninja."

"You were a Ninja the night you climbed on the roof to save Kyle and Stephen. That took guts."

He looked at me for a long moment. "So does this."

He reached for me—a Ninja move I did not see coming—and pulled me to him. He lowered his head and slowly raked his cheek against mine. Heat sliced across my chest, down my back. "What am I doing?" I murmured. "I don't even like you."

"Yes, you do." The faint web of lines around his eyes crinkled as he bent his head toward me and laughed. His voice rumbled like a war drum in my ear. "Maggie," he whispered.

A shadow slid across the edge of my peripheral vision, and I froze. "Somebody's here."

Eli was at the door and had it open before I could steady myself. A teenage boy wearing a black T-shirt took off running and sprinted down the handicap ramp to the driveway.

"Hey!" Eli yelled.

The boy disappeared around the side of the house, and Eli tore after him. By the time I made it off the porch, the kid was already jumping over a low privet hedge and pushing his way through the iron gate and into the backyard. He ran across the remnants of the crumbling patio and raced down the hill, plowing through the waist-high rhododendrons growing wild at the bottom of the property. The last thing he did before escaping across the street was to turn back and glance at me. *Travis.*

Eli trudged back up the hill. "Isn't that the kid who almost ran you over on his bike in front of the Art Factory?"

"Yes, that's Travis Walters."

"Is he stalking you? Could he be the one behind these pranks?"

"I hope not. I've known Travis since he was four years old. He's a good kid."

Eli raised his eyebrows. "He doesn't look like a good kid. If Les fired his father, and this boy is out for revenge, he could do anything. Including cutting your father's brake lines."

"That's pretty hardcore."

"Then why was he standing on the front porch looking in the window? And why did he take off like a bat out of hell when we saw him?"

"I don't know."

Eli held the door open for me. "About what happened before Travis showed up…"

I smiled. "You mean that little blip in the space-time continuum?"

"Oh, I think it was way more than a blip. When can I see you again? Tomorrow night?"

"The Art Guild Awards are tomorrow night."

"I hear the town's having a mural painted on the side of the courthouse."

"They are. And I'd love to be the one to paint it. The inheritance is frozen, and I can't apply for another teaching job while I'm a person of interest in a murder case. School boards frown on things like that."

"You can always come work for The Grayson Group. Maybe in the art department. I can still pull some strings there."

"I'll bet you can."

"Let me know when I can pick up the iris desk. I'd prefer you to be here. I don't want there to be any question about me taking something that doesn't legally belong to me."

"Don't be ridiculous. I trust you."

"No, you don't," he said softly. "You don't trust me at all."

I started to protest, then stopped. He was right, and we both knew it.

I didn't trust him.

Not one little bit.

Chapter 9

Horse Creek Landing looked like a downhome version of *A Midsummer Night's Dream.*

White fairy lights had been woven through the branches of low-hanging willow trees. Hay bales were stacked around the fishpond for extra seating. A wooden trestle table sat on the patio, piled high with tasty-looking finger foods. A dance floor and DJ station had been set up in the covered picnic area, promising fun for the winners and losers until the wee hours.

The finalists' paintings had been displayed on rose trellises. The six sculpture entries, all of them nudes, were lined up beside the judging table like guards at an upscale strip joint. Near the cash bar, where I was heading as fast as my three-inch heels would carry me, an emaciated Doc Moreland, looking more like the crypt keeper than a prominent family practitioner, sat at a portable keyboard merrily slaughtering a jazzy rendition of "Moon River."

I had begun Googling the names in Mrs. Grayson's address book, and so far, Dr. Herbert Moreland was the only person I had been able to unearth any information about. After going down a lot of rabbit holes, I'd found an article about him in the small Arkansas town where he had begun his practice. It said he had botched a procedure so badly, he was forced to give up thoracic surgery and go into family practice. Not the most shocking thing that could have happened in his career. But something he would want to keep under wraps.

I remembered Stephen saying he wouldn't send a dog he liked to Doc Moreland. Of course, I never knew if that were true or not. I never met a dog Stephen liked.

Jules had offered to escort me to the awards ceremony, but going to a fancy party with your gay best friend as your date is kind of like going to the senior prom with your brother. And I'd already done that. Jules was working behind the scenes helping to organize the ceremony, so I would have been on my own for most of the evening anyway.

I had dressed to kill in sling-back heels and a short black halter-top dress, which showed off my shoulders, accentuated my bust, and hid my surgery scar. I needed armor tonight to deflect the stares and whispers from a few of Florence's cohorts who doubted my innocence and a couple of women friends who felt sorry for me since losing my plus-one to another woman. I doubted if Stephen would be there to see the effort I'd made, which, in spite of everything, still stung. He had always encouraged me to try harder where my appearance was concerned, but I'd often found myself doing just the opposite to irritate him.

The place had filled up fast. People I'd known all my life milled around the enclosure. Florence and Delores were deep in conversation near the fishpond. Reverend Lyon was bringing in more chairs. The Byerly twins, with matching gray beards, flowing caftans, and handmade beaded necklaces, were eating off each other's appetizer plates. Snippets of conversation about the demise of the school's art department floated around, and I heard my name mentioned more than once.

This was the perfect opportunity to try and gather more information about Mrs. Grayson's death. I wasn't ready to question Florence just yet, not with so many people around, but Mayor Nash was on the premises. And Doc Moreland. And Mrs. Grayson's attorney, Percy DePaul with Mr. DePaul's secretary, Delores. My money was on Delores. She probably knew more than all the others put together.

I ducked inside the log cabin that housed the Horse Creek Pavilion and ran into Mayor Nash. Literally. "Sorry, Mayor," I said, moving out of his way. I hope I didn't spill your drink."

"It's all good, Maggie." Mayor Nash laughed. "I just saw the ocean painting you did. It's really beautiful. I might have to buy it for my living room."

"Thanks." I straightened my back and took a deep breath. "Mayor Nash—"

"You *are* allowed to call me Sherman, you know."

"Sherman." He did not look like a Sherman. "I wanted to ask you—Jesse saw you coming out of Grayson House day before yesterday. In the afternoon,"

His face turned ashen. "Yes, well…I—"

"I thought you might have left something there by accident. I know you met with Mrs. Grayson sometimes after Florence had gone home."

"That's why she gave me a key," he said a little too defensively. "So she wouldn't have to go downstairs to let me in. I didn't return it because I thought you would have had the locks changed by now."

"No, no, that's fine. I just thought if you'd forgotten something like a jacket or an umbrella, I could help you—"

"It was a notebook."

112

"Oh."

"Florence didn't know where it was. Mrs. Grayson may have found it and put it in her desk for safekeeping."

"What did it look like?"

"Just a small notebook. It had a few names and addresses in it, and some scribblings of mine. Must have fallen out of my briefcase. I can't seem to hang onto anything these days."

"I'll keep an eye out for it."

I believed him about sneaking into Grayson House looking for a notebook. I just wasn't sure the notebook he was after was *his* notebook.

"When do you take possession of the house?" he asked.

"I have no idea. Now that Mrs. Grayson's death is considered a murder, that's all up in the air while the investigation is ongoing." I had probably said too much, but I thought it might be interesting to throw out the word *murder* and see what his reaction was.

There wasn't one.

"I guess Dr. Moreland had a key too," I said. "He was in and out of Grayson House at all hours just like you."

"I wouldn't know." Nash's gaze shifted smoothly to my Bainbridge students' artwork strung across the stone fireplace on a fishing line. "Is that you?" He pointed to a portrait of a woman wearing a red beaded Native American outfit. Her long black hair hung to her waist and had been encircled with a feathered headband. Her large eyes were a deep chocolate brown.

"That's her," Jules said, coming to stand beside us with Eli right behind him, "before she chopped her hair off."

"I have a friend who is Native American," I said. "She wasn't able to come to my class, but she loaned me her great-grandmother's tribal dress to wear for the kids and pose for them. Then I had them draw their family trees. We had a long discussion about respecting each other's lineage and how important it is to be proud of who you are."

"So you were one of the cool teachers," Eli said

"*Were* being the operative word," I said.

"You kids have fun," Mayor Nash said. "I need to turn in these ballots."

Eli picked up a glass of wine from the table, sipped it, and winced.

"Nice tuxedo," I said to Jules. "I hear turquoise is the new black."

Jules made a face. "Nash loaned it to me. I look like the best man in a 1976 wedding."

"What are you doing here, Eli?" He had made an effort too, I noticed. His hair wasn't quite as wild and his dark suit coat had been tailored to fit his broad shoulders.

"I ran into Jules at Fat Daddy's last night," Eli said. "He said you were a finalist in the art show, and I didn't want you to feel bad when Stephen showed up."

"Stephen's coming?" I said.

"The girl he's with now also has a painting in the show," Jules said. "And Eli and I thought it would be nice to show him there are other men in the world who find you desirable."

I looked at Eli sideways. "So you find me desirable, do you?'

"You're the most beautiful woman here."

"He's good, isn't he?" Jules said. "That's why I invited him. I thought you needed a handsome straight man in your corner. Someone who knows the opposition."

As if on cue, Stephen and a tall, stunning Black woman walked in the door. Stephen steered her toward the wine bar, and I smiled, remembering what a wine snob he was and how much the wine he was about to drink tasted like palomino pony piss.

"Where's your painting?" Eli said. "I want to see it."

Jules pointed to the finalists' board. "It's the seascape."

The three of us avoided Stephen and walked down the hill past the pond. Eli stood for a long moment in front of my painting. "Not bad for someone who's never seen the ocean."

"I'm going to take that as a compliment," I said.

"You're from the coast, Eli," Jules said. "Does the water really look like that, or is it something she made up in her head?"

"Oh, it's real, all right," Eli said. "This has got to be at the Outer Banks. Nothing else looks like it. A strange iridescent light rolls across the water at the shoreline right before sunset. Not many artists can recreate that extraordinary light. But Maggie has nailed it."

"Why is it only at the Outer Banks?" Jules said.

"The Outer Banks is a long strip of land hugging the North Carolina coast separated from the mainland by three sounds. When the sun sets in the west, the land is so narrow, the light reflects on itself and makes the water on the eastern coastline shimmer with a kind of iridescence." He turned to Jules. "Are you sure she's never been there?"

"She says not. And it's always been a dream of hers."

"But why hasn't she gone? It's only seven or eight hours away."

"Oh, she's tried," Jules said. "But something always comes up. Her father needs her, her brother needs her, the dog runs away."

"I love it when people talk about me like I'm not here."

"Maggie is the go-to girl in her family," Jules said. "If she left, even for a week, none of them would know how to survive. It's been that way since her mother—"

"Okay, that's enough," I said.

"I'm going for more wine," Eli said. "Can I get either of you a refill?"

"I have to get to my post," Jules said. "They'll be announcing the winners soon."

I wandered back up the hill and stood outside the pavilion. The crowd was huge this year.

"We need to talk."

I spun around, almost knocking Stephen into the tall woman standing beside him.

"If it's about the toothbrush I left at your house, you can mail it to me." He grabbed my upper arm. "Or you could just throw it away."

I pried Stephen's hand away and looked at his date. All six feet of her. "My name is Maggie. You must be Rochelle."

"Call me Rocki." The woman pushed her shoulder-length hair back from her face with a graceful flick of her hand. Her blood-red nails sparkled beneath the fairy lights.

"I hear you have a painting in the art show," I said. "Which one is it?"

"Nudes on a Bus," Rocki said.

I looked at her with fresh interest. "You're R. Cunningham? I've seen your work. I love your work. How come we've never met?"

Rocki shrugged. "Maybe because you're a teacher, and I work at Hooters?"

"Well, I'm not a teacher anymore. I like your entry. You're really good."

"Thanks. *Nudes on a Bus* was inspired by a spring break trip I took to Myrtle Beach." She glanced at the finalist display. "Looks like we're competing against each other. The prize money's not much, but I'd sure like to win that month-long exhibit at the Marquis Gallery in Knoxville."

"Yeah, me too. Well, good luck, Rocki."

"I don't believe in luck." She ruffled Stephen's perfect hair then smiled. "We make our own luck, don't we, Stevie?"

Stephen took hold of my elbow and propelled me behind a bank of potted ferns. "Just so you know, Eli and I are going to contest the will. He doesn't want to, but he'll do it for me."

"That's your prerogative, Stevie."

"And the inheritance you stole from us could be tied up in court for a long, long time."

"I didn't steal it."

"What would you call it then?" he snarled.

"A gift from your grandmother."

"You knew before we went to DePaul's office that she had changed her will, didn't you?"

"Of course, not."

"I don't believe you. No one believes you. Maybe Florence is right: You wormed your way into our family. First, by dating me. Then sucking up to my grandmother by working in her garden. I should have seen right through you. Everyone else did."

"Stop yelling," I said. "Rocki can hear you. You've been dating for less than a week. Do you really want her to realize what a complete jerk you are this early in the game?"

He glared at me.

"How do we know *you* didn't try to kill your grandmother?" I said. "You had a key to Grayson House, right?"

"Yes, but—"

"And we both know you didn't have one ounce of regard for your grandmother, no matter how much you pretend to now that she's gone. I'm not saying you let yourself in the house and tried to smother her with a pillow, but you could have. You had the opportunity. And you definitely had a motive: you're drowning in debt."

"Stop it!" He lowered his voice. "I get that you're angry, Maggie. But you need to get over it. I'm not perfect. And maybe I didn't break things off with you as kindly as I could. But that's no reason to hold a grudge."

"I'm not holding a grudge. I'm finally seeing you for who you are." I knew I'd gone too far, but the look on his face made it worth it.

"Give the inheritance back." he said. "That money should have gone to my family, and everyone knows it. It won't be hard. All you have to do is go to DePaul's office and sign a paper. One little paper. Then you're off the hook, and life can go back to the way it's supposed to be."

I smiled at him. "Not a chance."

"Then you're going to be very, very sorry, Maggie."

His eyes narrowed. "Do you understand?"

Eli appeared at my side, holding two glasses of wine. "Everything okay?"

"Where've you been, sweetheart?" I said. "You promised me the next dance."

"That's right. I did." He set the glasses on the edge of a picnic table and looped his arm through mine. "Killer dress, baby."

"We're not done, Maggie," Stephen said. "You can't avoid this forever."

Eli led me down the sloped path to the makeshift dance floor.

"You don't have to dance with me," I said.

"Of course, I have to dance with you. They're playing "Brown-Eyed Girl." "

Eli swung me around and pulled me close as "Brown Eyed Girl" segued into "Moondance." My arms had nowhere to go but around his neck. "Smooth move," I said. "Where'd you learn that?"

"I'm making it up as I go along."

"How much of my conversation with Stephen did you hear?"

"Enough."

"Then you know he threatened me if I don't sign the inheritance back to the Grayson clan." I pulled back so I could look into his eyes. "You don't think...I mean, I know he's your cousin, and someone I sort of dated for a couple of months, but you don't think he could have..."

"Tried to kill our grandmother? No. He said he was home reading when she died, and I believe him."

"Not a great alibi unless he had company. I don't know. The way he looked at me just now when he told me I'd be sorry if I didn't give the money back gave me chills."

"That doesn't make him capable of murder."

"No, but it might make him capable of cutting the brake lines on a van he knows I drive to work every day just to make sure it's clear he means business."

A crash reverberated behind us. The music screeched to a stop.

People sitting at tables on the dance floor perimeter jumped to their feet.

"Nothing to worry about, folks." Jules' voice boomed through the loudspeaker. "Just a little accident up here near the finalists' display. Everything is under control."

Like hell it was. I could tell by the quaver in Jules' voice, that things were most assuredly *not* under control.

With Eli's help, I fought my way through the swarm of people and edged up the hill. Bodies crowded around the framed paintings, blocking our view.

"There she is," someone said. "There's Maggie MacGill."

"I'm sorry, Maggie." Jules sat crouched beside my seascape, holding his left hand. "Sonofabitch that hurts."

"Dr. Moreland is here," Eli said. "I saw him down at the—"

"Coming through." Doc Moreland pushed his way into the clearing. "What's going on, Jules? What have you done to yourself?" He took one look at Jules' hand and shook his head. "Looks like it might be broken. I'll call the ER and tell them we're on our way. Can somebody get me some ice?"

Jules looked at me. His blue eyes filled with tears. "I'm so sorry, Maggie. I'd just finished attaching the ribbons and was standing next to your painting.

Somebody shoved me—*hard*. My arm went straight through the canvas and rammed into the brick wall behind it."

A huge gaping hole had been ripped across the center of my seascape. Ragged strips of canvas flapped back against the splintered cross piece. A second-place ribbon dangled sideways from the corner like a red caution flag.

"Did you see who was behind you?" Eli said.

"No," Jules said. "Whoever pushed me knocked me off my feet. I ruined your painting, Maggie. Oh, God, I'm so sorry."

"Don't worry about the painting," I said. "I have an attic full of them."

"Come on," Eli said to Jules. "We'll follow you to the emergency room."

"Absolutely not," Jules said. "I just called my friend and he's meeting me there." He managed a weak smile. "It'll be nice for him to take care of me for a change. Just make sure Maggie gets home okay."

Eli turned to me. "What do you want to do?"

"I want to go home," I said.

He took my arm and led me to the exit. The music started up again. People filtered back to the dance floor. Others were laughing and filling their plates with steamed shrimp as if nothing had happened.

We crossed through the entrance archway and headed toward the parking lot.

"Who won first prize?" I said. "Rocki?"

"Yes, she won. That certainly was a big yellow bus she painted."

I laughed. "And there certainly were a lot of nudes onboard."

We started up the hill.

"I'd like to see those paintings you have stashed in your attic sometime," Eli said. "My mother owns a gallery gift shop in the town of Duck at the Outer Banks. Your painting was as good as anything I've ever seen for sale there. Would you like her to take a look? See if she can sell them?"

"I don't show my work to a lot of people."

"Then let *me* look at them." He stopped beside his truck. "Isn't that your car over there?"

"Yeah, that's Velma. Why?"

"Because something is swinging from the antenna."

I followed him to my Volkswagen Beetle. A blob of dark gray fur glistened in the moonlight. A long black tail curled around the chrome mast. "Is that a—"

"Dead rat." He picked up a stick and threaded it through the shoelace, then lifted it off the bowed antenna and flung it into the woods.

I shivered. "And the fun just keeps happening."

"Come on, Mountain Girl, I'll follow you home."

"No need for that. I'm perfectly capable of—"

"I know you're perfectly capable. You are the poster child for perfectly capable." He cocked his head and smiled. That unsure, slightly crooked smile that always clutched my heart. "But I'm following you home anyway."

Chapter 10

I unlocked the door to my loft.

The tang of turpentine and freshly ground coffee hung in the air. Eli stood on the threshold and peered inside. His gaze slowly flicked around the room: from the rectangle skylight cut into the pitched roof, to the old farm sink, to the kitchen table I'd inlaid with blue and gray mosaic tiles, to my unmade bed.

He crossed the room to my easel and glanced at the round plastic table filled with jars of brushes. He touched one of the scallop shells I had strung across the window, slid a painting out of the wooden bin beneath, and smiled. "Another seascape. Wild and windblown. You sure you've never been to Kitty Hawk?"

"Not in this lifetime."

"It's always windy there. Which is why Orville and Wilbur set up camp down the road for their first flight." He glanced at the canvases drying against the wall. "The dog portraits are great, by the way."

"I sell them on the Internet. Any first-year art school student could crank them out."

"You're not giving yourself enough credit." He pointed to the small oval frame on my bookshelf. "Is this your mother?"

"Yes. That's Sarah MacGill."

"You have the same eyes."

"You mean the kind that can bypass the bullshit and

slice right through you?"

"I meant brown." He watched me fill the kettle.

"Do you realize that every person whose name you wrote on that list in the attic room was at the art show tonight? Except for Miss Starnes, who's in a nursing home. I thought that was interesting."

"That is interesting."

"And none of them ever tried to help you get out of Grayson House?"

"Reverend Lyon had the guts to come to the house once to see if my claims of mental abuse had any merit. But he couldn't get past Florence. She told him I was exaggerating and everything was fine. I stood in the foyer that night with Reverend Lyon's hand on my shoulder, and I saw in Florence's eyes that she knew how much I hated her for lying to him. How much I would always hate her."

"Do you think she could have tried to kill your grandmother? She's strong enough physically. She had full access to the house. And according to my father and Trude, because of the way she was treated, she hated Mrs. Grayson with a passion."

"I never understood why Florence kept working for her."

"Her name is in the address book. Maybe your grandmother had something on her."

"That's a possibility. I may go see her tomorrow. She might talk to me."

"Well, she won't talk to me."

He stood beside the kitchen counter, taking his usual stance—legs apart, arms crossed over his broad chest. What color were his eyes tonight? Blue-green? Green-gray? Painting them would be a challenge for any artist, but capturing the wicked twinkle and the blistering intelligence would take more skill than I had acquired painting springer spaniels.

The scent of his aftershave drifted toward me like bait.

"Did you know I sat behind you in Algebra?" I said.

"You did?"

"You were so smart and funny. I loved the sarcastic things you used to say under your breath. I may have even had a little crush on you. Until you started calling me that awful nickname—Frankie. Then I kept my head down and tried to be invisible."

"We were in high school. All anyone does in high school is change out one façade for another until they find one they can survive in."

"When you surprised me in the locker room that day, you didn't even know who I was. Until you saw my chest."

"I was a seventeen-year-old straight guy. Women's chests took up a lot of real estate in my brain. But you're right. I didn't know you sat behind me in class. I should have turned around." He smiled. "God, I wish I'd turned around."

The sound of splintered glass cut through the night. A crash exploded beneath us.

"Maggie!" my father screamed.

I was out the door first, swinging around the corner railing, rushing and stumbling down the steps. I flung the back door open and ran through the kitchen to the living room. My father lay on the floor beside the couch, his arms over his head.

"Pop!"

"I'm okay." He pushed himself up on one elbow. "It

sailed right over me."

Eli ran through the room and out the front door, slamming it behind him.

Pop picked up the jagged gray rock that had missed him by a few feet. "Whoa! This sucker is heavy. It could've knocked me into next week."

Ten minutes later, while I was picking up shards of glass and putting them into a cardboard box, Eli came back in.

"Did you see anything?" Pop's voice shook.

"Just some kid running away," Eli gasped. "I'm pretty sure it was Travis."

"Why would it be Travis?" Pop asked.

Eli and I exchanged looks.

"Tell me," Pop said.

"Travis almost sideswiped me on his bike a couple of days ago. It seemed deliberate. I wondered if he was trying to get back at us because you fired his father."

"I can't believe it." Pop rested his cast on the ottoman. "Travis has always been so polite. I paid him to mix paint for me and tape off woodwork. He's a pretty good painter too. Bob was proud of him."

"Tell him the rest," Eli said. "He needs to know."

Pop's tired eyes rested on me. "The rest of what, honey? The fact that someone in this town has it in for me and cut the brake lines on my van?"

"Yes," I said.

"When did you find out?" Eli said.

"Roone Kesterson posted it on Facebook. I'm over sixty and stuck at home. You think I don't check Facebook every two hours?"

"I was trying to keep you from worrying," I said.

"I know, honey," Pop said. "But I busted my ankle,

not my brain."

"Exactly what I keep telling her," Eli said.

"She's been like this since her mother left. Always trying to protect Jesse and me from the bad things in life. Always trying to solve our problems so we won't have to worry."

"She also found a dead rat hanging from her car tonight," Eli said.

"And someone pushed Jules into my painting at the art show."

"This is not good," Pop said. "Why would someone sabotage the van? Because Mrs. Grayson named Maggie as the main beneficiary in her will?"

I sat on the arm of the sofa. "If anything happens to me, the revised will automatically reverts to the previous one." I looked at Eli. "Which you've seen, right?" He nodded. "So what was in it? Who did she leave the money to? I think Pop and I have a right to know."

"The will made provisions for Kyle's son Alex. At the time, Grandmother believed Irena and Kyle had been legally married, so she left him one third of the estate, with Stephen and I receiving the other two-thirds. Florence got a very small stipend."

"That could be a motive for Irena to commit murder," I said.

"I'm sure Irena had no idea the will had been changed," Eli said. "If she had, I would have heard about it. You've met her. She's not one to keep her feelings hidden."

"I didn't mean she had a motive to murder your grandmother," I said. "I meant she had a motive to murder me. With me out of the picture, the will reverts back to Alex receiving one-third of the estate. Then Irena could afford to stick him in a pricey boarding school, skim enough inheritance money off the top for herself, and go live her best life."

"But it was your van that was targeted, Les. If Maggie was the intended victim, it had to have been sabotaged by someone who knew she was going to drive it."

Pop picked a stray piece of glass off the sofa. "Everyone in town knows I got hurt and will be laid up for weeks. If you don't believe me, look at the get-well posts on social media."

"Not everyone cares about social media," I said.

"And we don't know when the van's brakes were tampered with," Eli said. "Before Maggie drove it that morning, when was the last time anyone used it?"

Pop thought. "After my accident, Maggie didn't go back to finish painting the bed and breakfast for a few days, until she thought I could stay here by myself."

"Maybe someone had seen the revised will," Eli said, "and knew Maggie would inherit."

"But who?" I said. "The lawyer? The witnesses? Unless Mrs. Grayson told someone, who else would know what it said?"

"I'm not sure the witnesses read the terms of the will," Eli said. "They are only there to make sure the client isn't being coerced into signing something she doesn't want to sign. I doubt if they were privy to its contents."

"Delores Goldstein is Attorney DePaul's secretary," I said. "She would have had to enter the changes into the computer, so she would have known."

"Delores has worked for DePaul for years," Pop said. "She prides herself on being indispensable. She would never breach attorney-client privilege."

"Or what about Doc Moreland?" I said. "He was there. And I found information about him on the Internet that Mrs. Grayson could have used to blackmail him."

"Oh, that's old news," Pop said. "Everybody knows about him having to switch from surgery to family practice because of a mistake he made. He wouldn't hurt Mrs. Grayson. He was grateful to her for giving him a job. Where else would he have been able to get one?"

"Maybe Florence knew what was in the revised will," I said. "She could have overheard Mrs. Grayson and DePaul talking the day it was changed and blabbed it to someone." I glanced at Pop. "Like maybe her daughter Trude?"

"If Trude was involved, then why come after you, Les?" Eli said. "I thought you guys were a couple. Besides, Maggie is the one who inherited the estate, not you."

"As of this afternoon, Trude and I aren't together anymore." Pop shook his head. "I'm not sure we ever really were."

"Could Trude have tried to kill Mrs. Grayson?" I said. "She hated the way Mrs. Grayson treated her mother. Maybe she found out Florence wasn't going to be remembered in the will after Mrs. Grayson died and let her temper get the best of her. She does have a temper, Pop. We've both seen it."

"I know she does," Pop said wearily. "I just can't believe she would physically hurt someone like that." He yawned. "Maybe we're all overreacting. Maybe that rock through the window tonight was just another prank."

Eli glanced at his watch and moved toward the door. "If these *are* pranks, then they're hardcore pranks carried out by someone with a serious grudge against one or both of you. Counting the rat—which, I have to say, was a little juvenile—and Velma's tire getting slashed, five of these stunts have happened in the last week."

"Six if you count me falling off the scaffold."

"When was your accident, sir?" Eli said.

"Wednesday before last," Pop said.

Eli blew out a sigh. "That's the same day Grandmother changed her will."

"After hashing this out tonight, I'm convinced this raft of pranks directed at us is all about the inheritance," I said. "Someone must have seen the changes in the new will before we met at DePaul's office. They knew I going to inherit, and they knew I'd be driving your van because you weren't able to. It had to have been planned."

"Does someone really want me dead?" Pop's voice had dropped until I could barely make out the words. "Or worse, my sweet girl." He hadn't called me that in years. "What if someone wants *you* dead?"

Eli's phone dinged. He pulled it out and checked the text message. "I have to go. Stephen has called a family meeting in my room at the Blue Ridge Motel in about twenty minutes." He looked up and sighed. "I cannot wait to see what he wants now."

Chapter 11

I pulled into the Blue Ridge Motel parking lot and cut Velma's lights.

A few cars were scattered about, but Eli's giant blue truck was easy to spot. The old motel, which had been around since the early '60s, never seemed to change. Every few years, someone tried to spruce it up with a fresh coat of paint and some new shrubs. The sign beside the one-story structure, a hand-painted mountain logo, looked sweetly vintage. I'd never been inside the motel and wondered if it was still a favorite hideout for students from the local community college whose dates had sampled one too many mango margaritas at Fat Daddy's.

The night air, thick and fragrant with honeysuckle, swirled around the globe lamps hanging beside each door. Fog had begun to roll in from the river. Clouds tumbled across the dark sky as the wind picked up. It felt like rain.

I'd called Jesse to come over and stay with Pop. And even though it may have been the first time I'd ever asked him for a favor involving the care of our father, he agreed without sighing first and didn't ask why or where I was going. Maybe he had taken one look at my determined face and known when to back off.

As I drove around looking for a discreet place to park, I tried coasting to keep Velma's motor quiet. I probably should have driven Pop's old Honda, but when

I decided to follow Eli to the motel and spy on his family, I wasn't thinking too far ahead.

After scoping out my options, I parked in a small space beside a utility building away from the lights. I got out and pulled my gray hoodie closer around me. I spotted a picnic table at the edge of the woods beneath a weeping cherry tree positioned directly across from the corner room, up a slight hill, and so deep in the shadows, no one could detect me without a pair of night-vision goggles.

I couldn't believe I was actually doing this. Or what, exactly, I hoped to discover.

All I knew was that two people—three, counting Eli—who had a viable motive, means, and opportunity to get rid of the one person who'd been holding them back were going to be in the same motel room that night. And I had to find out the reason why.

I sat on the damp picnic table, glanced at the time on my phone, and shivered. 11:05.

Luke Prichard's SUV roared into the parking lot and pulled in beside Stephen's Jaguar. Luke got out of the driver's side. A few seconds later, Irena emerged and helped Alex climb out of the backseat. The little boy looked sleepy, rubbing his eyes and holding a stuffed penguin under his arm. "Come *on*," Luke yelled. "What's the matter with you?"

Alex wiped his eyes with the back of his hand and clutched his penguin tighter.

Irena knocked on Eli's door. It opened immediately, and Stephen ushered them inside.

I slid off the table to the ground then retraced my steps back to the motel, careful to stay in the shadows. I'm not sure who I thought I was hiding from. Everyone in the Grayson family was already inside Room 102. And unless they were standing at the window looking out, they would never see me skulk down the hill in my dark gray sweatshirt.

Had Stephen called this emergency meeting so they could put their heads together and think of the best way to recover what they thought was rightfully theirs? Or was it a brainstorming session to decide, once and for all, how to deal with me? I crouched behind the cars and skirted the perimeter of the parking lot. At least Eli's room was situated on the end and would provide shelter in case I needed to duck out of sight.

I tried to stay calm, but my head was spinning.

Mrs. Grayson's time of death had been estimated between 8:00 and 10:00 p.m. Did any of these people have alibis?

Stephen said he'd been home reading while I was at Comfort and Joy busing tables, but who knew? And what about his new girlfriend Rocki? Could she be his alibi? Not unless Stephen had lied about meeting her two days after Mrs. Grayson had died.

Eli was supposedly on the road driving in from Kitty Hawk when she died. He said he'd talked to Mrs. Grayson around 7:45. Had Sheriff Conley checked the pings off the cell tower records to verify that? Eli also claimed he'd been tied up in a traffic jam near Winston-Salem waiting for a jackknifed tractor-trailer to clear the interstate. Had Conley bothered to verify that too? Or ask what time Eli got back on the road? A witness might have seen him at a gas station or a fast-food joint. CCTV footage could have photographed him at a rest stop. I was trying hard to find a way to prove the guy's innocence. But it troubled me that he could have arrived in

Wrenhaven much sooner than 1:17 a.m., let himself into his grandmother's house, replanted the key in the planter, left and come back, then pretended he'd only just arrived.

I had no idea about Irena's whereabouts when Mrs. Grayson died. Was she on Conley's list of suspects as well? Did he even have a list of suspects?

If Eli had tried to smother his grandmother—which I didn't believe for a second—what would his true motive be? Was he desperate for money like Stephen? Had Mrs. Grayson told him she'd changed the will and was cutting him out of it? Had he never recovered emotionally from the mental abuse he had suffered at her hand as a teenager? People had killed for much less. And if Eli thought he had killed her, why would he return to her house? To remove a piece of evidence he'd forgotten? To throw suspicion off himself by finding her dead body? To keep up appearances because Florence had known Mrs. Grayson was expecting him?

I did not—could not—believe Eli was capable of murdering his grandmother. Or anyone else, for that matter. But as he had said himself, "People aren't always who we think they are. Especially the ones we're closest to. Everybody has secrets."

I stood in the shadows feeling queasy.

Eavesdropping wasn't something I was comfortable with. I'd done enough of it growing up: hiding at the top of the stairs, listening to my parents argue about things I didn't understand when they thought I was fast asleep. I'd long ago concluded that the worst thing about hearing someone else's private conversation was that you could never unhear it. The words you weren't supposed to hear would be seared into your soul forever.

I glanced around. My car was close enough that I could make a run for it if I had to, but Velma wasn't exactly a car that could fly under the radar. Everyone knew who owned the little black Volkswagen Beetle with a 1967 Flower Power sticker on the rear window. Most of them recognized Velma and loved her. She was the town's pet car. But she wasn't the quietest pet car on four tires.

The motel room curtains were drawn, and I leaned near the window. The voices coming from inside weren't as loud as I'd hoped. I could only catch a few words and sentences.

Irena said, "Alex." Then, "your proposition."

Through a gap in the lined curtain, I could see Irena's face. Her streaked blonde hair had been pulled back, making her look young and vulnerable. Her simple pearl earrings and lack of makeup gave her an air of innocence that had been missing at the reading of the will. Her bottom lip trembled. If this was a performance, it was a good one.

"Permanent guardianship." Luke raised his voice. "Comes with a price."

"How much do you want?" Eli countered. "What makes you think I can get my hands on that kind of money?"

"It's your fault he's deaf," Irena shouted.

"You can't blame that on Eli," Stephen shouted back.

"My poor Alex," Irena wailed.

I listened closely, trying to make out the words, even pressing my ear against the windowpane. I wanted to turn up the volume. But between the yelling, all I could hear was mumbling. And more mumbling.

Luke yelled, "You can't talk to her like that!"

"This is extortion!"

Thunder rumbled in the distance.

I'd heard enough to know I had no idea what was going on. Did Irena blame Eli for Alex's deafness? Was someone extorting money from someone else? Eli had mentioned the possibility of petitioning the court for permanent guardianship of Alex, but would he actually pay Irena to let him do it? And where did Mrs. Grayson's death fit into all this?

The voices on the other side of the window stopped abruptly.

My heart slammed into my throat.

I ducked around the corner and slid back against the side of the building. Before I could dig my keys out of my pocket, the door to Eli's room opened and Irena, Luke, and Alex filed out. I cowered deeper into the shadows. Once Luke's SUV pulled onto the highway, I could leave.

"Why are you still letting Irena make you feel guilty about Alex's deafness?" Stephen asked. "There was no way you could have known the kid had an ear infection."

"I was supposed to be looking after him," Eli said. "He was only eighteen months old. It was on my watch."

"He couldn't have lost his hearing from having an untreated infection for one weekend. He had to have been sick for days, or weeks before that. This is not your fault. Irena is to blame."

"I know that."

"You do not know that," Stephen said. "Guilt is plastered across your face every time you look at the boy." Eli didn't answer. "I saw you and Maggie dancing tonight at the Art Guild Awards. She was looking at you like—well, she never looked at me like that."

"I like her, Stephen. I didn't expect to like her this much, but I do."

"That's good. Because that will make getting our inheritance back so much easier. If she's sweet on you— and I'm pretty sure she is—you can use it to your advantage. She's got a brain and she's not gullible, so it could be a little tricky. But I'm sure you can convince her not to accept the inheritance."

"How am I supposed to do that?"

"Oh, come on, Eli. You're a good-looking guy. You've got moves; I've seen them. You don't have to sleep with her. Unless you really want to. She's sarcastic, but she's smart, and really funny sometimes. Her chest would be a solid ten if she didn't have that godawful scar on it. I saw that scar once when she was changing her necklace. It looked like somebody had taken a knife and slashed her with it."

"Well, technically, they did."

"What a turnoff," Stephen said. "It made me realize I never wanted to get to second base with her." He laughed. "But you could always do it in the dark, right? Or with your eyes closed. Take her out a couple of times. She's a cheap date. The only place she ever wants to go is that beer joint called Fat Daddy's." His voice hardened. "I don't care what you do, Eli, just make sure you get her to agree to sign the inheritance back to us. I don't think either of us can afford to contest the damn thing. Not now, with you shelling out big bucks to Irena for that kid."

Hot tears burned behind my eyes.

I leaned against the building and gulped in a ragged breath. I looked down at my hand pressing against my chest, covering my scar. And just like that, after spending years learning to love my less-than-perfect body and feel genuine pity for the handful of guys who weren't men enough to see past it, it all fell away. In one crushing moment, listening to a man I didn't even like ridicule the way I looked, I was seventeen-year-old Maggie MacGill again. Hiding in the back of the girl's locker room. Feeling like a freak.

"Why don't we make it worth her while?" Stephen said. "She just wants enough money to keep her brother's restaurant and her father's painting business from going under. We can afford to give her that much."

"I don't think she'll go for it."

"Then we'll have to take her to court; we won't have a choice. You know that, right?"

A pause, then, "I know."

I wasn't sure when it had started to rain. The cotton hoodie I was wearing clung to my shoulders. Water ran down my face in little rivulets. My short hair had plastered itself to my scalp and the hood I'd pulled over my head smelled like a dryer sheet.

"Somebody killed our grandmother," Eli said, "and I'm going to find out who."

"Well, good luck, but leave me out of it. My life's enough of a shitshow without playing detective for someone I'm glad is dead." He strode across the parking lot to his silver Jaguar, popped the trunk, flung his leather messenger bag inside, and slammed it shut. Seconds later, he was screeching onto the highway.

I had never been so glad to see anyone go.

As I stepped back, my heel crunched against a bottle cap, scraping it softly against the gritty concrete.

"Is someone there?" Eli said.

I didn't dare answer. I stood with my back to the wall, my heart thumping in my chest.

The wedge of light jutting across the entryway to Eli's room was still visible. He stood listening for a few more seconds until finally, the light disappeared and the double click of the door lock sounded in the night.

Driving home through the mist and rain, Eli and Stephen's words echoed in my head. I wasn't any closer to finding out who killed Mrs. Grayson, but at least I knew where I stood with the Grayson family. I was a glitch. A hiccup. A bump in the road. I was their smart, funny, physically unattractive, insurmountable problem to solve.

And after tonight, there was something about being Eli and Stephen's problem that made me want to dig in my heels and become an even bigger problem.

Chapter 12

The next morning, halfway through a long sweaty run, I stopped by the sheriff's station.

Sheriff Conley wasn't in, but one of his deputies, Allen-something, yet another guy I'd gone to high school with who still called me Frankie, listened patiently to my questions about cell tower pings and the best way to contact the Winston-Salem Department of Transportation. He assured me, without ever actually making eye contact, that Sheriff Conley was doing everything he could to find the attempted murderer of Mrs. Grayson, and I should just back off and let them do their jobs. Kind of made me glad I hadn't showered first.

I spent the rest of the day finishing Caroline's Bed-and-breakfast and doing some serious soul searching. I was still on the fence about accepting the inheritance. At least all of it. But I wasn't sure how much was too much to keep. Or how to decide that. Or how to proceed. I also couldn't help thinking about Alex.

Did Irena really not care about the boy like Eli claimed? Or was she just terrified of screwing up his life and a little—all right, a lot—clueless when it came to doing what was best for him? I decided to offer my help. As a teacher, I was aware of resources she and Eli might not know about. And even though I was pretty sure my help would not be welcomed, for Alex's sake I had to try.

I'd thought of broaching the subject with Eli first, but after listening to his conversation with Stephen the night before, I needed to put some space between us until I figured out how I felt about things. Like the sweet almost-kiss in the Grayson House foyer. And the fact that I was suddenly desperate to trust him.

I pulled into the parking area behind Giles Hardware. Still wearing my cutoffs and an oversized shirt covered in latex splatters, I looked like the runner-up in a game of Paintball Wars. The tiny lot was empty except for the hardware store truck. Mr. Giles prided himself on being the last of a dying breed: a store owner who still offered free home deliveries. I'd always wanted to order a one-dollar paint can opener just to see if he would load it on his truck and bring it over.

The wooden stairs leading to the little apartment Mr. Giles rented had weathered to a soft Dove Gray. The door at the top, once a bright Cosmic Blue, had been repainted with warm Spun Honey. I always wondered how many glasses of wine some marketing expert had to guzzle to come up with paint brand color names.

I climbed to the landing and stopped. I didn't want to upset Irena—I knew she didn't think too much of me—but if she was planning on leaving her child in the permanent care of a relative, I wanted to make sure she knew she had choices.

I knocked on the door and waited. When no one answered, I cupped my hands over my eyes and peered into the tiny square door window. Sheets and blankets tumbled together on an unmade sofa bed. Alex's stuffed penguin, its black and white fur matted with years of bedtime hugs, lay on the lumpy pillow. The zippered pocket on the penguin's back was pulled open with one leg of Alex's Spiderman pajamas spilling out. Fast food cups, greasy burger wrappers, and crumpled cans of Blue Ribbon beer covered a small table between the stove and fridge.

"Can I help you?"

I swung around. Mr. Giles stood on the landing below me, his wiry arms crossed over his chest.

"It's me, Mr. Giles. Maggie MacGill."

He squinted up at me. "Maggie? What are you doing up there?"

"I stopped by to see Irena. I thought she might be home."

"She and the boy left half an hour ago. She came in the store to pay the rest of the week's rent, and said they were headed out."

"Do you know where they went?"

"No telling." He slid a toothpick out of his shirt pocket. "That girl comes and goes at all hours." He squinted again. "Are you and she friends?"

"No, I teach her son at the Art Factory. I wanted to talk to her about his progress."

"Well, Irena seems like a nice girl—a little high-strung, maybe." He grinned. "But she sure is a looker. That man who hangs out with her—Luke? Now, him I don't like."

"Why not? I've met Luke. He seems okay."

"Well, he ain't okay in my book. He yells at the kid all the time. Calls him *stupid* and *dumbass*. Says some pretty rough things to Irena too, but I reckon she can take care of herself. Sometimes they both yell at the kid. Don't know why. He can't hear either of them."

"Luke is from Wrenhaven. Had you met him before?"

"I know he's Annie Prichard's boy and used to work at the printing press down by the river—the one that closed last month—but I think now he's hired on with a local moving company." He shook his head. "I heard he pulled his family out of poverty working two jobs and took care of his dying mama for years. But he's a bully with the little deaf boy. That's why I make it my business to keep an eye out for the kid. Never could stand a bully.

"I don't think Irena will be here much longer. She says she's goin' to Hollywood to be an actress." He chuckled. "Can you imagine that? But I swear, I believe she'll do it."

"You said Irena comes and goes at all hours. Does she leave the little boy—Alex—with Luke? Or does she take him with her?"

"Mostly she goes off by herself. I guess she just needs time alone."

"How about a week ago last Saturday? Do you remember if Irena was here at the apartment, or did she go out? Say, between the hours of eight and ten. I was at Jesse's restaurant that night busing tables or I would have been at Fat Daddy's listening to the band."

"They do have good music on the weekend, don't they?" Mr. Giles grinned. "Yes, sir. Me and the Missus love to go—why, that's where we were last week. I remember now. And I did see Irena. She waved to me when she came in. I think it was about 8:30 or 9:00. She sat at the bar and ordered one of those fancy pink drinks with the sugar on the rim. Then me and the Missus got up to dance, and I didn't see her no more." He chewed on his toothpick. "I've never eaten at Jesse's restaurant. Is it good?"

"You should come down and try it. Jesse would love

to see you."

"I heard they had chicken livers cooked three ways. Is that true?"

"Yes, they do."

"See, that's what I don't understand. Why go to all that trouble, when frying them in bacon grease is what people around here want?" Mr. Giles looked past me and smiled. "Why, here comes Irena now." She parked a blue Toyota beside the row of trashcans. "Yes, sir," he said before trundling off. "She sure is a looker."

Irena got out and gave me a look that would have stopped a less seasoned person in their tracks. But I was a teacher. I was used to scowls and glares and flip-offs behind my back.

"Why are you here?" Her eastern European accent had suddenly become more pronounced. "Checking up on me for Eli?"

"Eli doesn't know I'm here. I wondered if you had a few minutes to talk. About Alex."

"Alex is not your problem."

"I thought I could...maybe help."

Irena was right. Alex wasn't my problem. He was just another kid whose parent wasn't strong enough to cope with his disability. Just another kid who was going to fall through the cracks unless someone stood up for him. "I know you're planning on leaving town without him. I just wanted to make sure you've thought this through and know what you're doing."

Irena frowned. "And why do you care?"

"My mother walked out on me when I was fifteen because she couldn't handle a child who wasn't perfect. I was much older than Alex, and didn't need her as much as he needs you, but when she left, my world imploded.

Even with my father trying his best to fill in the gaps, nothing was ever the same. From that day on, every thought I had of my mother was colored with what-ifs. What if she'd been stronger? What if she'd learned to take my health problems in stride? What if she'd had the courage to look at my scar and not burst into tears? What if she'd stayed?"

"What if you mind your own business?"

"There is help out there if you want it. There are scholarships to schools that can take the burden off you and give Alex a place to learn how to feel safe and navigate the world as a hearing-impaired person. How long is he going to feel safe when he can't speak or communicate?"

"You've got some nerve," she said.

"I just want to help. I'd be glad to give you the names of some—"

"I don't have time for this. I need to change then pick up Alex and drop him at Eli's. They're spending some quality time together so Eli won't take me to court for being a bad mother."

"*Are* you a bad mother?" Irena's amber eyes flashed, and I knew I'd gone too far. "Look, I know it can be overwhelming. And it's got to be the hardest thing you've ever done. But walking out of Alex's life could do him more harm than good. I'm sure Eli will help you financially whether you give him permanent guardianship or not."

I thought I was getting to her, but she tossed her hair and threw the ball back into my court. "Tell me, Maggie, how does it feel to be the person everyone wants gone?"

"Excuse me?"

"We were all there when the lawyer read the will. If

something happens to you then the new will reverts back to the old one where all of us were left something. We have talked it over and agree our lives would be so much better if you were out of the mix."

"Out of the mix?" I stopped to let that sink in. "You mean if I were dead?"

"Well, yes. I guess. Theoretically speaking."

I stood there. Speechless.

When I had driven to Giles Hardware, the only thing I could think about was trying to convince Irena not to give up her son. But after listening to her say that everyone wished I could see my way clear to taking a powder, she didn't seem quite so deserving of my sympathy. Maybe Alex *was* better off without a mother like her in his life. No matter how many years he had to go to therapy.

"So, tell me," Irena asked with a smile. "*Did* you kill the old bat?"

"I did not." I started to leave. "But I'm going to find out who did."

"Then you might want to check out the girl who's about to marry your father."

I turned around. "You mean Trude? Gertrude Claussen?"

"That's right. Florence's daughter. The one who sneaks in and out of Grayson House when she thinks no one is looking." Irena laughed. "I was there a lot these last few weeks, and I saw her leaving the house with that big bag of hers plenty of times. And it never looked empty."

"You think Trude was taking things from Grayson House?"

"Sure looked like it to me."

"What about Florence? Did she know her daughter was stealing from Mrs. Grayson?"

"Oh, I think she knew," Irena said. "Nothing gets by Florence."

****

Florence Claussen's one-story ranch sat two miles out of town on a dirt road skirting the south pasture of Henry Marsdale's goat farm. Henry hadn't started his goat business when Florence moved there as a young divorcee with her four-year-old daughter Trude, or Florence would have kept right on going. Trude said the view from their front porch, of baby goats hopping around like Jack Russell Terriers on crack, was fun to watch. But in the middle of summer, when the wind was out of the west, the stench was so strong, it permeated your skin.

I steered Velma over a rocky strip of ground that served as a makeshift driveway. I'd thought about calling first, but I was afraid Florence would hang up on me. Or tell me not to come since she had branded me a murderer.

Her white clapboard house looked neat and inviting. Red petunias cascaded over painted window boxes. Two green rockers sat on the porch. A hand-painted sign that said *Welcome, Friends* hung beside the front door. I wondered if Florence had any friends. Did her gal pals drop by and bring slices of homemade pound cake? Did they sit on the porch in the evening after Florence got off work and drink lemonade? Or maybe something a little stronger like homemade wine or apple pie moonshine?

Florence and I had never talked about anything personal. Neither of us had mentioned the fact that Trude, a mind-boggling eleven years younger than me, was engaged to marry my father. I wondered if Florence knew they had broken off their engagement.

I parked beside Florence's burnt orange Subaru. The two black and white cats on the porch scattered as soon as I stepped out. Florence must have heard my car because she banged open the screen and stood in the doorway, scowling. Her denim skirt hung loosely on her narrow hips. Her quilted vest in alternating squares of giant sunflowers and yellow checked gingham looked way more cheerful than the expression on her tired face.

"What brings you out here?" Florence said. "I thought you'd be moving your things into Grayson House by now."

"Not yet."

Her eyes shone like the stones in my black onyx ring. "Course, I don't rightly know where you'd put anything else in that house. I've never seen such a mess of useless stuff." I refrained from pointing out that most of the useless stuff I'd seen in Grayson House was covered with at least six months' worth of dust she had been paid to remove.

"I'm sure it'll all work out for you," she said. "Stephen says that was the plan all along."

"I didn't kill her, Florence."

Florence's dark eyes looked away, then lasered back to me. "But I saw you holding—"

"You saw me after I'd picked up the pillow on her loveseat and found her makeup smeared on the back of it. Literally two seconds later. I was only looking at the pillow because my mother used to have one similar to it, and it reminded me of her."

"I remember Sarah," she said softly.

"I would never have tried to hurt Mrs. Grayson. Never. Not for any reason. I was as shocked as you were seeing that pillow."

Florence nodded, which was probably all the understanding I was going to get. But at least, she wasn't reaching for her shotgun or her phone to call the sheriff to come and arrest me.

"So I would appreciate it if you would stop telling people I caused Mrs. Grayson's death."

"Is that all? Or did you drive out here to accuse me of stealing from Grayson House? Because I never took that diamond and pearl choker. No matter what she said in her will."

"And I never worked a day in her garden hoping she would name me as a beneficiary. No matter what Stephen said." I sighed. "Look, Florence, I'm just trying to find out the truth before somebody else gets hurt. You didn't take the diamond and pearl choker, but I think you know who did."

Florence stared at me. I was fishing without any real evidence, but I could tell from the expression on her face I'd hit pay dirt.

"It was Trude, wasn't it? Irena said she saw Trude sneaking in and out of Grayson House carrying her big canvas bag full of things. Did Mrs. Grayson know Trude was stealing from her? Trude said you hated your job at Grayson House. Is that why you stayed? Did Mrs. Grayson threaten to have Trude arrested if you didn't keep working for her?"

"You need to leave."

"Tell me who was at Grayson House the Saturday Mrs. Grayson died, then I'll go. I know you were there. And Doc Moreland. Was Percy DePaul there with his secretary Delores?"

"No, they came on the Wednesday before. The day

Mrs. Grayson changed her will."

"What about Stephen? And Irena and Alex?"

She nodded.

"I know Trude was there too. Who else was there?"

She crossed her arms over her chest. Her dark eyes bore into mine.

"Who else, Florence?"

"That doctor who runs the Art Factory and his secretary."

"Dr. Harold Gatz and Kath?"

"They were only there for a few minutes. I saw him hand Mrs. Grayson some papers which she threw in the trash as soon as he left. Irena's boyfriend, Luke, was there. I don't think he ever came inside, though. Just sat on the porch. I offered him some iced tea, but he didn't want any."

"What time did you leave to go home that night?"

"I always took Mrs. Grayson's dinner tray up to her around 5:30, then I usually left by 6:00. The next morning, I would bring Mrs. Grayson her newspaper and coffee around 9:00 and collect the tray from the night before."

"Did you take a dinner tray up the night she died?"

"It was different that day. In the evening, Mrs. Grayson usually stayed in her little sitting room reading a book. I never cared for reading much—too boring—but that's what she liked to do. That night, she hadn't been feeling well so she didn't leave her bedroom. She didn't want anything to eat, but I had made chicken salad with grapes—her favorite—and I told her I'd leave it in the fridge with some cut up watermelon. I was supposed to leave around 5:00 p.m. Mayor Nash was expected—he has his own key—and I felt like he could take it up to her on a tray if she got hungry. But then, Irena showed back up. I thought she'd left with Luke; they'd all been sitting on the porch talking. Stephen had already come and gone."

"Why did she come back?"

"She said she left her sweater in the parlor—don't know why she'd brought a sweater; it was sweltering hot that day—and she went inside to get it."

"Do you know of any other enemies Mrs. Grayson might have had?"

Florence cackled. "Like I told Sheriff Conley, that woman had enemies crawling out of the woodwork. And I had to fix ginger tea for all of them."

She hiked up her skirt and sat in one of the rockers, then motioned for me to join her. It felt like some kind of truce offering. She would never apologize for accusing me of murder.

I sat down. A hot, sticky wind swirled around my shoulders. Typical Tennessee mountain weather—chilly in the morning, hot as hell in the afternoon. Pop always said it was one of the inconveniences of living in a valley surrounded by a range of mountains whose sole purpose was to block the horizon and hog the breeze.

"Nobody liked Mrs. Grayson," Florence said. "Except maybe you sometimes. I listened when the two of you talked about books, and you weren't afraid to stand your ground with her. She liked that. She said you reminded her of someone called Elinor Dashwood. And that you might be the only person in this town who had any sense."

Florence fanned her face with the bottom of her apron. "I guess she's with the Lord now, standing in line waiting to find out where she'll spend eternity. I'd be willing to bet there are some pretty tall flames nipping at her heels."

"Eli said Mrs. Grayson was mentally abusive to him and Stephen the summer they stayed with her."

"And Kyle." Her eyes misted. "Poor little Kyle. Hard to believe he's gone." She shook her head. "Eli got the brunt of it because he was the oldest. And because he shouldered the blame to protect his brother and cousin."

"Did she hurt them physically?"

"I would have called the authorities if she had. But she was too strict. Her rules were ironclad, and anyone who broke them suffered the consequences. No noise after dinner. No running in the house. No food or drink anywhere but the kitchen. No going outside—she didn't want the neighbors gawking." Florence stopped. "Prayers and Bible verses every day. She made them memorize long passages and recite them until they were perfect. It was hard for the little ones. Eli used to write them on Stephen and Kyle's arms so they wouldn't forget. Because if they forgot…"

"What?"

"She'd make them go without supper. Or she'd lock them in the attic room. We didn't have cell phones then, and she never let Eli call his mother. If your father hadn't found Eli and helped him off the roof that night when he tried to escape, he might have fallen to his death."

"You should have told someone how she treated them."

"Who was I supposed to tell? I was alone in the world with a child to raise. I couldn't afford to lose my job." Florence leaned forward. "Besides, she never hit those kids. All she did was put them in time-out and make them memorize the Lord's word."

I shook my head. It was useless to argue with her. But at least she was talking to me.

"What were you doing in Mrs. Grayson's bedroom when you walked in on me holding the pillow?"

"I know I wasn't supposed to be there, but I was looking for the little notebook she kept hidden. She dug up as much dirt as she could on people—some of them friends of mine—then threatened to print it in the Wrenhaven Gazette if they didn't do what she wanted. Little stuff. Big stuff. I don't know how she found it all out. Someone must have been spying for her. I know she kept it all written down; I just didn't know where. That day, I thought I could go up the back stairs, sneak into her room, and give that iris desk a good going over. I'm sure that's where it's hidden."

"That is where she kept it." I pulled the address book out of my purse and handed it to her. "There's no information in it. Only names."

"This isn't all," Florence said. "She had papers and newspaper clippings stacked beside her when she wrote in this. I saw them. Are you sure they aren't in the desk too?"

"They're not there. Eli and I looked."

"Well, they've got to be somewhere."

"Maybe someone scanned them for her. Maybe the information she gathered is on a disk or a thumb drive."

"She doesn't have a computer."

"Then it has to be written on the papers you saw when she was sitting at her desk. And they've got to be somewhere." I gazed at the clouds and sighed. "I just have to figure out where."

Chapter 13

I doubled back to the Art Factory.

Florence had said Dr. Gatz and his secretary Kath were at Grayson House the day Mrs. Grayson died, and I wanted to know why.

I didn't believe Harold Gatz had anything to do with her death, but he had been a fish out of water in Wrenhaven ever since he'd come there. He'd never hidden the fact that he despised shilling for an organization, however charitable, that he didn't care one whit about. I'd always thought he was a strange choice to helm the Factory, but Mrs. Grayson had handpicked him for the job at Mayor Nash's request. And hoping for a generous benefactress, the always low on funds Art Factory couldn't afford to say no.

Harold may not have been able to say no either.

As soon as I stepped inside the atrium, the sound of muffled sobbing echoed through the room. It was late. All the kids had left for the day, so I knew it wasn't a student emergency. I peered through the glass window fronting the administration office. Kath Davis, the admin assistant, was sitting in the black ergonomic swivel chair she'd bought with her own money, leaning over the desk, weeping. I'd never seen Kath shed a tear before, much less cry into a towel like the world was coming to an end.

"Kath?" I said softly. "Are you all right?"

"He's leaving," Kath wailed. "He's in his office

right now packing all his stuff, and he's…he's leaving."

"Who's leaving? Harold?"

Kath nodded between sniffs. "I thought he liked me. I thought we had a future together. And now he's in his office throwing files into a cardboard box like the FBI is after him."

"What happened?

"He said running this place has been nothing but a time suck. He said he's going to find another charity to helm where all he has to do is show up at a banquet once a year, get his picture in the brochure, and write a check."

"I thought that's all he did now."

"He said Constance Grayson is dead, and he doesn't have to do this anymore."

"Why don't I talk to him? See what I can find out."

"No!" Kath grabbed my arm. "He made me promise not to tell anybody he was leaving until after he's gone."

"Okay."

"Have you found another job yet?" Kath balanced her thick glasses on her nose.

"Not yet. I've updated my resume, so I'm going to start applying for teaching positions soon. If I'm chosen to paint the town mural, the income from that should be enough to get me through until fall. But that's a long shot."

"I have some more bad news." Kath looked down, avoiding my gaze. "We can't let you volunteer at the Art Factory anymore. At least, not for the time being. Some of the parents have threatened to take their children out if you're here. We can't afford to lose the revenue. I just think it's best for you, and the Art Factory, if you stay away until this thing blows over."

"Until what thing blows over?"

"Until they find out who killed Mrs. Grayson." Kath's brown eyes met mine. "And it isn't you."

The thing about holding in anger for a long time is that when it seeps out—and it will—you can't always control who's going to be on the receiving end.

"Well, Kath," I said quietly. "I appreciate the vote of confidence. But there are other suspects running around out there besides me. You and Harold, for instance. Florence said the two of you were at Grayson House the day Mrs. Grayson died. Want to tell me why?"

Kath looked a little taken aback. "I-I was hoping to persuade her to get behind the Art Factory financially. Harold didn't want to go with me, but I told him I needed his support. Mrs. Grayson has always donated enough money to keep up appearances, and she gave us Harold as our spokesperson, but the Art Factory needs so much more. I know your mother created the Art Factory, and I might have been overstepping a bit, but I'd drawn up a proposal—and yes, it included changing the name to the Constance Grayson Art Center, which I thought she might endorse—but then, she died."

"Yeah," I said softly. "She sure did."

****

I drove to the rear of the Art Factory, parked behind a huge hydrangea bush, and waited.

Once Kath left for the day, I was going back inside and talk to Harold. I doubted if he would tell me if —or what—Mrs. Grayson had been holding over his head in order to keep him in Wrenhaven. But I had to try. Now that Mrs. Grayson was gone, he might be more forthcoming. Was I naïve not to consider Harold a suspect? I didn't know him that well, and although he was a bit of a blowhard, he seemed harmless. But people could surprise you. If Mrs. Grayson knew he had a secret that could destroy his career, and threatened him with it, it might have pushed him over the edge.

Kath slammed open the side door and made her way down the steps to the staff parking lot. When she got to her car, she stopped and gazed back, as if deciding whether or not to go inside and give it another go with Harold. I thought she was going to relent, but she shook her head sadly, slid beneath the steering wheel, and in a few seconds drove out of the lot onto Fairlane Road.

Before I could grab my purse, the Art Factory door banged open again. Harold made his way down the steps holding a medium sized cardboard box. He glanced around, then satisfied no one was watching him, flung the box into the open dumpster and hurried back inside. I slid down in the car seat and held my breath. A few minutes later, he came out again and headed for the only car left in the parking lot, a big black town car that looked like it should have been parked outside the Shady Rest Funeral Home.

I watched him in my rearview window until he had cleared the intersection, then I drove Velma to the dumpster and left her door open and the motor chugging. If I had to get out of Dodge fast, she would be close by and ready to roll. I slid open the door to the small commercial dumpster and peered inside. It wasn't as gross as the one at Fat Daddy's, but it still smelled like something had died and not left a forwarding address.

The box Harold had been carrying lay at the far end, just out of my reach. He must have hurled it at the back wall. After a few tries, I managed to grab one of the cardboard flaps and pull it toward me. Before I stashed it on Velma's front seat, I checked inside to make sure

Harold hadn't packed something strange in it like a pipe bomb or a dead cat. I closed it up, drove down one of the long tree-lined streets behind the courthouse, and parked near the woods. If Harold had second thoughts about dumping the box and decided to retrieve it, I didn't want him to catch me going through its contents.

I skimmed through the papers inside, most of them bank statements and tax forms, until I pulled out a clipping from a four-year-old issue of the *Austin Times Herald* featuring a photo of Dr. Harold Gatz with the name Jon Erik Vanderhook printed beneath it.

CHARGES DROPPED IN VANDERHOOK CASE

Dr. Jon Vanderhook, convicted of fertility fraud, used his sperm to inseminate a patient while having an affair with the patient and her twin sister.

It went on to say that Vanderhook had let his patient's husband believe his sperm were viable, then charged him a fortune to have them harvested even though he knew the guy had been shooting blanks for two years. When the husband left his cheating, and by then, very pregnant wife, he sued Dr. Harold for fertility fraud and alienation of affections.

"Whoa," I said softly.

It wasn't hard to figure out why Harold had changed his name and moved to a town the GPS had a hard time finding on the map. Wrenhaven had needed an OB-GYN, and shrewd Mrs. Grayson had found one. Somehow, she'd tracked down a doctor who needed a job and a fresh start. Jon Vanderhook/Harold Gatz was the perfect candidate: a brilliant obstetrician with cutting-edge skills and a shady past that could destroy his career. Continuing the work he loved at a hospital where he wouldn't have to furnish references or be subjected to a background check probably seemed like the answer to his prayers. But I'd bet the farm he hadn't counted on having to beg for donations for a small-town children's art center to keep his past from being exposed. No telling what else he'd had to do.

I didn't understand how Harold thought changing his name would keep his secret safe. No one could hide in this day and age. Not with the Internet and face recognition software and the cold hard fact that everything a person has ever done in their life that made it into print will survive forever.

I decided to wait until the next day to head back to Grayson House to search for the evidence Mrs. Grayson had stockpiled. It seemed like the next logical step. And with any luck, I would be the only one there. The last thing I wanted was to have to explain myself to anyone. Or find Eli Grayson hyperventilating in the attic.

****

By the time I finished painting a nursery for the expectant parents down the street, it was late in the afternoon when I turned into the Grayson House driveway. I drove past the rhododendron hedge and cut the motor. I wasn't trespassing; the house was still mine. Stephen could complain all he wanted, but I wasn't leaving unless he convinced the sheriff to show up with a warrant and drag me out.

I had my hand on the door handle when my phone rang. "*Maggie?*"

"Hey, Mayor Nash." My mind started buzzing with questions to ask him.

"I wanted to let you know the Downtown Wrenhaven Association has chosen you to paint the mural on the courthouse wall. I've emailed you the contract. They came up with some extra donation money at the last minute, so it's a very sweet deal. They'll furnish the paint, of course. Just called to make sure you're still onboard."

"Of course, I am." Relief and happiness flooded through me. "I'm very honored, Mayor. Please thank the committee for me."

"I also want to make sure you're available to ride on the Art Factory float for the Founder's Day Parade again. I know you're usually on it with a bunch of kids, but this year we—the DWA—would like to honor you as the chosen artist. We're going to blow up some of the sketches you entered and display them behind you. You'll do it, won't you?"

I sighed. Every year that I rode through the middle of town on that rickety float, I swore it would be my last. "Sure," I said. "Be glad to."

"They'd like you to get started on the mural as soon as possible. And when you're done, I have a cocker spaniel for you to paint. Not the actual dog." He laughed at his little joke. "I thought I'd give my daughter Holly a portrait of Snickers for her birthday."

"I'd be happy to paint Snickers." I took a breath, not sure where I was going next with the conversation. "I stopped by the Art Factory a little while ago and found Harold packing. Did you know he was leaving town?"

"No, but I'm not surprised. He's been wanting to go for some time. He's never been a good fit for the Factory, Maggie, and he'd be the first to tell you that. I've often wondered how Mrs. Grayson kept him in Wrenhaven as long as she did."

I knew. And she may have been killed for it.

Did she have something on Mayor Nash as well?

Something he was desperate to keep hidden? Now that Mrs. Grayson was dead, was Nash planning to tender his resignation to the city council and leave a town he loathed like Harold was doing?

Desperation was the wild card no one could predict, even from someone as seemingly nonthreatening as Mayor Nash. It could cause an otherwise normal human being to take a step back from reality and slip off the edge. I had to tread carefully.

"Mayor Nash?" I said. "Pop and I were talking the other day, and we couldn't remember your wife's first name. I know I met her once before she got sick."

There was a long pause.

"Jayne," he said. "Jayne with a 'y'. Her name was Jayne."

"Oh, that's Holly's middle name, isn't it? How sweet."

It suddenly occurred to me how to delve into Mayor Nash's past without giving him the third degree. Although, if he had changed his name like Dr. Harold, it might not be so easy.

I thanked him again, quite profusely, for the chance to paint the mural on the Wrenhaven Courthouse wall. After I ended the call, I immediately called Jules. He was good friends with the administration office secretary at Bainbridge Elementary. She had access to students' files.

"Let me get this straight," Jules said. "You want me to ask my friend Maureen if she'll check Holly Nash's birth certificate? What are you looking for, proof of paternity?"

"No, I'm pretty sure the father's name is going to be Sherman Nash. I just need to know his daughter's city of origin—where she was born, which hospital, attending physician, whatever you can find out."

"And you need this information because…"

"It's important, Jules. Please."

"Okay, hon. You got it. But I'm sure she'll want to wait until she's at work on Monday, so it won't look suspicious. When she pulls Holly's file, I'll text you."

Unless I found the information first.

I gazed at Grayson House towering above me. In the gathering dusk, I half expected to see lightning bolts shoot down from the weathervane while a wolf howled. The evidence Mrs. Grayson had collected was somewhere in that house. All I had to do was try to think like a sharp-witted, eighty-six-year-old woman who wanted to keep something hidden from her meddlesome housekeeper, and find it.

I stood in the foyer and let my gaze wander—to the parlor, to the top of the stairs, through the arched opening leading to the dining room. Where would Mrs. Grayson hide something she didn't want to be found? Where would Florence never think to look for it?

Following the dust trail might work. It couldn't be that hard to spot fingerprints and smears where Florence had searched; the woman hadn't dusted since Halloween. And I was pretty sure she had searched again. She'd probably driven over as soon as I'd left her house and rummaged through the place room by room. I'd thought of asking her to give the key back, but I didn't want to alienate her any more than I already had.

I took my time walking through the parlor looking for antiques with potential secret compartments, but I didn't think Mrs. Grayson would have hidden something so far away from her bedroom. Florence said she didn't wander far afield in the big house, preferring to stay down the hall in the sitting room near her books and TV.

I made my way to her sitting room and switched on the Tiffany lamp. A blue and gold tapestry chair sat in the center of the room like a throne, flanked on both sides by mahogany tables. One table held a small ceramic tray, and the other held a magnifying glass, a crossword puzzle book, several remote controls, and a vase of silk flowers. Directly across, sat a wooden loveseat. I imagined that was where the unlucky person who was taking a meeting with her had been forced to sit. Like having an audience with the queen.

I read some of the titles on the bookshelf by the fireplace: *Wuthering Heights*, *The Collected Works of Jane Austen*, *The Woman in White*, *Jane Eyre*, *The Great Gatsby*—all classics. I wondered if she kept her pulp fiction collection in another room away from prying— wait a minute. *The Great Gatsby* was one of my favorite F. Scott Fitzgerald novels. In the book, wasn't Jay Gatsby's real name James Gatz? Like Dr. Harold Gatz?

I pulled the book off the shelf and opened it. A small sheaf of newspaper clippings slid out and fell to the floor. They were the same ones I had found in the box Harold had stashed in the dumpster. Mrs. Grayson had kept Dr. Harold Gatz's ill-reputed past neatly filed inside the pages of *The Great Gatsby*.

Of course Mrs. Grayson would hide things in her books. What better place? What safer place? Florence, who admitted she found reading boring, would never look inside a book. It would never occur to her.

Doc Moreland had had to give up surgery because of a fatal mistake he'd made. Where would Mrs. Grayson hide information about him? In a book about doctors?

I scanned the bookshelves searching for Doctor

titles. *The Island of Dr. Moreau? Dr. Zhivago? Dr. Seuss? Dr. Doolittle?* I finally opened *Dr. Jekyll and Mr. Hyde* and found the information I had discovered about Dr. Moreland online.

Next up: Mayor Nash.

I took a deep breath and rubbed my aching neck. *Mayor Nash. Mayor Nash.* What was his first name— Sherman? No one called him Sherman. Everyone just called him Mayor—I stopped. I knew exactly where she'd hidden it. "Don't let me down, Mrs. Grayson. We talked about this book once because we both love Thomas Hardy." My fingers skimmed across a lovely dark green leather bound collection until I came to the volume I'd been hunting for. I pulled *The Mayor of Casterbridge* off the shelf and opened it.

An article from the *Richmond Times-Dispatch* had been placed between the pages near the back. *Oliver Sherman Nashton Won't Serve Time*, the headline read. I glanced over the article. It seemed that Wrenhaven's fine upstanding mayor, Sherman Nash, who had changed his name from Nashton, had been charged as the antagonist in a road rage incident resulting in the death of a beloved town icon.

Oliver S. Nashton was driving north on Monument Avenue in Richmond, Virginia, when a blue Subaru carrying three rowdy teenagers cut him off, forcing him into the median. Mr. Nashton proceeded to chase the driver, swerving in and out of traffic, while, according to witnesses, blowing his horn and screaming obscenities. Tearing through the double red light, he veered left to miss another vehicle and hit and killed an elderly homeless person, Tiberius Releford. Many of our readers will remember Tiberius as a familiar and much-loved fixture on some of Richmond's busiest street corners, dispensing sage advice, good cheer, and messages of hope from his wheelchair to all who were kind enough to stop. Mr. Releford's death has been ruled accidental, and the charge of manslaughter against Mr. Nashton has been dropped. Mr. Nashton's reckless driving charge, a class-one misdemeanor, still stands, punishable by a fine and the completion of a two-month anger management course.

I whistled through my teeth.

This information wasn't exactly earth-shattering, but I was sure Mayor Nash, AKA Oliver Sherman Nashton, wouldn't want it broadcast to his constituents. Threatening to expose it would be the perfect hold over someone in the esteemed and useful position of mayor. It would allow Mrs. Grayson to call the shots where the town was concerned. How many of her pet projects had he helped push through? The Riverwalk Festival? The new pavilion at Horse Creek Landing? Demolishing an entire neighborhood to build a park and name it after her? Mayor Nash must have influenced all those decisions.

Why had he stayed? His wife had passed on. Was it because of his daughter Holly? Now that his little girl had found the help she needed at the Art Factory and was finally starting to thrive, is that what kept him in Wrenhaven living under an old rich woman's thumb?

Being treated like a flunky by the town's demanding matriarch must have felt demeaning. And beyond humiliating. Everyone knew Mrs. Grayson had the mayor's ear, but was it degrading enough for him to kill her to make it stop? Or had he found out she'd changed her will and left nothing to the Art Factory as promised?

I put the books back on the shelf and went

downstairs. There were many other names in the address book, but I didn't look for them. Finding out the deepest, darkest secrets of people I had considered my friends made me feel like I needed to go home and take a shower. It wasn't helping me find out who tried to kill Mrs. Grayson. It only established a motive for the few people I suspected.

I climbed in Velma and closed the door, then sat for a few minutes checking my phone.

The wrought iron gate swung open to my left. A long, tearing screech, like graveyard ghosts make when they want to give you a heart attack.

I glanced in the side mirror expecting to see the mailman but instead spotted Travis Walters skulking behind the thick hedge. I dove beneath the car window and lay my head on the passenger seat. Travis had to have seen my car parked in the driveway, so probably assumed I was inside the house. I eased my hand up and unlocked the passenger door. If he tried to open it, and I was sure he would, I was going to be ready for him.

I waited, hunkered down in the seat, watching the steam from my breath fan across the basket weave seat cover with my heart pounding in my throat. After a few seconds, the handle on the passenger's side clicked softly. The Volkswagen door swung open.

I rose up, just far enough to see the stunned look on Travis Walters' young acne-scarred face, then roared like a wounded buffalo. He yelled a one-word obscenity, then turned and bolted across the lawn.

I shoved the driver's door open, scrambled out of the tiny front seat, and took off down the hill after him. He scaled the stone wall at the bottom of the garden in two easy strides, landed on the concrete sidewalk with a thud, and glanced behind him. I opted not to leap over the wall, a move I had neither the skills nor the nerve for, and detoured diagonally through the perennial bed beside the birdbath. The shortcut dropped me less than ten feet behind him. A maneuver that, judging by the look of astonishment on his face, he had not anticipated.

He ran down the sidewalk past the houses on Victorian Row. He was fast, as only a wiry sixteen-year-old kid can be, but I managed to keep up. My leisurely jogs around the neighborhood hadn't prepared me for a sprint like this, but so far, I was holding my own.

"I'm a runner, Travis," I shouted, ignoring the twinge in my side that was beginning to pinch. "I jog every day, and I can keep going for hours." I wasn't sure that was the absolute truth, but it sounded convincing enough to make him glance back to check my progress. He sped up, and so did I. "I mean it, kid," I panted. "I won't stop chasing you until you turn around and talk to me. And I know where you live. The white house with green shutters on the corner of Birch Street. Big honeysuckle bush blocking the porch. I run by it every day. So stop, already."

The boy slowed down.

"Please, honey. I promise I won't tell your dad what you did. I won't tell anybody. Just quit running and talk to me."

He stopped abruptly. On a dime, abruptly. It was all I could do not to crash into him. "Okay," he gasped. "What do you want?"

"Just to ask you a few questions."

He stared at me sullenly. "Like why did I hang the dead rat on your car?"

"That's one of them. Another one is: why did you

throw a rock through my father's living room window? And don't deny it, I have a witness who saw you fleeing the scene." I was bluffing, but from the sudden, panicked expression on his face, I knew he was guilty.

He pushed a lock of light brown hair out of his eyes. "I didn't throw it."

"Yes, you did. And I want to know why."

"Please don't tell my dad, Miss MacGill. You promised."

"I won't. But you've known our family since you were a little kid. You've helped my father paint. You trick-or-treat at our house. Why would you do something like that?"

He looked at me defiantly. "Because your dad took my dad's job away. And now my dad stays home all day and sits in front of the TV and drinks beer. Lots and lots of beer. I can't even talk to him." His voice cracked. "He's like a different person now because *your dad fired him.*"

"I'm sorry, Travis."

"At least when he was painting for Hit the Wall, he wouldn't drink until after dinner."

"He was drinking all day at work," I said gently. "People were complaining. That's why my father had to let him go."

"He drinks and drinks. And he's so sad all the time. He pulls out these old pictures of my mom from when she was alive, and just sits there, and looks at them and drinks."

"He needs help, honey. We need to get him some help." I put my hand on his arm. "We just need to figure out how." Travis looked up. The tough exterior he'd wrapped around himself like armor began to crumble.

His eyes glistened with tears. His lower lip trembled. It was all I could do not to put my arms around him and tell him it was going to be okay. But I knew better. He was a sixteen-year-old boy whose world was falling apart, and the last thing he would put up with was sympathy.

"Travis?" Dread washed over me. "Did you cut the brake lines on my father's van?"

His head shot up. "No way!"

"Are you sure? Because you're a smart kid. You could find out how to—"

"No! I swear! I didn't touch his van. I wouldn't do that." He wiped his eye with his fist. "I wouldn't, Maggie. I swear."

"Okay. But you're going to have to tell Pop about the window. And then you're going to have to figure out a way to pay for it. Agreed?"

He nodded.

"Okay." I stepped back. "That's all. You can go home now."

Travis started up the sidewalk. But this time he wasn't running. This time his shoulders were hunched and his head was bowed, as if going home was the last thing in the world he wanted to do. I stood for a moment watching him go, then blew out a long sigh. "Travis?"

He turned around.

"You still remember how to mix paint?"

"Yes, ma'am."

"Well, starting tomorrow, I'm going to be painting the town mural on the side of the courthouse wall, and I sure could use some help. They're paying me a lot more than I'm worth, so I'll have enough money to hire an assistant. Are you interested?"

A wide grin spread across his face. "Hell, yes,

Maggie! I mean, yes, Miss MacGill."

"Okay, then, meet me at Marvin's Paint Emporium—I still can't believe he named it that—on Monday afternoon at one o'clock sharp. Wear old clothes. You're gonna be a mess by the time you get home."

He nodded solemnly. "Thanks, Miss MacGill. You won't regret this."

"I hope not." I turned and started the slow jog back to my car. "I really hope not."

By the time I arrived at Grayson House, it was almost dark. Even in the middle of July, night came early in the mountains. Once the sun dropped behind the hulking presence of Blue Wolf, the air cooled, humidity dropped, and the streetlights popped on in self-defense.

I was taking the shortcut through the garden to my car when I received a text from Eli.

—Irena is letting me take Alex for an early dinner tonight. I'm meeting them at your brother's restaurant in a few. Join us?—

I stared at the text and took a slow, deep breath. Did I really want to do this? Did I really want to see him again? Was this crazy anticipation wrapping itself around me like a cool breeze what happy felt like?

—Sure— I texted back. *—Can I bring a date?—*

—Plus ones are optional— he answered.

I laughed but didn't reply. Let him think about that one for a bit.

Chapter 14

I parked my father's Honda in the tiny parking lot behind Comfort and Joy. Velma was a fun car to drive, but totally impractical for transporting a grumpy six-foot-three man with a broken ankle and two bruised ribs.

Pop had jumped at the chance to get out of the house and visit Jesse's restaurant, and I couldn't blame him. Everyone at Comfort and Joy loved Chef Jesse's father. The cast on his leg was sure to be oohed and aahed over while he was treated like a king. I wheeled him down the tree-lined street to the front entrance so Dottie, the effusive Black woman who seated customers at the front of the house, could fawn over him.

Dottie did not disappoint.

"Now, you come right on in here, Jesse's family," Dottie gushed, "and let me give you a hug. How's that leg of yours, Mr. MacGill? Heard you tried to fly off a scaffold." She winked at me. "You might want to lay off of those funny cigarettes for a while."

"Don't believe everything you hear, Dottie," Pop said.

I spotted Eli at a table for four in the back. "We're meeting someone, Dottie. I see him."

"Mrs. Grayson's grandson, Eli?" Dottie's dark eyes twinkled. "We had a nice long chat. He's nicer than the last Grayson grandson you dated. *Much* nicer."

"We're not dating," I said.

"Um-hmm." Dottie grabbed a couple of menus. "Well, I think he's a sweetheart. You could do a lot worse." She laughed again. "What am I saying? You *have* done worse."

"Thanks, Dottie."

I pushed Pop to Eli's table. The crowd was sparser than usual for a Saturday night, but the aromas enveloping me were an onslaught to my senses: steak sizzling on the grill, baked cinnamon bread, tangy Memphis barbecue, grilled chicken pot pies. Jesse's cooking never failed to surprise and delight me. Very comforting and joyous, indeed. I felt like I'd come home.

Eli helped Dottie remove a chair to accommodate Pop's wheelchair.

Eli grinned at me. I looked into his eyes—grayer than green tonight—and everything around me seemed to fall away: the din of voices, the soft clatter of plates, the easy strum of bluegrass music in the background. It all disappeared. If I didn't watch myself, I could be drawn to him like still water to a divining rod.

"Where's Alex?" I said.

"Irena's going to drop him off. She should have been here by now."

Pop picked up the paper printout with the day's specials. "I wish Jesse would get some decent menus. I like to know what my food's gonna look like before I order it."

"Use your imagination," I said.

"What's your favorite food, Eli?" Pop peered at him over his wire-frames. "You're a beach boy, so seafood, I bet."

"Soft-shelled crab, sir. Add a cold beer and a bowl of hush puppies with warm brown sugar dipping sauce, and I'm a happy man."

"Looks busy back there." Eli pointed to Jesse and another cook shoving plates under the warming light.

"Jesse likes to call it controlled chaos," I said.

Eli's gaze wandered around the dining room. From the collection of antique candy tins swinging from the overhead beams, to the hand-carved black bears beside the brick wall, to the cut stone fireplace where a painting of the Appalachian Mountains shrouded in a dreamy haze of fog hung over the mantle. "Is that one of yours?" he asked.

"It is. I gave it to Jesse the day he opened this restaurant."

"Nice to know you can paint mountains just as brilliantly as you can paint the sea."

"I expected the restaurant to be more crowded tonight," Pop said.

"Business is down," I said. "Probably because your fiancée's mother publicly accused me of murder."

"Ex-fiancée," Pop said. "And Florence has a vindictive side to her. Just like Trude. Damn, that reminds me. I hope Trude remembered to cancel Family Haul Movers. They're supposed to pick up some things from her storage unit and store them in my garage."

"Hello." Irena stood to the left of Eli holding Alex's hand. "Sorry we're late."

The image of her holding a pillow over Mrs. Grayson's face shot through my brain for an instant, and I tried to dismiss it. I also tried to dismiss the fact that she'd said everyone would be better off if I could just find it in my heart to jump off a swinging bridge somewhere.

"Luke's not with you?" Eli said. "I thought the two

of you were joined at the hip."

"Still at work," Irena said. "I'm meeting him later."

Alex ran to me with his arms outstretched. I hugged him and then signed "hello." I pointed to myself, then to Pop, and signed the word, "father."

Alex grinned, placed his foot on the wheelchair's metal footrest, and pivoted onto Pop's lap like he'd been doing it his whole life.

"He's used to my mother's chair," Eli said.

"Your mother's still in a wheelchair?" Pop said.

"She still needs to use it sometimes. Alex stays at our house in Kitty Hawk while Irena goes to—well, we don't know exactly where you go, do we, Irena?"

"And that just makes you a little bit crazy, doesn't it?" Irena chucked him playfully under the chin. "Oh, look, Eli has mashed his lips together. He does that when he wants to hide his thoughts." She tapped the top of his head. "Probably because it's so scary in there."

Eli's gaze settled on the stained glass sun catchers hanging in the window. Then on the salt and pepper caddy. Then on my face. His expression softened.

"There was a time when I had both Grayson boys fighting over me," Irena said, "and I had to decide which one I wanted." She smoothed the hair back from Eli's forehead. "I chose well when I picked Kyle, don't you think?"

Eli caught her hand, stopping it. "That's enough."'

Irena lowered her voice to a sultry whisper. "You have two days to decide if you will accept my final offer."

Eli's gray eyes turned to steel. "Sorry you have to leave now. I'll be sure and get Alex home before nine."

After she'd gone, Pop shook his head and laughed.

"That is one serious broad."

"I know Irena loves Alex," Eli said. "But she doesn't care about his education. He seems too young to send off to school by himself."

"You don't have to send him away," I said. "He could catch up with a tutor and then attend regular school. That's why the IDEA exists."

"The what?"

"Individuals with Disabilities Education Act. It provides children who have disabilities the same opportunity for education as children without disabilities. If Alex qualifies, most public schools are required to provide an education for him, whether he's blind or deaf or has dyslexia or ADHD. Alex has choices. He can either go to a school for the deaf or one that's mainstream. I'm not sure I'd want to be the only deaf kid in a school full of hearing children, but it is an alternative to separating him from his family."

"How do you know so much about this?"

"Because she's a teacher," Pop said. "And a damn good one."

"How long has it been since Alex has been evaluated by a doctor?" I said. "Technology has made great strides in the last five years—cochlear implants, special devices to help them read lips. One of the hearing impaired kids in my class learned SEE instead of American Sign Language."

"Signing Exact English. I've read about that."

"So there are options. And more help out there than you realize. You should make Irena aware of that before she decides to give up her child for money. It's the right thing to do."

"Oh, man," Pop said. "Here comes trouble."

Trude Claussen strode through the restaurant and stood beside Pop. Her long blonde hair frizzed around her face. Dark brown eyeliner was smeared beneath her left eye. She looked like she'd been crying. For hours.

"Who was the lady who was just here?" Trude asked.

"Irena Belka," Eli said. "She's my nephew's mother."

"She hangs around with a guy called Luke, doesn't she?" Trude said.

"She does," I said. "I think they're engaged."

"They are? Really?" Trude' face crumpled. "I didn't know they were serious."

"What are you doing here, Trude?" Pop said. "What's wrong?"

"I used to see her all the time at Mrs. Grayson's house. She and Luke—" She stopped. "I thought they were just friends. But then I saw her come in here, and I thought maybe Jesse knew her. But then I saw her talking to you, and I just want to know what's going on between them."

"She was dropping her little boy off," I said. "She and Luke are meeting later."

"I've got to go," Trude said abruptly. "If Irena comes back, don't say anything about me being here, okay? I don't want her to think I'm stalking her."

"I won't," Pop said. "But you need to tell me what this is about."

"I'm gonna miss you, Les." Trude leaned over and kissed the top of Pop's head. "We had a good run, didn't we, babe? But like you always said, 'Life is what happens when you're making other plans.'"

"Actually, that was John Lennon," I said.

Trude shot me a look. "You want to know what I won't miss, Frankie? *You.*"

The waitress brought our drinks, a basket of mini sweet potato biscuits, and four little crockpots full of flavored butters.

When I glanced up, Eli was staring at me. "How did you know Irena is considering accepting a monetary gift for giving up custody of Alex? Did Stephen tell you?"

"No, I overheard you arguing about it at the motel." I met his gaze without flinching. "While I was hiding in the alleyway beside your room. Eavesdropping."

"I thought I heard something out there. That was you?"

"That was me. Maggie MacGill, Girl Detective."

Pop brushed a few crumbs off the table and leaned back, pretending not to have heard the exchange between us. "So what's your bliss, Eli?"

Eli looked startled. "My bliss?"

"Your bliss. Your passion. What's your favorite thing to do when you're not being an education consultant?"

"I work on my father's old fishing boat. I walk the beach. I borrow my neighbor's Jeep and ride to the north end of the Outer Banks to see the wild horses."

"Are there really wild horses there?" Les said.

"Oh, yeah," Eli said. "They live in a fenced area, but it's so huge, they don't even know they're being protected. Guided tour companies take tourists out to see them. I always wanted to be a wild horse tour guide." Eli grinned. "Or a wild horse."

"It's not too late," I said. "We could go to the feed store tomorrow and pick up something for dinner."

He laughed then, crinkling the little lines around his

eyes.

My peripheral vision slammed into focus.

A man in a mask and dark blue hoodie was circling the seating area. He reached into his pocket with a gloved hand, spritzed the air with a small atomizer, then hurled four glass vials, one after the other, onto the floor. He shoved Dottie aside as he pushed his way through the double front doors and catapulted into the street.

People sat in stunned silence as the stench of sulfur and manure filled the air.

I pulled Alex onto my lap. My eyes had begun to water. "What's happening?"

"Stink bombs," Eli said.

The restaurant erupted.

People coughed. People laughed. People held their noses. They threw down money for their meals, grabbed up their children, and made a frantic, jostling dash for the door. I tossed my napkin on the table and stuffed my phone into my purse.

Eli flipped the brakes on Pop's wheelchair. "Can we take your father out the back way?"

"Yes, go. I've got Alex." I looped my purse strap across my chest and hoisted the five-year-old onto my hip. The boy whimpered and buried his face in my shoulder.

"It's okay, honey." I patted him on the back. "It only smells bad. It won't hurt you."

Eli handed Pop a folded cloth napkin. "Hold this in front of your nose, Mr. MacGill."

"What kind of stink bomb is that?" Pop rasped. "It smells like three-day-old roadkill."

Jesse pushed open the swinging door leading to the kitchen. "Pop! Are you—"

"Over here!" I yelled.

I followed Eli as he wound his way through the maze of tables to the kitchen door. The staff had already evacuated, leaving half-filled salad bowls and abandoned entrees ready for pickup strewn across the Formica worktop. Jesse held the swinging door while Eli navigated the wheelchair through the narrow opening. We made our way through the storage area and out into the fresh night air. A breeze blew toward us from Blue Wolf Mountain, and we drank it in.

"What the hell's going on?" Jesse cried.

"Somebody set off a couple of stink bombs," Eli said.

"But why?" Jesse pulled his black cook's cap off and slapped it against his thigh. "I mean, a few eggs thrown against the side of a restaurant because someone doesn't like their omelet is one thing, but…stink bombs? In my dining room? Why would somebody do that?"

"Someone wants me to give the inheritance back," I said.

"But why target my restaurant?" Jesse said. "The old bat didn't leave her friggin' money to *me*."

Alex snuggled his face into my shoulder. The line cook stood beside the brick wall, smoking, while Dottie and the two servers huddled together near the dumpster. The cook extinguished his cigarette then crossed the parking area to where we were standing. "Dottie called the sheriff, Jesse. He's on his way."

"Thanks, man." Jesse shook his head. "Look at the people running for their cars. This could ruin me. Who would want to ruin me?" I had never seen him look so vulnerable. "This restaurant is everything to me, and the only thing that can save it now is a miracle." He laughed.

"Maybe a Food Network star will show up in a red convertible and put it on TV."

"Stranger things have happened," Eli said. "I'm Eli Grayson, by the way."

"I know who you are," Jesse said.

"I'd like to help," Eli said, "but first, I need to get this little guy away from here. He doesn't understand what's going on."

"Neither do I," Jesse said.

Eli held out his arms and I transferred Alex to him. "It's okay, sport," Eli murmured, rubbing the boy's back.

"Is this your kid?" Jesse asked.

"Alex is Eli's nephew," I said. "He's hearing impaired. He's one of my students at the Art Factory." I touched Alex's shoulder. When he glanced up, I pointed to Jesse then touched my right index finger to my temple, signing the word "brother."

Jesse looked dazed.

Eli turned back to him. "Maggie won't like what I'm about to say, but make her tell you what she and your dad have been going through." Then, with Alex still nestled into his shoulder, he picked his way through the crowd of onlookers filling the narrow street and left.

"What's he talking about?" Jesse said. "The rock somebody chucked at Pop's window?"

"That was Travis Walters. He admitted he threw it because Pop fired his father."

"Pop?" Jesse said. "Did you know about this?" Pop stared at the ground. "Will the two of you please stop keeping me out of the loop and tell me what is going on?"

Sheriff Conley screeched to a halt beside the curb, blue lights flashing. He and a deputy jumped out and pushed their way through the crowd. "Stand back, folks.

We're coming through. You okay, Les? Jesse?"

"We're fine," Jesse said. "At least I remembered to turn the burners and the fryer off, so I won't have to watch all my hopes and dreams blow up in my face."

"Who called this in?"

"I did," Dottie said, walking up. "Some man in a hoodie went through the restaurant dropping stink bombs. One of the waitresses got a glimpse of his face before he covered it."

"Let me check inside first," the sheriff said. "Can you find that witness for me, Dottie? I want to talk to her." He lumbered down the street, huffing and puffing with each labored step, parting the throng of people like Wyatt Earp strolling into the O.K. Corral.

"What are you keeping from me?" Jesse said.

"Calm down," I said.

"Calm down?" Jesse shook his head. "My restaurant smells like a toilet that's been set on fire. No one who ordered food in the last twenty minutes is going to pay for it. Word that this place is bad news will rip through town like a freakin' fireball. And you're telling me to calm down?" He wiped his forehead with the back of his wrist. "What did Eli mean? What are you not telling me now?"

"Can you kids take this around back?" Pop said. "There's another crowd forming, and they're looking at you. I'll send Dottie for you when the sheriff gets back."

I followed Jesse around the building to the alleyway. Dark clouds streaked across the pink and gold sky. The heavy scent of honeysuckle growing thick beside the weathered fence hung in the air, reminding me of Mrs. Grayson's bedroom.

Jesse's eyes narrowed. "The fry cook told me about

your wild ride through town with no brakes. Is that what you don't want to tell me?"

"Sheriff Conley said the brakes were cut deliberately."

"Seriously?" Jesse sighed. "I am so over this, Maggie. You don't tell me anything. First, you get yourself fired, like what, a week ago? And I had to hear it from your principal. Then I find out you were driving through town with no brakes from the restaurant hostess."

"You've got a lot on your plate right now. I didn't want to add to the—"

"I can't believe we're having this conversation—*again.* Aren't you ever gonna realize I'm part of this family too? You and Pop keep everything from me—*everything*—and I'm sick of it. I want to know what's been going on, and I want to know now. Spill it."

I took a deep breath.

Once I started talking, spilling wasn't so hard. As long as I kept my eyes on the back of Sam and Dan's shop across the alley and not on Jesse's face. I listed it all: the brakes and the rat, Velma getting trashed, the rock through Pop's window, someone shoving Jules into my painting. I tried to relay the terrible feeling I had that if I didn't give the inheritance back, something awful was going to happen to one of us, and it would be my fault.

Jesse's eyes had grown as dark as the sky. "What about Pop's fall from the scaffold? What about that?"

"I don't know. The day he fell was the day Mrs. Grayson changed her will, but I was the one who inherited. Why would someone target our father?"

I followed his exasperated gaze down the alley. No

sign of Dottie.

"Jesse, I know I should have said something, but I wanted to keep you—"

"—from worrying."

"You say that like it's a bad thing."

"I'm tired of you deciding when I can and can't worry about our father." He glanced at the restaurant's back door. "When do you actually get your share of the inheritance?"

I pinched off a honeysuckle blossom. "It all depends on Mrs. Grayson's murder investigation. Until my name is cleared—"

"Cleared? Are you a suspect?"

"I'm a person of interest."

"But when you get the Grayson money, you won't have to—" He stopped. "Oh, my God. You're not gonna take it, are you? All that money and you're not—"

"I'm scared, Jesse. I'm scared for all of us. What if they never find out who killed Mrs. Grayson? What if the person who made sure she didn't live to see another day is going to make sure I won't be alive to inherit?"

"You're blowing this all out of proportion, Mags. Somebody's pissed off at Pop. It's as simple as that. Probably that stupid kid whose dad got fired for drinking on the job. He hung a dead rat on your car antenna. How lame is that? Sounds like something Stephen would do." He started to laugh. "Was the rat wearing a cashmere sweater and holding a martini glass?"

"I was never going to keep all the money anyway. Just enough to get us over this financial bump in the road and secure our future for a few years. That's fair, right? I want to donate some funds to the Art Factory and give some to Alex. The boy got cut out of the will because his father and mother weren't legally married, and that's so unfair. There are things and opportunities he will never be able to afford without this money. It will change his life."

"He's not your kid, Maggie. He's not even Eli's kid. What about your own family's needs? What about me and Pop? What about changing *our* lives? If someone is trying to frighten you into giving back the inheritance, I'll help you make them stop. You've never been one to back down from a fight. Don't start now."

It suddenly all seemed so hopeless.

Like life was testing me and I was failing miserably. Maybe the Universe was telling me to grow up and solve my own problems. That I needed to work harder to make my dreams come true instead of having them handed to me on a Grayson House silver tray.

"What if I did give the money back?" I asked quietly. "We could still survive. We could put our heads together and figure out a way to save the restaurant and pay off Pop's debts. We're MacGill's. We're smart. We're resourceful. We're—"

"—broke."

My idea was gaining steam. "We can do this, Jesse. You're a great chef. All we need to do is get the word out about Comfort and Joy, and I can help you do that. Until I find another teaching job, I can devote more time to my pet portrait business. Eli's mother owns a gift shop at the beach, and he thinks she might be able to sell some of the seascapes in my studio. My artwork could help pay for—"

"Your artwork is a joke."

I stepped back as if I'd been slapped. "What?"

"How many pet portraits have you sold online?"

"I don't know. Twelve."

"How many paintings of the ocean have you sold?"

"None, but I haven't tried to—"

"It's time to stop kidding yourself and face reality. You're never gonna make any money selling those stupid paintings. I gave up culinary school for…what? So you could go to art school? So you could get a teaching degree you didn't really want, teach art for four years, and get canned? So you could live in Pop's attic for the rest of your life and paint pictures no one in their right mind will ever, *ever* want to buy? It's bullshit, Maggie. Your life is bullshit."

My eyes filled with tears. The knot in my throat threatened to choke me.

But Jesse wasn't finished.

"Cooking was all I ever wanted to do. If I hadn't given up my college fund and gone to a culinary school, I could be living in Knoxville, or Asheville, or Denver. I could be working as an executive chef for some big restaurant in some big city. I'd have a following by now."

"I thought you gave me your college fund so I could have corrective heart surgery."

"I did it because Pop asked me to. There were all kinds of charitable organizations that would have footed the bill, but he was too proud to ask them. You and your damned heart operations screwed me out of the life I wanted to lead. So, thanks, Maggie."

I put my hand on my chest and pressed against the vertical scar. My heart—my poor mended heart that had been the cause of so much resentment for so many years—thudded along as if nothing had happened. As if my brother's words hadn't broken it again.

"I'm sorry," Jesse said. "I didn't mean that."

"Yes, you did. And you're right. My work is a joke. I'm wasting my time painting seascapes and dog portraits when I should be concentrating on the things I do best like painting walls and woodwork and kitchen cabinets."

"Jesse?" Dottie stood at the front of the alley. "Sheriff Conley is ready for you now."

"Coming." Jesse turned back to me. "I'm sorry, Mags."

I nodded to Dottie then walked past Jesse around the side of the building.

"No real damage done," Sheriff Conley was saying to my father. "But it left one hell of a stench. I don't know what this world is coming to. Where does somebody buy stuff called Liquid Ass? Off the Internet, I guess."

"Could I have a word with you first, Sheriff Conley?" I said.

"Sure, Maggie."

We stepped to the side and turned our backs to the crowd. "Dr. Harold Gatz is leaving town, and I have proof that Mrs. Grayson had information on him that may have resulted in her blackmailing him to stay here. The same goes for Mayor Nash."

"Honey, these men are two of the most upstanding citizens in Wrenhaven. I can't haul them in for questioning if I don't have any evidence."

"Mrs. Grayson kept a list of names in an address book I found. She hid incriminating information about the people on that list in the books in her sitting room. I'm sure the killer is someone in that book. Someone she kept on a leash. Someone who was tired of living in a town they hated and being bossed around by a woman they hated even more."

"Maggie," he said tiredly.

"I also have reason to believe Florence's daughter, Trude, was stealing from Mrs. Grayson and—"

"Do you have proof of that?"

"No, but Florence didn't deny it when I asked her about it."

"You've been talking to Florence?"

"Yes, and there's something else. Trude came into the restaurant tonight before the stink bombs got thrown. She looked like she'd been crying. I think she'd followed Irena there. She seemed really upset to find out Irena was engaged to Luke, so I don't know if anything is going on between the two of them. Do you think Trude could know something about Irena and Luke and Mrs. Grayson's death? Something she's been hiding?"

He shook his head and sighed.

"I'm not allowed to volunteer at the Art Factory or apply for a teaching job until Mrs. Grayson's death is resolved. You know about Pop's brakes and the broken window and my art show painting. You see what happened here tonight. My family is being targeted by someone who wants us to leave Wrenhaven, Tennessee, and never come back."

"I know, but if whoever tried to kill Mrs. Grayson finds out you're looking for evidence, it will only make things worse. Trust me."

"Ready, sweetheart?" Pop said.

"Go home," Sheriff Conley said to me. "Be careful, but let me deal with it."

I helped my father into his car then slid behind the steering wheel.

"Did you and Jesse clear the air?" Pop said.

"He's angry. He wants me to keep the inheritance."

"And you don't want to?"

"I just want to keep us all safe, Pop. That's all I've ever wanted." I turned onto Fairlane Road. "What was the matter with Trude tonight? I've never seen her like that."

"Neither have I. But it got me thinking: Before Mrs. Grayson died, Trude had this crazy idea I was going to be named sole beneficiary for Mrs. Grayson's estate. She kept talking about it as if it were a sure thing. Then when the woman only left me a car and lawnmower, she stopped pretending she liked me. I don't know where she got the idea I was going to be rich."

I stopped at the red light on Main Street. "Pop, if you thought Mrs. Grayson was such a terrible person, why did you let me work in her garden?"

He took his glasses off and polished the lens with the corner of his shirttail. "Because you're a grown woman, Maggie MacGill. You have to get to know people and judge them for yourself. Who knew you and Mrs. Grayson would find common ground with flowers and books? I'm glad you discovered a side of Mrs. Grayson worth knowing. Not everyone would try to do that." He squeezed my shoulder. "I'm proud of you."

My eyes misted with tears. How many times does an adult daughter get to hear her father say he's proud of her? "And Pop? Thanks for never calling me Frankie."

"You're welcome." Pop grinned. "And thanks for never calling me Leslie."

I pulled into the driveway and parked beside the trash cans lined up against the fence. "Tomorrow is trash pick-up day, right?"

"Right. You'll have to haul it out for me this week." He turned to me and laughed. "What is this? I haven't seen such a determined look on your face since you were nine years old and decided you were never going to eat peas again."

"And I never did. It was something Jesse said tonight. It made me realize it's time to clean house."

Chapter 15

I'd known what I was going to do the moment Jesse said my artwork was a joke.

His words had cut me to the quick. But at least he'd told me the truth.

"You have so much talent," my artist mother had said. And I had believed her. I should have known it was an exit line. When Sarah MacGill had said those words to me, she already had a packed suitcase hidden in the closet, a full tank of gas, and her passport tucked into the side pocket of her new leather purse. She hadn't meant what she'd said about my artwork. She'd only wanted to leave her daughter with something positive. A sweet, warmhearted memory to keep me from wasting money on a lifetime of therapy.

I held up the small seascape I'd been working on. Jesse was right. Painting pictures no one wanted to buy was a ridiculous waste of time. And somewhere in my heart of hearts, I think I had always suspected that was true.

The knot in my chest ached.

I pulled two seascapes from the wooden bin and propped them against the wall. I gathered an armful of canvases and stacked them beside the door. I poured myself a glass of wine and added forty-two more to the pile. The larger ones, I'd have to slide across the wooden railing and down the banister one by one.

The dog portraits were something I was obligated to finish, and even though they were easy to bang out, I was proud of them. In the morning, I would check my computer for any new customers, then close down my Etsy account. Then, a person of interest or not, it was time for me to start the long arduous chore of applying for teaching positions.

I opened the door to the deck and began hauling the paintings down to the street. I worked methodically well into the night making trip after trip, careful to move quietly through the yard beneath my father's bedroom window so I wouldn't wake him. Once I was done, I looked at the canvases leaning against the trashcans, stacked neatly against the curb, and blew out a long, shuddering sigh.

What would Eli say when he found out I'd thrown my life's work in the garbage? Would he understand? Or would he tell me I should have thought it through more carefully? And why did I care what he thought? Except for the occasional little zaps of electricity sparking between us, we'd never really been on the same wavelength. The only thing we ever agreed on was the fact that life didn't always turn out like you wanted it to. Sometimes it never came close.

After a few restless hours of sleep, full of dreams about Jesse and the restaurant and bears roaming wild on Blue Wolf Mountain, I brewed a cup of strong coffee and quietly let myself out the side door. I hadn't bothered to change out of the leggings and sweatshirt I'd slept in, but I was anxious to know if the trash truck had picked up my paintings. It wasn't that I was having second thoughts; I just needed to know where they were. Sitting beside the front curb for the neighbors to see or on their way to the county dump.

I walked down the drive. Dew glistened on the overgrown lawn like ice crystals. Dappled sunlight shone through the neighbor's trees. The morning air felt like velvet against my face. I rounded the curve and took a deep breath.

The parkway was bare. Both garbage cans stood empty with their tops gaping open like baby birds waiting to be fed. The trashmen had taken everything: every canvas, every sketchbook, every watercolor. All of them—gone. The narrow rectangular depressions in the wet grass were the only indication anything had ever been there.

Well, that was that.

No looking back. No regrets. Onward and upward.

It was all for the best. I knew that as well as I knew my own name. Both of them. So why did I feel like the gaping hole I had just blown into in my life would never close again?

I started back up the driveway.

The latch hanging on the garage door looked bare without a padlock. Where was the padlock?

Wait a minute. Wasn't some moving company supposed to drop off Trude's things from her storage unit and store them in our garage? Pop had mentioned he hoped Trude had cancelled Family Haul Movers. Had he forgotten to remind her? Or had Trude just forgotten on her own? It would be so like her to forget. Or get the day wrong. Or decide to call it quits with Pop and still let the movers haul her stuff out of a storage unit she had to pay for. Pop was a nice guy. He would never charge Trude to keep her crap in our garage, and she knew it.

I searched along the gravel path behind the climbing

roses, then beside the white fence where the garbage cans were stored, but the silver padlock was nowhere to be found. It was probably inside the garage sitting on a shelf.

The garage door stood slightly ajar. I pushed it the rest of the way open, curious about the things Trude had sent over. I didn't really know Trude, but she had never hidden her disdain for me. She seemed to relish embarrassing me, especially when my father was in the room. She liked to ask me questions. Personal questions. Mostly about my sex life, or lack of it. Fun times.

There had been no love lost between the two of us, and I could honestly say, I was not going to miss Trude one little bit.

I flipped the switch by the door, flooding the interior of the old double-car garage with fluorescent light. My father's work area took up most of the room, consisting of a large wooden farm table and eight floor-to-ceiling steel shelves lining the walls. His tools resided on one side, painting supplies on the other, with everything arranged in a seemingly haphazard fashion known only to him. Which drove the methodical part of me crazy. When he saw the stacks of plastic containers and cardboard liquor boxes holding the belongings of the woman he was no longer going to marry encroaching on his space, he was not going to be happy.

Some of Trude's boxes looked like they'd been dropkicked across the street. Some hadn't even been taped shut. But that was typical Trude. She was always in a hurry trying to pull herself together—grabbing her shoes, putting on lipstick, fluffing her already fluffy hair. Half the time she forgot to fasten the front of her shirt. Or maybe that wasn't an accident.

I lifted a cardboard flap and peered inside the box. "Holy—"

"Whatcha doing?"

I jumped and spun around.

Eli Grayson stood in the doorway holding a cardboard container with two sleeved coffee cups from Mac's Diner. "Sorry, I didn't mean to startle you."

"Where did you come from? I didn't see Big Blue parked on the street."

"Big Blue," he said. "I like that. Not as catchy a name as Velma, but it works."

"These boxes are from Trude's storage unit. They were delivered yesterday, even though she and Pop have called off the wedding." His eyebrows raised. "Okay, I know I shouldn't have opened one, but my curiosity got the best of me, and—" I grabbed a fistful of necklaces and held them up. "This is what I found."

Eli set the cup carrier down. "Let me see."

He raked his hand through the jewelry—pearls, garnet necklaces, jet beads, gold chains, tangled together like a nest of shiny snakes, and all of them looking old and expensive. "I think this jewelry belonged to my grandmother. What was Trude going to do with it?"

"Sell it."

"You don't sound surprised."

"Irena told me she'd seen Trude sneaking in and out of Grayson House with a bag, and thought she might be taking things. I mentioned it to Florence, and judging from her reaction, I think she knew it was true."

"I talked to Florence yesterday after you did, but all she said about Trude was that she was sad Trude wasn't going to marry your father and finally settle down."

"She knows about their breakup then. I wasn't sure."

I looked at the stacks of boxes. "Wonder what else Trude stole from Grayson House?"

"Let's find out." Eli reached for another box and opened it. He pawed through a cluster of plastic grocery bags and held one up to the light. "These items are from my grandfather's Civil War collection: white lead bullets, Union and CSA belt buckles, brass buttons with eagle insignias. There are also pieces from his Civil War chess set." His eyes met mine. "I wonder how long Trude's been stealing from my grandmother and hiding it in her storage unit?"

"I don't know."

"What about your father? Do you think he knows Trude is a Class A thief?"

"I'm sure he doesn't have a clue about any of this. If he had suspected Trude was stealing from Grayson House, he would have said something."

"Or maybe Florence stole it and hid the loot in Trude's storage unit? Remember what Grandmother claimed in her will? That Florence had filched her missing diamond choker?"

"Or do you think Florence was covering for Trude?"

"Maybe. If Grandmother found out about this and threatened to turn Trude over to the sheriff, Trude would be desperate to keep her quiet."

"And it would be one hell of a motive for murder." I helped him close the boxes. "What should we do first? Talk to my father or call the sheriff?"

"What's in there?" He pointed to an old flat-topped steamer trunk sitting beneath a stack of containers. "Does that belong to Trude?"

"It's not ours."

"Then I think we should open it."

Eli lifted the plastic containers off the trunk and set them on my father's work table.

I didn't know much about steamer trunks, but this one had been cared for meticulously. The aged dark wood had been polished to a rich patina, the studded leather straps were still unbroken and pliable, and the two brass hinge locks looked shiny and smooth.

"Let's do it, then." I flipped the hasps and lifted the lid.

At first, I thought a mannequin had been stuffed inside the trunk. One of the old ones that used to grace department store windows with wigs that always sat slightly askew and arms screwed into their torsos, positioned into weird angles no human could ever achieve. I wondered why this one had been folded into a fetal position and wrapped in a blue plaid blanket that looked vaguely familiar.

"What's in there?" Eli came to stand beside me. "What are you—oh, shit."

I stared at the dead body, listening to the seconds tick by on an alarm clock my father kept on the shelf. Long blonde curls wound around the woman's face. The matted hair on the side of her head looked wet. Her bare toes, the nails painted a strange aqua color that I had only ever seen on one other person, were calloused from being smashed into pointy-toed heels.

I was vaguely aware of Eli's arm sliding around my waist and pulling me back. I wasn't sure how long it took me to realize the mannequin was Trude. Or how many more seconds to realize she had been murdered.

But what I did know, without question or uncertainty, was that once I closed the trunk lid and went to wake my father, nothing would ever be the same.

****

Pop sat at the kitchen table with his ankle cast balanced on a vinyl chair, looking as shaken as I felt. "I can't get my head around this. Are you sure it's Trude? I mean, are you absolutely sure it's her?"

"Yes, Pop," I said. "Sheriff Conley is out front talking to Eli. The medical examiner has already arrived. We didn't touch anything except the trunk and the jewelry and a few boxes."

"Holy hell," Pop said.

"After the movers delivered Trude's stuff, you didn't go out there and touch anything, did you?"

"I never went in the garage." He picked up his coffee cup and put it back down again. "I don't understand. Did Trude steal all that jewelry from Mrs. Grayson? And the Civil War artifacts too?"

"Eli recognized most of it. Stephen will have to identify the rest of the collection."

"How did Trude die? Do we even know how she died?"

"It looked like she was hit on the back of the head. There was blood in her hair and on the front of her knees."

Pop shook his head. "Poor little Trude."

"I called Jesse."

"Now, why did you do that? You know he's busy cleaning up the restaurant from the stink bombs."

"Jesse doesn't think I keep him in the loop. So I'm keeping him in the loop."

"What about Florence? Did anyone call her?"

"Sheriff's going out to her place after the medical examiner finishes. "

"But you recognized the—you're sure it was Trude,

right?"

"It was Trude, Pop." My eyes misted with tears. Not because I would miss Trude. But because it was such a ghastly, shocking thing to happen in your own garage.

I sat in the chair opposite my father. "I'm sorry, Pop."

"Honey, me too." He sighed, then gave a little laugh. "Not as sorry as Trude, though."

"Does Trude still have any of her belongings here? I know she used to keep a few things in your bathroom upstairs. Are they still there?"

"She was supposed to come by yesterday and get her stuff, but she never showed up. She still has some clothes in the closet and her travel-sized toiletries in the bathroom. She keeps a cardboard file box in the cedar chest at the bottom of the bed. Not sure what's in it. Some kind of papers. I saw her looking through them one day."

Sheriff Conley came into the kitchen.

"Coffee, sheriff?" I said.

"No, thanks. Eli's gone to find Stephen. I just wanted to let you know the M.E. is finished, and they're taking the body to the lab in Knoxville. We don't have the facilities here in Wrenhaven to process it properly. I'll drive her mother down to make an identification." He pulled a white handkerchief out of his pocket and wiped his brow. "I sure dread telling Florence what's happened to her girl. She's going to be heartbroken. Trude was all she had."

"It's a sad day," Pop said.

"We have evidence that Trude was killed at her storage unit," Sheriff Conley said. "Then her body was moved here in the trunk. I'm still gonna have to ask you a few questions, Les."

Pop nodded.

"I understand you and Trude had parted ways."

"A few days ago," Les said. "She said she wanted out of the relationship, but I was ready to break it off with her too."

"She died sometime last night," Conley said. "Maggie said you talked to Trude at Jesse's restaurant. Did you come straight home after you left?"

"Yes," Les said. "Maggie and I both did. I went to bed but couldn't sleep. Maggie was upstairs dragging those damned canvases back and forth across the floor half the night."

Conley nodded. "What time did the movers deliver Trude's things yesterday?"

"I'm not sure," Les said. "They called around four and said they were running late. I called Trude to tell her to call them off, but it went to Voicemail. So before Maggie and I went to dinner, I hung the garage key on the hook beside the back door for them in case they showed up. I forgot to check on it when we got back."

"You said she was killed at the storage unit," I said. "What was she doing there if all her stuff had been moved to our house?"

"Oh, she still had things left," Conley said. "An old mattress, a bottle of Jack Daniels whiskey, some more boxes. And a bronze horse head sculpture thing."

"Maybe she was meeting someone," I said. "Mattress? Bottle of Jack? Not exactly a suite at the Hilton, but private."

"Do you know of anyone who'd want to hurt Trude?" Conley said.

"Nobody," Les said. "She was a fun-loving gal.

Young. Happy. Lots of friends. Her shop, Smiles for Miles, was ready to go under—she was in debt up to her ears—but talking to her, you'd never know it."

Conley crossed his arms over his chest. "And you knew the shop was failing when you got engaged? You weren't worried about going halves on that kind of debt?"

"I figured she'd declare bankruptcy, and that would be that. But yes, I wanted her to close it before we were married."

"How about you, Maggie?" Conley said. "Know of anybody who would do something like this to Trude?"

"I don't."

"How did you feel about having a stepmother so many years younger than yourself?"

"Pop was happy, so it wasn't something I thought about too much."

"Still, it can't have been easy. My wife Janine said she heard Trude complaining to somebody down at the Bear Claw Bakery that she and your dad didn't have any privacy."

"Bull," Pop said.

"Trude knew I was planning to move out before their wedding," I said. "I'd been looking for a place."

"So why'd she call off the engagement, Les? Had she found somebody else?"

"Pretty sure that was the case," Pop said. "She hung on as long as she did because, for some strange reason, she thought I was going to inherit the Grayson estate. When I didn't, she was done."

"I'm still not sure why Mrs. Grayson left her estate to you, Maggie," Conley said.

"Neither do I," I said. "Unless she did it to teach her

grandsons and great-grandson not to count their chickens. She'd led Stephen to believe that he and Eli were in the will. Stephen moved to Wrenhaven and spent years trying to stay in her good graces."

"And then she left him a walking stick," Conley said.

"A pretty rare and expensive one, as it turns out. But not what he was expecting."

"He was surprised he didn't get more," Pop said. "At the reading of the will, his face turned purple. I thought he was going to explode like that girl in Willy Wonka who turns into a blueberry."

"Violet," the sheriff and I said at the same time.

Sheriff Conley grinned and shrugged. "I have kids."

"That was my excuse for years," Pop said. "Then I had to face that fact that I love Willy Wonka, and own it."

Conley laughed. "You're a man's man, Les."

"Any leads on who dropped the stink bombs at Comfort and Joy last night?" I asked.

"Not yet. But we lifted some prints from a canister we found in the alley. Hopefully, we can match them." Conley sighed. "Liquid Ass stink bombs. I'm getting too old for this." He stopped at the door. "Whoever killed Trude must have been as strong as an ox. She was bludgeoned on the back of the head, so she had to have been dead weight when they stuffed her in the trunk and moved it to your garage. We all know Trude wasn't exactly skin and bones."

"No," Pop said, tearing up. "But she sure had a way about her."

After Conley left, I couldn't get to Pop's bedroom fast enough.

The towering four-poster he'd slept in with my mother stood empty in the corner of the room. The giant futon he used now was shoved sideways against the far wall. It seemed sweet, and a little romantic, to imagine a man couldn't sleep alone in the bed he'd once shared with the love of his life. But Pop had never struck me as romantic. Instead of searching for another Grand Passion, his forays into the dating world with women half his age seemed like something he did just to pass the time.

I found the box Trude had left in the old cedar chest under two pillows and a green thermal blanket. I'd had the presence of mind to grab a pair of latex gloves from the kitchen drawer before I left Pop staring into his third cup of coffee, and I pulled them on.

I opened the cardboard box and lifted out a sheaf of papers—mostly computer printouts with paperclipped handwritten notes. As I rifled through them, many of the names in Mrs. Grayson's address book jumped out at me. The names had been run through search engines and background check sites like Truthfinder and Intelius. Pop had said Trude was a whiz when it came to computers, and here was the proof. Trude had been doing Mrs. Grayson's research for her. Probably as a way to keep Mrs. Grayson from having her arrested for stealing.

I closed the box and stuffed it back in the chest. I thought about calling the sheriff, but so far, he hadn't seemed to care much about any of the pertinent information I had discovered. But I still felt morally obligated to tell him what I'd found of Trude's, whether he blew me off or not.

Before I tracked down Conley, there was one more place I needed to visit. One more person I needed to talk to who probably knew more than any of us. And I was going to need one very large salted caramel toffee blondie to do it.

Chapter 16

I'd spent all day Sunday dreaming of the ocean and wishing it were Monday.

By the time it *was* Monday, and I'd swung by Bear Claw Bakery and arrived at Percy DePaul's office, I was two espressos in and impatient to finish what I'd come to do.

I'd called Delores and set up the earliest meeting possible under the guise of signing back the inheritance to the Grayson family. I didn't like misleading her, but I needed her advice as soon as possible, and I knew she would make me a priority if it sounded urgent.

I'd survived another sleepless night, which had been exhausting but productive. I'd made lists. Charted timelines. Tried to weed out suspects. And thought long and hard about the Grayson inheritance and the risks I was willing to take to keep it.

My family came first. That was the bottom line. And even though Jesse had injured my ego by criticizing my artwork, he'd said something in the alley that night that had resonated with me so deeply; I couldn't stop thinking about it. He said I had never backed down from a fight.

I'd never really thought of myself as a wounded warrior, but I guess that's what I had become. I'd gone to bat for my father when the bank wouldn't give him a loan. I'd badgered the insurance company until they'd agreed to pay for my grandmother's cataract surgery. I'd stood up to Greg Harwell in the middle of Fat Daddy's and warned him if he ever called me Frankie again I was going to learn Jujitsu and change him from a bass to a soprano. Little insignificant fights to be sure. But fights I hadn't backed down from.

I swung open the door to Attorney DePaul's office and ducked inside.

The light brown box with the Bear Claw Bakery logo made Delores' eyes sparkle. "Oh, my," she said in her breathy little voice. "What have you got there, Maggie MacGill?"

"These are for you, Delores." I handed her the toffee blondies. "Just a little thank you for seeing me on such short notice this morning. I know how busy you are."

Delores peeked into the box and sighed. "What a glorious surprise. I'm going to save these for my break." She smiled up at me. "Now, how can I help?"

"I want to run something by you about accepting Mrs. Grayson's inheritance. I've had second thoughts about refusing it, and I trust your judgement, Delores. I need to know if you think my new proposition is feasible, and what I need to do to start the ball rolling."

"I'd be happy to help," Delores said.

"Oh, good. Pop said you were the best."

"Oh, that Les." She blushed. "How sweet of him."

I pulled the notepaper from my purse and unfolded it. I explained my plan to keep the house and its contents but only retain part of the business inheritance: two years of profits from The Grayson Group instead of five, with the stipulation that Alex be included as an equal recipient for the remaining three years. This would give him a nice nest egg for the future and assure that he'd be taken care of. I'm not sure why I felt so protective of him. But if Eli was right about Irena's greediness, I didn't want her to be able to cash in on her son's birthright.

If Delores had been surprised by the proposition I had just presented her, she didn't show it. But as she turned to scan and copy the list on her printer, I caught the tiniest smile and a nod of approval. She assured me that she would have the papers drawn up and ready to sign by the afternoon. I could drop by whenever it was convenient.

"And Delores?" I said. "Keep this just between us, okay?"

"Well, of course, Maggie. I'm a professional."

Now that the attorney/client part of the visit had been completed, Delores didn't waste any time pumping me for information about Trude's death. I should have known that finding a dead body on our property would be headline news, and Delores loved news. She peered over her round glasses and twisted her face into a mixture of curiosity and concern. "So how is Les? I couldn't believe it when I heard his *fee-yon-say* was found stuffed in a trunk in his garage."

"Yes, it's been awful. But they had broken off their engagement several days before."

"You don't say." Delores looked incredibly happy. "Such a shame."

I had always suspected the majority of single straight women over forty who lived in Wrenhaven—and for a small town, their numbers were legion—harbored a secret crush on my father. Several of them had tried to strike up a friendship with me in the hopes it might further their cause. Single straight over-forty Delores Goldstein was the leader of the pack.

"Poor Florence," Delores said. "She's had her hands

full with that daughter of hers. Growing up, Trude was always in trouble. And wild. Florence worried that someday she would get into a dangerous situation and come to a bad end. Maybe that's what finally happened."

"I can't imagine who would want to hurt her."

"Florence was sure Les would be a stable influence in Trude's life, but I had my doubts. Oh, the stories Florence would tell about that girl when she was working late."

"Working late? At Mrs. Grayson's house?"

"No, here. She cleans our offices after hours twice a week."

"She does?" *How did I not know this?*

"Florence would leave Mrs. Grayson's house, run home to feed the cats, and get here by 6:30. But now that she isn't working for Mrs. Grayson, she comes in around 5:00."

"Would she have access to keys and things? Could she look up a file if she wanted to?"

Delores pushed a thatch of gray permed curls back from her face. "I suppose she could if she knew where to look. Most of our files are digital now and password protected. But some are still on paper stored in filing cabinets. Wills mostly. A lot of our clients are elderly without home computers, and we still use paper for them. Of course, we scan the documents too."

"What about Mrs. Grayson's original will?"

"Oh, it was definitely on paper. Of course, it wasn't the original will, even though we keep calling it that. A codicil was added after her great-grandson Alex was born. But that's the version it would revert to if you refuse the inheritance." Delores dropped her voice to a whisper, even though she and I were alone in the office.

"In the old will, she was *very* generous to her family, including her great-grandson. Not like the revised one."

"That's what Eli said. Do you have any idea why she changed it?"

"I haven't a clue. But she was most insistent we go to her house that afternoon and get everything squared away. I had to cancel a hair appointment to accommodate her."

"Did she mention me? Did you know she had decided to leave everything to me?"

"Well, yes. I mean, I had to type it up, so I was aware."

"Did she say why?"

Delores thought for a minute. "She said you were very sensible. And good with flowers. And a great reader. I guess she admired that."

"One more question: Why would someone read the revised will and have the crazy idea that my father was going to inherit instead of me? I thought the wording was very clear."

"Because both of you have the same first name and middle initial. I can't remember what they are right off the top of my head, but—"

"Leslie M. MacGill. I'm Leslie Margaret and my father is Leslie Malcolm."

"That's right. When I was typing the names into the document for clarification, I remember thinking how unusual that was. Sounds very British."

"So if someone glanced at the will and zeroed in on Pop's name instead of mine, they would naturally assume he was the one named as beneficiary."

"Yes." Delores frowned. "But who would do that? Not Florence, surely. We keep our files under lock and key. Mr. DePaul is very careful about security here."

"I'm sure he is." I smiled and stood to leave. "But it is something to think about."

****

After leaving DePaul's office, I turned my phone back on and checked my messages.

Only one. From Jules. *Call me ASAP.*

"You're right, Maggie," Jules said. "According to Maureen, something looks very fishy about Holly Nash's birth certificate. The scanned copy on file lists Oliver Sherman Nash as her father, but if you look closely, you can see that letters beside the word *Nash* have been covered with a white-out pen. And not a very good one. Looks like his name was Sherman Nashton, and he shortened it to Nash."

"Thanks, Jules. And please thank Maureen in the office. I owe you both one."

So, the info in Holly's file corroborated the evidence I had found in Mrs. Grayson's copy of *The Mayor of Casterbridge*. Good to know Trude's research had been spot-on.

I wasn't sure what to do next.

I still had a few hours before I was scheduled to meet Travis at the paint store. I thought about trying to talk to Florence again—I wanted to ask if she had been snooping through DePaul's files and seen Mrs. Grayson's original will. But now was not the time. Florence had just lost her daughter. I couldn't barge in asking questions. Not yet.

I'd always found it strange that Florence had encouraged Trude to cozy up to my father. Delores thought it was because she hoped Pop would be a stabling influence in her daughter's wild life. But I was beginning to think Florence might have given her approval so readily because she thought Pop would inherit the Grayson fortune. If Trude married into that kind of money, they would both be set for life.

Back at Pop's house, I was surprised to see Jesse's car parked out front. And even more surprised to see him and my father sitting on the sofa, waiting for me.

"Have you heard anything else about Trude's death?" Jesse said.

"Nothing," I said. "What about you, Pop? Has Conley called?"

"No, but I keep wondering if her killer knew that trunk was gonna end up in my garage? How long did they think Trude would stay hidden before anyone found her?" Pop shook his head. "Poor Trude. Strange how things turn out sometimes. So different from what you expect."

"Pop," Jesse said, grinning. "Can I change the subject to something…good?"

"You've been about to bust a seam since you got here. What's going on?"

"I've got some news," Jesse said. "And for once, it's great." He laughed and sat down. Then, unable to contain himself, jumped up again. Without his stiff chef's coat covering up his *No Crying in the Cooler* T-shirt, he looked like an overgrown kid.

"It's freakin' amazing," Jesse said. "I went back to my office last night to work on the menu for this week and saw that I'd missed a call on the restaurant's landline. I hardly ever use that phone, but the number is still on some of the flyers, so I've kept it alive. Anyway, a producer from the Food Network had called and left me a message. They're putting together a new show called *Dish Jockeys*." He gulped in a breath. "It's about a group of talented young chefs who are trying to open their own restaurants and make their dreams come true."

"And you're going to be one of the talented young chefs?" I asked.

"Yes," Jesse said. "I mean, there's a chance. They said they'd heard great things about Comfort and Joy, and if everything checks out, and they like the food as much as they think they will, they want to feature me on the premiere episode."

"Oh, Jesse, that's wonderful." I threw my arms around my brother. "It's exactly what you wished for. How did they hear about you?"

"I don't know," Jesse said. "I was so excited, I forgot to ask. They must have seen the review in the *Knoxville News Sentinel*. Or maybe the one in the *Asheville Citizen-Times*. I don't know." He whooped. "I don't care. They're sending a crew out in a couple of weeks to interview me and taste my food."

"I'm so proud of you, son." Pop took his glasses off and wiped his eyes.

Jesse laughed. "I was so bummed Saturday night with the stink bombs and all. But today, everything is great." He smiled. "Right now, it's close to perfect."

"Don't get too cocky," Pop said. "The minute you think your life is perfect is the minute it decides to kick you in the ass."

Chapter 17

"Sheriff Conley," I shouted from the rooftop. "Hold up a minute."

I swung my leg over the drainpipe and climbed down the ladder leaning against the side of the courthouse building. "Go ahead and start the base coat, Travis. I'll be back in a minute."

"Looks like you've got a good helper there," the sheriff said. "I understand why Les had to let Bob Walters go, but I think it's nice you're helping his son."

I wiped my hand on my overall strap. "Have you had any leads on Trude's death?"

"We know she was hit with that bronze unicorn head. Forensics found blood on it."

"Eli said it used to sit on the mantel in Mrs. Grayson's sitting room."

"Only one of the indoor security cameras was turned on at the storage unit, but we found a reliable witness who saw someone go into the building with Trude on Saturday night. They couldn't tell if the suspect was a man or a woman, but they said Trude was talking and laughing. So it doesn't look like she was coerced in any way."

"Do you think she was with the guy she was cheating on my father with? Have you been able to find out his name?"

"Not yet. But we have a couple of leads."

"Was the witness able to give you a description?"

"White guy. Average build and height. Baseball cap. Super helpful, huh?" He laughed. "Stephen looked through the stolen items recovered from your garage. He's sure there are still things missing from Grayson House that haven't been accounted for."

"Trude kept a box in a cedar chest in Pop's bedroom. It contains printouts of incriminating material she'd gathered on some of the residents in Wrenhaven. The names seem to correspond with the names in the address book I found in Mrs. Grayson's desk. You know, the one you didn't think was relevant? I'm sure Trude was researching people's lives for Mrs. Grayson." I took a deep breath. "I told you there was a file on Mayor Nash. A few years ago, he—"

"Are you talking about the automobile accident he had?"

"Is that what you're calling it?"

"I know all about Sherman Nash. I had him checked out the minute Mrs. Grayson started pushing the council so hard to appoint him as mayor."

"Then you know Nash isn't his real name."

"Of course, I know. Don't look so surprised. I weighed the risks very carefully before I gave him my endorsement to govern Wrenhaven."

I stared at Sheriff Conley. "Seriously? I thought you swore an oath to protect the people of Wrenhaven from—"

"From what? From a man who made a mistake and is trying to atone for it? From a man who lost his wife and is raising a special needs child on his own? From a man who—like all of us might someday—deserves a second chance?"

Eli came out of Sam and Dan's Ice Cream Parlor with Alex in tow. He looked at our faces and stopped. "You guys were talking about Trude's death, weren't you?"

"She was killed by the unicorn," I said.

"Such a waste," Eli said. "I knew Trude the summer I stayed at Grayson House. We were kids, but she was fearless. And funny." Eli shook his head. "Things like this aren't supposed to happen in a small town. People move to small towns to get away from things like this. How's Florence doing?"

"Not good," Conley said. "I'll check in with you later, Maggie. I need to get back."

"Have you looked at the sky lately?" Eli said. "There's a storm coming."

"We're trying to get the base coat on," I said. "I brought a plastic tarp to pull over the paint if it rains." I glanced at the gray clouds sweeping low over the mountain. "I'd say we've got at least another half hour before the heavens open."

"Are you always this optimistic?"

I laughed. "Not usually."

"Alex now knows how to sign 'ice cream.' " With his free hand, Alex pretended to hold a cone and lick it.

"Amazing." Eli was holding Alex's hand and a cone of butter pecan ice cream, grinning at me. That, and the little crinkles around his blue/green/gray eyes, made me open my mouth and blurt, "Since the restaurant is closed tomorrow, Jesse is cooking brunch at Pop's house before the Founder's Day Parade. Would you like to join us?"

He looked pleased. "Are you sure it's okay?"

"Well, you are the guy who pried a dead rat off of Velma. So that kind of automatically secures you an invitation."

"That would be great, then." He glanced up. "Who's your assistant on the roof?"

"That's Travis Walters. Remember him? Hey, Travis," I yelled. "Say hello to a friend of mine."

Travis lifted his hand to wave, then recognized Eli and blanched.

"Hey, Travis." Eli laughed. "I'm sure glad you're up there and not on a bike."

"Travis is sorry about almost running us down the other day, aren't you, Travis?" I said.

"Yes, Miss MacGill," Travis said.

"And he's never going to ride his bike that recklessly again, are you, Travis?"

"No, Miss MacGill." Travis grinned and picked his way around the paint supplies stacked on the roof. He reloaded his roller and continued to paint over the rough brick.

"Asking Travis to help you," Eli said. "That was a nice thing to do."

"He's a good kid at heart. Just like you, Alex." I made a face at the little boy and pretended to gobble his ice cream.

"We've been taking an ASL crash course together online. We're working on signing to each other, aren't we sport?" He signed the word "happy" to Alex. Alex grinned and signed it right back.

"I'm glad to know he has you in his corner."

"I plan to always be in his corner. I know you don't think I'm going about it the right way, but look at him."

"Well, he could use a napkin, but—"

"No, I mean, *really* look at him. He's wearing dirty clothes. He needs a bath. His shoes are too small. He looks neglected. And ignored. I told Irena I would have the money ready for her tomorrow, but even if she backs out, I've got a solid case to petition the court for custody."

"Aren't you afraid she'll convince a judge you're just being vindictive?"

"Oh, I'm not worried. Irena has a heart as black as pitch. She'll show her hand. She always does." He glanced at the dark clouds racing across the sky. "We'd better go. And you'd better hustle if you're going to get that base coat on before the storm blows in."

I watched the two of them disappear down the street. Eli's shoulders, usually so straight and unflinching, were hunched over his nephew, shielding him from the wind. There was no mistaking they were a family.

"You think we're gonna finish before the storm hits?" Travis said.

"You go on. There's just one little section left. I can do it." I climbed the ladder, reloaded my brush, and started cutting in the side border. "Founder's Day is tomorrow. Once I get the base coat on, I can cover it with a tarp and forget about it. Go on. It's almost seven."

"I'm supposed to meet Zara." He smoothed the beginning of a scraggly brown goatee. "Are you sure? I can text her. She lives over on Afton Street."

"Go." I laughed. "I'm not standing in the way of true love. Put your brush in the bucket and go see Zara."

He wiped the paint off his hands with a utility cloth. Then pulled on his backpack and stood beside the guardrail.

"See you day after tomorrow, Travis."

"I need to tell you something." Soft thunder rumbled in the distance. "I want to thank you for giving me this job."

"You're a hard worker just like your dad. Pop always said Bob Walters was the fastest painter he knew. And the neatest. He never spilled a drop."

"He's sick."

"I know, honey. I wish there was something I could do to help."

Travis nodded. "He's trying to get sober. He's going to AA meetings."

"That's good. That's a good start."

"I was really angry when your father fired him. But I guess now I understand why."

"When your dad gets back on his feet, I'm sure Pop will have his old job waiting for him. Everyone deserves a second chance."

"If you want to fire me, I'll understand." He looked down at his feet and took a deep breath. "I moved the scaffold. The one Mr. MacGill was standing on."

"That was you?"

"I didn't mean to hurt him. I swear. It's just—my dad always set up the scaffold for Mr. MacGill, and I wanted him to miss having my dad around. I wanted him to miss him so much, that he would hire him back. I thought he had locked the brake, and it would only slide a little bit. Just enough to let him know he needed my dad's help. But your dad hadn't locked it. So when he landed on it, it rolled with him, and he fell."

"Pop didn't tell me that part."

"Zara said if I worked for you, I had to tell you upfront. Wouldn't be right not to."

"I like this Zara." I glanced at the darkening sky. "Go on. If you hurry, you can make it before the rain starts."

He hoisted his backpack on his shoulders and swung his leg over the rail.

"And Travis? I'm not firing you. Everyone deserves a second chance."

I felt the first tiny drops of rain hit my arm. "Well, almost everyone."

****

I tamped the paint can lids with a rubber hammer then wrapped the wet rollers in small plastic trash bags. I would deal with them tomorrow. I gathered my tools and chided myself for not stopping work sooner. It had been foolish to try to finish the base coat on the side of a brick building in one afternoon. The brick was rougher than I'd anticipated. It had taken forever.

The wind suddenly picked up. Gravel dust from the flat rooftop swirled around my ankles. I cupped my hands over my eyes and squinted upward like Dorothy scanning the heavens for a tornado. A jagged streak of lightning cut across the sky followed by a sharp crack of thunder.

I spread the plastic tarp over my supplies and threaded a rope through the grommets. Then I looped the nylon cord around the metal bar and tied it to the bottom of the guardrail to batten down the hatches. Where was my jacket? Had I left it in the car?

Before I could decide if I had time to run back for it, the rain began in earnest. It pelted my high-necked top beneath my overall straps. Beat against my back. Pricked the bare skin on my shoulders like needles. I moved my phone to the inside zippered pocket to keep it dry.

Thunder crashed overhead, deafening me.

I glanced around to make sure I hadn't forgotten to secure anything then held onto the tarp-covered wall and edged toward the ladder, ducking my head into the wind.

The first thing I was going to do when I got home was sink into a hot bath. I might even get around to using that almond-scented bubble bath Jules had given me last Christmas. I wiped the rain out of my eyes, smearing mascara onto the back of my hand. After a long soak, I'd make myself a cup of chamomile tea. Super sweet with cinnamon and an extra glob of honey.

I reached the corner of the roof and held on to the drainpipe. Water spilled over the side of the gutter, splashing the front of my overalls. I grasped the wet railing with both hands and tried to gauge how far down I would have to stretch my leg to reach the ladder rungs. Water ran in rivulets down the back of my neck. My short hair plastered to my face like wet sticks. I rubbed the rain off my forehead and swung my foot over the side where I'd left the ladder.

Except there was no ladder.

I looked down, gulping in air, staring in horror at the empty space beside the huge circulating fan. No ladder. *No ladder?*

Where the hell was the ladder?

Had it fallen over? Had the wind swept it off the roof? Had Travis moved it?

Travis wouldn't have stranded me on a roof in the middle of a thunderstorm. Would he? Not after the heartfelt confession he'd shared so poignantly. A confession I'd swallowed hook, line, and sinker. Had the boy been lying to me? Had he wanted to get down the ladder and speed away on his bike so he could do the same thing to me that he'd done to my father? No. I had not been wrong to trust Travis. And I could not, *would* not believe I'd misjudged him.

I pulled my foot back, then held my hand over my eyes and peered over the side of the building. The extension ladder lay on the ground parallel to the courthouse wall, missing the Wrenhaven Garden Club's prizewinning Floribunda roses by a scant foot.

I backed up and huddled against the brick. Rain pelted me from all sides. *Eli.* I reached into the depths of my overall side pocket and pulled out my phone. I would call Eli. He would drive back and—*no*. I couldn't bother Eli. He was with Alex. Why did I automatically think of calling Eli first? Jesse was the one I should call to help me down.

Thunder cracked above my head. Lightning flashed. Rain slapped me in the face from all sides. If I hadn't been so terrified, it would have been funny.

I had never experienced a raging thunderstorm so up close and personal before, and I had to concede that between the torrents of rain bouncing off the roof, the relentless thunder booms that shook the encroaching night, and the sky lighting up every ten seconds like a detonated nuclear blast, it was pretty apocalyptic.

A high-pitched buzz sawed through my ears, and I glanced up. White sparks from the transformer on the corner rose into the air then showered down from the utility pole, hissing and fizzling like sparklers.

My phone flew out of my hand.

I blinked away the rain and watched my one connection to the outside world sail over the edge of the roof and tumble into the dark. The next flash of light caught me off guard. I held onto the edge of the tarp and faced the street, trying to get my bearings. Down below, beside the courthouse entrance, a man scurried away with his head down.

A short round man.

"Mayor Nash!" I cried. "It's me, Maggie! I'm up here! *Help!"*

The mayor glanced behind him but didn't slow down.

"Mayor Nash!"

He pulled a folded newspaper from under his arm and held it over his head, then turned toward the parking lot and ran.

"Mayor Nash! Please!"

It was no use. My voice was swallowed by the roar of the wind. I could barely hear it myself. There was no overhang. No ledge sticking out from the upper story. I was exposed on all sides to the elements. Even the huge sycamore tree growing beside the building had decided to turn its branches in the other direction.

I couldn't let myself panic.

Sooner or later the power company would send a crew to repair the transformer. Once they arrived, I could figure out a way to get their attention. Throw a can of Seashell Gray paint over the side if I had to. In the meantime, the tarp was my only option for protection. I untied the corner, scooted beneath it, and yanked the rope hard to close the gap. I crouched next to the wall, grateful for the break from the lashing rain.

Water streamed down my neck. My tank top clung to me like a second skin. I shivered and held my hands over my ears to block the sound of the rain. I'd always loved listening to rain on a tin roof. I just never thought my head would *be* the tin roof.

There was nothing to do but wait. If Jules were here, he'd probably pass the time by breaking into an uplifting chorus of "My Favorite Things." But that was Jules.

Always looking on the bright side.

What had Mayor Nash been doing outside the courthouse? Where was his car? Didn't he have a parking space with his name painted on it fifty feet from his office at City Hall? How many other people in Wrenhaven knew he was living under an assumed name? Mrs. Grayson had known, of course. And Sheriff Conley. And now, me. And Jules. I would also bet a long, luxurious hour sitting beside a cozy fire in dry clothes that Florence knew it too.

A couple of times, I reached into my pocket to check the time, then remembered I had no phone. My phone was on the ground. In the mud. Probably in eight pieces.

I wrapped my arms around my legs, pulling them close, and tried not to notice how much I hated the suffocating smell of plastic tarp. Then I laid my head on my damp, denim-covered knees and closed my eyes. "Hmmmm…"

Chapter 18

A sharp clap sounded below me.

What had I heard? Something banging against a metal stick? A car door slamming?

If someone was down below, maybe I could get their attention. Then get them to help me off the roof. Or at least call Jesse.

I picked up one of the clean roller trays—not sure why I hadn't thought of that before—and held it over my head as a shield. I hurried to the edge of the roof and peered over. Luke's white SUV sat parked next to Velma with its lights on. I banged the metal roller tray against one of the exhaust pipes over and over, screaming, *"Luke! Luke!"* Until finally, he flashed his lights to let me know he'd seen me.

The door to the SUV opened. I had never felt such relief. Luke Pritchard had been sent by my guardian angel to rescue me for the second time that week.

"Maggie! Maggie are you up there?"

My head jerked around. *"Eli?"*

The tops of two ladder rungs clanked against the guardrail running the length of the roof. The ladder pulled back and wavered in the air for a surreal moment before slamming against the gutter.

"Maggie!"

"I'm here! I'm here!"

I threw down the roller tray and ran to the roof's

edge. Eli's head popped up between the ladder rungs. "Are you okay?"

"I'm fine."

Eli clasped my hand in his, then waited for me to maneuver around and feel for the ladder with my foot. He wrapped his arm around my waist to steady me and we climbed down, one slippery step at a time.

At the bottom, he took my hand. "My truck's out front. Let's make a run for it."

"Yeah, we wouldn't want to get wet."

He laughed. "Wouldn't want that."

Luke suddenly appeared behind us with an umbrella. He held it over my head, and for the first time in what seemed like hours, I could open my eyes without squinting into the rain."

"Where did you come from?" Eli said.

"Side parking lot," Luke said. "I went to Sam and Dan's to get a pint of pistachio for Irena, but they had already closed. I was getting ready to leave when I heard a banging sound coming from the roof. I couldn't believe it was Maggie up there."

"My phone flew off." I pointed to the rhododendron hedge. "It landed somewhere in there."

"I'll get it." Eli left Luke and me huddled under the umbrella and rooted around in the bushes. Luke wiped the rain off his face with the back of his hand. A few minutes later, Eli came back clutching my phone to his chest. "It was wedged between two branches. Never hit the ground."

"It'll probably still work," Luke said. "These days, phones are pretty water resistant."

"How did you know I was still here?" I asked Eli.

"We cut our visit with Stephen short because Alex

is afraid of lightning."

"Yeah, he hates it," Luke said. "I always feel sorry for that kid in a rainstorm."

"I was on my way back to the motel when I noticed your car still here," Eli said. Thunder crashed above us. "You're shaking. My motel is just around the corner. Come to my room and dry off before you go home."

"I'll let you two go, then," Luke said. "I'd better get home to Alex and Irena. They'll be worried about me."

"Thanks for coming to my rescue again, Luke. I hope this is the last time." I tried to give the umbrella back to him, but he motioned for me to keep it.

"Just glad you're okay, Maggie," Luke said. "See you guys later."

Once we were in Big Blue, I tried my phone, and—miracle of miracles—it came to life right away. I checked on my father and was relieved to learn Jesse had come over to stay with him. Pop was even less crazy about storms than I was.

Eli handed me a tissue, and I wiped the water off my face. Laughter bubbled up in my throat. "You should see yourself. Little rivers of water are streaming down your dimples."

"Oh, I'd talk," he said. "You look like you fought a ten-foot king wave. And lost."

He reached behind the seat and pulled out an OBX sweatshirt that smelled of salt. "Wrap this around you."

"Did you s-see the transformer blow?"

"No, but I heard it. Power's off all over town." He pulled into the motel parking lot. "Looks like it's off here too."

We scrambled out of the truck and ran through the rain to his room. A plastic grocery bag hung on the doorknob, whipping back and forth in the wind.

Eli unlocked the door and waited for me to go inside. He switched on his phone light and held up the bag. "I hope it's something to eat; I'm starving." He pulled out two fat candles, a pack of matches, and a peanut butter granola bar, compliments of the motel. "The Blue Ridge Motor Lodge has just moved to the top of my list. I'm never staying anywhere else."

I laughed. "You light the candles. I'm going to dry off in the bathroom."

"Wait." He opened a dresser drawer and pulled out a folded T-shirt and a pair of gray drawstring sweatpants. "These will be way too big for you, but at least they're dry." He stopped. "What's the matter? Why are you looking at me like that?"

"I never saw anyone actually use the drawers in a motel room."

"Oh, I use everything—chairs, bed, shampoo, body wash. If I get lonely, I line up the little bottles on the sink and talk to them." He lit a candle and handed it to me. "Go take a shower. There should be enough hot water left to revive you."

I stopped to catch my breath. "Thanks for coming back for me."

"What happened with the ladder?"

"Somebody had to have moved it. When I went to climb down, it was lying beside the rose bushes. If it had fallen over on its own, it would have been pointing in the other direction."

"Do you think Travis—"

"No, I watched him ride away on his bike. He's not completely innocent, though. He confessed to throwing the rock through our front window and hanging the dead rat on Velma. But he d-denies cutting the van brakes, and I b-believe him." I didn't mention he had also moved the scaffold.

Eli put his hands on my shoulders, sending a little jolt of electricity buzzing down my spine. "I know you're worried about tonight, but we'll get to the bottom of this. I promise." He pressed his lips against my forehead so softly I could have closed my eyes and not been certain he'd done it. Then he turned me around and pointed me toward the bathroom. "Go on. Get warm. Once your teeth stop chattering, we'll talk."

Thunder boomed outside the window. Lightning flashed white behind the half-closed curtains. Eli slid his hands into his pockets. Then took them out again.

"I think I should go home," I said.

"You don't want to take a shower?"

It had been a long time since I'd been brave enough, or foolish enough to let someone glimpse the vulnerable side of me. I had bitched and moaned to Jules about Stephen not trying to make a move on me, but in my heart of hearts, I was relieved he had kept his distance. I had been burned one too many times by saying yes to someone I thought I could trust.

And yet, here I was: cold and wet and shivering. Standing in the middle of a motel room with Eli Grayson, a man I had hated, then didn't hate, then liked a little more than I thought I should. It was clear where the night was going if we were both willing. I just wasn't sure I was ready to believe he was the person I wanted him to be.

Which is why I was making a list of pros and cons in my head while he stood there, smiling his crooked smile, looking at me like I was one of the chocolate silk pies sitting in the display case at Mac's Diner.

He squeezed my hand and pulled me toward him. "Don't be afraid, Maggie MacGill. It'll be just like jumping off a pier."

"Are storms like this at the beach?"

"They're worse." He smoothed my short wet hair back and held my face in his calloused hands. Then he kissed me. Gently. Tenderly. As if I were made of glass.

Eli pulled off his wet T-shirt and threw it across the room. He drew me down beside him until we were sitting on the edge of the lumpy mattress.

"You're beautiful. I hope you know that." He kissed my throat, pulling my high-necked tank down to trail his mouth along the sensitive ridge of my scar. "You get to kiss mine next."

"Kiss your what?"

"My scar. I fell off the end of a sailboat when I was eight and had to have four stitches."

I laughed. "Let me guess. It's somewhere near your inner thigh."

"No, but you're close." He leaned back and grinned.

"I see a lot of fumbling in my future." I stopped, wishing I had a couple of tequila shots under my belt. "But, you know what? Maybe we could just—" I looked at him. "This is really nice. And we all know everybody looks fabulous by candlelight. But I'm exhausted. Could we just not—"

"Absolutely."

He scooted to the middle of the bed and stretched out. Then he pulled half the bedspread back for me to climb in. Once I had nestled into the warm crook of his arm, with my head on his chest and my hand resting on the waistband of his damp jeans, the world blurred. The flickering candles sprayed golden light around the room, on and off, off and on, as if they were dancing to music.

I closed my eyes, ignoring the sticky clothes, and let sleep pull me up into the night sky.

The last thing I thought about was Irena. I wondered how upset she was that she didn't get her pistachio ice cream.

****

I opened one eye.

A column of sunlight shone through the gap in a pair of flowered drapes that looked like they'd hung there since Reagan was president. I raised up on one elbow and watched the man sleeping beside me. A tiny jagged white scar creased his right shoulder. His tousled brown hair grew uneven across the back of his neck. When he moved his arm, a couple of muscles rippled like waves beneath his smooth tanned back. I'd touched that back the night before. Lightly skimming it with my fingers after he had turned over, when I was sure he was asleep.

I eased out of bed, hurried into the bathroom, and flipped on the light. Which, thank goodness, was working. I ran damp fingers through my short stubby hair and rinsed my face. When I came out, Eli was standing at the foot of the bed in a pair of dry jeans and a clean unbuttoned shirt.

"The power's back on," he said. "I can run out and get us some coffee. Or I have a couple of bottles of water if—"

"Water's good." I slipped on my shoes.

"You're frowning. What are you thinking about? Are you wondering who could have moved the ladder last night?"

"I was wondering where you put the granola bar." I

looked up. "You know, a week ago, I would have accused Trude of moving the ladder. She was strong enough to lift it, and she would have had so much fun stranding me on a roof in the middle of a storm. But she's dropped off the suspect list."

"That's one way of putting it."

"The attacks on my family are escalating. I have to find out who's doing this to us before our lives completely tank. I've been banned from volunteering at the Art Factory until they prove I didn't kill your grandmother. Comfort and Joy is hanging by a thread. Pop is trying to make sense of Trude's death. How is this all going to end?"

"Sweetheart—"

"Pop and I are sure that everything that's happened—all the ugly little pranks and sabotages directed at us—stem back to your grandmother's revised will."

"I agree." He sat on the end of the bed. "Someone must have known what was in it before we ever went to that lawyer's office."

"Florence worked after hours cleaning DePaul's office. She could have found the original copy and known who was included in the will before Mrs. Grayson changed it. But do you really think she's that technically savvy? Could she crack a password code and pull up a file on an attorney's business computer?"

"I don't know," Eli said. "But there's not a doubt in my mind she knew the contents of both wills. Florence knew everything that went on in Grayson House. She was always sneaking around eavesdropping. And she's not beneath listening at keyholes, either. I've seen her do it."

"If Florence had read both wills, she could have passed that information along to Irena or Mayor Nash. Or to Stephen; he was there every other day. She thought my father was the lucky new recipient." I explained about our matching initials. "I think that's why Florence was so keen to marry off her daughter to him."

"Makes sense."

"How did Stephen fare in the will that was amended after Kyle died? Delores said there was a codicil naming Alex as an heir. Was it an even cut between the three of you?"

"Yes, and it was a considerable amount of money. Stephen always needs money. He got fired from his job. Did he tell you that?"

"Jesse heard he was in debt, but I didn't know he'd lost his job. You said you don't suspect him, but—"

"I can't believe my cousin would kill our grandmother. Or anybody else, for that matter. In the old will, she'd left quite a bit to charity, including a generous donation to the Art Factory. Which, as we both know, is very important to Mayor Nash."

"And speaking of Mayor Nash…" I started to tell him about Nash changing his name and moving to Wrenhaven at Mrs. Grayson's request, but something stopped me. Maybe it was the lack-of-trust thing rearing its ugly head again. Or maybe my heart had softened toward Eli more than I realized and I didn't want to involve him anymore in what was turning out to be a very dangerous situation.

"Mayor Nash?" Eli said. "What about him?"

"Just what you said. He's another person who would have benefited greatly from your grandmother not changing her will." I leaned against the edge of the TV table. "We have to figure out why she changed it. If she woke up one morning and thought, *Hey, it might be fun to leave my house and a large chunk of money to the girl who weeds my flowerbeds,* then I want to know why. Why did she pick me and not the mailman or the pizza delivery guy?"

"Because you're prettier?"

"She told Delores she thought I was sensible. And I am. But that's not a reason. No one alters their will at the end of their life unless something happens to trigger it. Constance Grayson wasn't impulsive. She was a shrewd, calculating businesswoman. Everything she did, she did for a reason. Something lit the fuse. And I want to know what it was."

"Or who."

"I think we can pretty much eliminate Trude as a suspect," I said. "Although, if she was marrying my father because she thought he was going to inherit, I'd say she was counting on there being no prenup. Something Irena may have alerted her to."

Eli thought for a moment. "If you're right about Florence knowing, she may have told Irena that Grandmother had decided not to provide for Alex. The will stated it was because Kyle and Irena never married. Which is a stupid, stupid reason. But she was old-school. She wanted to teach Irena a lesson."

"You should ask for a DNA test to prove Alex is Kyle's son and a true Grayson."

His eyes met mine. "Do you want to know why I think she left the estate to you?"

"Yes."

"Because she thought you wouldn't keep it. She knew that changing her will at the eleventh hour would tear the family apart. It would force us not to take the Grayson money for granted. Teach us some humility. She was very big on humility. Leaving it to you would make us crazy, but then you'd give it back, and we'd all be better people for it."

"Why was she so sure I *would* give it back?"

"Because your father worked for her for years and never accepted any compensation. Because you never expected payment to take care of her garden. The MacGills are a proud, wonderful family, and she knew that. She took advantage of it."

"But why didn't she just leave it to my father?"

"Perhaps she didn't want Trude trying to influence him to keep the house and the money. And from everything you've told me about Trude, she would have."

That was my opening. The moment I should have told him about my decision to give part of the inheritance back to the Grayson's with a few stipulations and keep the rest for my family. Now, after he'd spoken so sweetly about my family's pride, and with such assurance that I was going to return the inheritance to him and Stephen. It was wishful thinking on his part. He didn't know my family well. He hadn't counted on the kind of loyalty and love we shared. Or the fierce protectiveness I felt toward them. Or the fact that when my family desperately needed something that was in my power to give them, pride flew out the window.

Three sharp raps sounded on the door. "Eli, it's Stephen."

"Just a minute." Eli pulled the comforter over the sheets and tried to smooth it out.

"Saving my reputation?" I said.

"Something like that."

Stephen walked in holding a cup of takeout coffee. "I just talked to Irena." He glanced at me. Then at the bed. His left, perfectly groomed eyebrow shot up half an inch. "Looks like you two survived the storm."

"Hello, Stephen," I said.

He nodded then turned back to Eli. "I was down at The Coffee Nook just now picking up my standing order for—"

"—one decaf sugar-free soy latte with an extra shot of cream," I said.

"Right." Stephen huffed a disapproving sigh in my direction. "Irena was there, and she couldn't stop talking about selling you permanent guardianship of Alex. I think she thinks what you're doing is legal. Thank God she waited until we were outside; the place was packed."

"What did she say?" Eli asked. "That if I don't hurry, the price is going to double?"

"Triple," Stephen said and laughed. "Irena always was a greedy girl."

"I wish you had recorded her," Eli said. "It would be irrefutable evidence in a custody case to prove a parent agreed to give up their child for money. Irena thinks this is going to happen overnight, but it's not that easy. A person assuming permanent guardianship can't just sign a few papers and walk away with the child. They have to file a petition in court, then go to a hearing. It's quite a process."

"Irena only wants two things," Stephen said. "To finally be rid of Alex, and money."

"And she wants it in cash," Eli said. "That's why it's taking so long."

"You're right about recording her, though." Stephen

sipped his coffee. "Luke was still inside the shop, and she kept shushing me so he wouldn't hear what we were saying. That relationship doesn't stand a snowball's chance. Once you agree to Irena's terms, and she has the money in hand, she'll ditch Luke and go to California by herself." He glanced at me. "Eli told me about your brother's restaurant getting stink bombed. Any idea who did it?"

"Someone who doesn't want our family to stay in Wrenhaven."

"People are still wondering if you killed our grandmother," Stephen said. "I overheard a six-top talking about it today at the Coffee Nook. I think they were taking bets."

"And I'm sure you set them straight," I said. "I'm sure you told them there was no way such a warm caring person like Maggie MacGill could do something so heinous. Did you tell them you believed I was innocent? Did you stick up for me?"

"Well, no," Stephen said. "I didn't think to."

"I didn't think so." I grabbed my purse and looped it over my shoulder. "I'd love to stay and chat, but the Founder's Day parade is at 3:00. I promised Mayor Nash I would ride on the Art Factory float again."

Eli followed me outside. "Let me take you to your car."

"I can walk."

"I know you can walk, but the courthouse is two blocks away."

"I like walking."

He sighed. "You regret coming back to the motel with me last night, don't you? I thought it was nice. You said it was nice. I thought you were beginning to like me again."

"I *do* like you."

"But you don't trust me. Other than a thoughtless, stupid nickname I gave you in high school, why don't you trust me?"

I turned back to him. "Your grandmother's autopsy. Did you request it? Or did Stephen?"

"I did," he said. "Why?"

"Because the person who held a pillow up to Mrs. Grayson's face watched her die of fright before touching her with it. They must have hated her."

"And you think I'm that person? Because I hated her? I've never tried to hide how I feel about my grandmother. Or what she did to cause it."

"I don't—"

"You think I asked for an autopsy because I knew I hadn't touched her with a weapon and she died of natural causes? And it would prove that I didn't cause her death?"

The look on his face stopped me cold. "No. Of course, I don't think that. I didn't mean to sound so accusatory. I'm just trying to look at things from different points of view. Fill in the blanks. Think of questions no one has asked. I'm just trying to—"

"Solve the murder. Got it."

I reached out and took his hand, then looked into his eyes. "I don't think you tried to kill your grandmother. I don't."

"Then, what is this about? I hurt your feelings seventeen years ago, so you'll never trust me again?"

"I'm just normally a suspicious person. Always have been. I'm cynical and guarded. I'm a worst-case-scenario girl. And I have a hard time trusting anybody."

I forced a laugh. "It's just so much easier to be that way, you know? Trusting someone takes a lot of work."

"Actually, it's the other way around."

"That's what Jules says." I took a breath and laughed. "Look, I know I invited you to brunch today, but I don't want you to feel like you have to come."

"Of course, I want to come. I wouldn't miss it." He beamed at me.

I never trusted anyone who beamed at me.

I walked across the motel parking lot. My overalls, still clammy and cold from the night before, flapped against my legs, reminding me of the ordeal I'd survived on the courthouse roof. After being stranded twenty feet up in a raging storm, I was afraid of what might happen next. I was a girl without a plan, and that made me feel helpless.

I rounded the corner and was relieved to see that the blue plastic tarps I spread over the paint cans had survived the rest of the night intact.

I didn't want to go home. I wanted to climb on the courthouse roof like I'd climbed back on the pony that had thrown me in seventh grade. I wanted to block everything out and lose myself in painting the mural. Painting was my solace. My happy place. It was the thing that let my mind roam free to do my best thinking and planning.

And oh, baby, I needed a plan.

I also needed an attitude adjustment.

It wouldn't kill me to look on the cheerful side of life more often like Jules. Why did I feel so resentful I was expected to sit on a float for two hours because I was painting the town mural? But I couldn't get out of it; I had promised Mayor Nash. I wondered what kind of expression would flit across his face if I called him by his real name. Now, *that* was looking on the bright side.

I unlocked Velma and realized I was starving. I vowed to stay cheerful and ignore the slow, icy dread that had begun to snake its way up my spine.

I did not have a good feeling about Eli coming to brunch.

And no matter how many times I hummed "My Favorite Things," it would not go away.

Chapter 19

When I got to the house, my family was waiting in the living room. Pop's wheelchair sat beside the couch pointing toward the front entrance and Jesse stood beside the wing-backed chair near the fireplace.

"This looks serious," I said. "What's going on?"

"We're waiting for Eli," Jesse said. "His truck just pulled up."

"Why aren't you in the kitchen cooking?"

"Pipe down, Mags," Jesse said. "I have something to get off my chest first. Something I think you'll be very interested to hear."

Eli knocked on the door.

"Come on in," Pop yelled.

Eli came through the foyer and stood in the arched entranceway.

Except for the mouthwatering aroma of Jesse's bacon and hash brown casserole simmering in the oven, it seemed more like a courtroom than a family brunch. My brother and father weren't smiling. Neither one made a sound.

Pop motioned to the empty chair.

"So what is this?" Eli asked uneasily. "An intervention?"

"Sit down, son," Pop said.

"With all due respect, Mr. MacGill, I have something to say first." Eli ran his hand back through his unruly hair, a nervous gesture I had come to know well. He smiled at us. Trustingly. Like the family dog who doesn't realize he's been dropped off at the vet to be neutered.

Jesse jumped to his feet. "I don't care what you've got to say, Grayson. I have a bone to pick with you."

"Jesse, please," Pop said. "Don't get angry. He was only trying to help."

"What are you talking about?" I asked.

"The restaurant," Jesse said. "*My* restaurant." He took center stage. "Would y'all like to know why Comfort and Joy is suddenly on the Food Network's radar?"

"That's what I wanted to tell you," Eli said excitedly. "So you know about the Food Network calling? They've already contacted you?"

"Yes, I know about it," Jesse said. "I also know *why* they called." He turned to us. "Did they call because of the four-star reviews in the *Knoxville News Sentinel?* No. Because of the great reviews on *Yelp?* No. Because of the incredible word-of-mouth? *Hell*, no. The only reason my restaurant is being considered for a spot on the show *Dish Jockey* is that Eli set it up."

"I don't understand," I said.

"Eli just happens to know one of the show's producers," Jesse said. "She called to make sure the network had all my contact information and said you were a friend of hers."

"We're not friends," Eli said. "She vacations with her family on the Outer Banks every summer. She owed me a favor."

"A favor?" Pop said. "What kind of favor?"

"She bought a painting at my mother's shop a few

years ago and wanted another one. The artist was a recluse. I helped her connect with him. She said if I ever needed anything—"

"So you used your favor to help Jesse's restaurant?" I said.

"Why not? He's Les MacGill's son, who I owe a great debt to. And he's your brother."

"I thought I got it on my own merit," Jesse said. "Because I deserve it. Because my food is the best."

"You did get it on your own merit," Eli said. "I mean, you *will* get it as soon as the production team tastes your food. I only helped get your foot in the door. That's how things work in television. It's who you know. I'm sorry if your ego is taking a hit, but—"

"You're basically saying I could be serving slop out of a bucket," Jesse huffed, "and I'm in the running as long as I know someone who can get me on the show?"

"I wouldn't have recommended your restaurant if I didn't think it was good enough to impress them," Eli said. "Your food is extraordinary. I haven't actually eaten it yet, except for those little muffin things they brought out before the stink bombs went off, but I trust Maggie's judgment. I didn't call in a favor to piss you off. I did it to help you."

"That's not all you did," Jesse said. "Tell Maggie why she was chosen to paint the town mural. Tell her how you bribed the mayor."

My head shot up. "You what?"

"I don't mean to hurt you, Mags," Jesse said, "but you need to know this. Eli told Mayor Nash he would funnel some of the money from the Grayson Group's charity fund to pay for our city's mural. If—and *only* if—they chose you to paint it."

"You didn't," I said to Eli. "Tell me you didn't."

"I still have some sway with the Grayson Group," Eli said, "even if I wasn't handed any of the profits for the next five years. I've already run it by the house committee, and they think it's a great idea. They're always looking for charitable causes in towns where we do consultant work. It's good business."

"Now I'm a charitable cause?" I said.

"You said you'd love to paint the mural," Eli said. "You said you'd sent them sketches. In the end, I'm sure they would have chosen you. I only nudged them a little." He took a breath. "Maggie, you're so talented. And you don't believe you are. I thought it would give your self-confidence a boost."

"So you went behind my back and offered Mayor Nash money because I'm not good enough to get the commission on my own. Do you Graysons think you can buy off everyone?"

"Not cool, Eli," Pop said.

"Wrenhaven is a community full of respected artists," I said. "If people find out you bribed the mayor to let me paint the mural, I'll be a laughingstock."

"I did it for you," Eli said hoarsely. "For both of you." He turned to Pop. "Sir, I owe you so much. I wanted to help your family and make things easier for them. And for you too." He glanced at me sitting on the edge of the sofa, my eyes brimming with disappointment. "I swear, Maggie, I only had good intentions."

"You wanted to make our lives easier so I would give back the inheritance." I got up and walked to the fireplace, my head held high. "I heard you and Stephen talking at the motel that night. When he advised you to suck up to me. Why didn't you tell me you were going to do this? These are our lives you're messing with."

"I should have warned you," Eli said. "I know that now. But I was sure this would make your family happy. I wanted to make you happy."

"You know what?" I said. "I need to get out of this room before my head explodes. So I'm going upstairs to my little loft, and I'm going to try not to think about having to sit on a purple float this afternoon in front of the whole town and pretend I'm honored and grateful to have been chosen to paint Wrenhaven's freaking mural." I picked up my purse and glared at Eli. "And don't you follow me."

I went through the kitchen, pushed open the screen door, and went outside. With Eli right behind me.

"Maggie, please. I wasn't thinking when I talked to the mayor. You're an incredible artist. I just want the world to appreciate how good you are. I know your feelings are hurt, and my good intentions—"

"Enough with the good intentions." I spun around on the landing and glared at him. "I know this is my wounded ego talking, but you need to back off. I have too much on my plate right now to worry about any of this."

"Let me make it up to you. I can call my friend at the Food Network and—"

"Don't you dare call the Food Network. Getting Comfort and Joy on TV is the best thing that's happened to Jesse in a long time. His pride is hurt right now, but when he cools off—and he will—he'll realize this is an opportunity he can't pass up."

"Please, Maggie." He reached for me, but I dodged him. "Just listen to me for one minute."

"No," I said. "I want you to shut up, Eli Grayson. Before you abscond with any more of my artistic self-esteem. And believe me, there ain't much left."

"Abscond? You make me sound like a pirate."

"I have things to do. People to wave at. My family to protect." I started up the stairs. "And most importantly, I have a murder to solve."

****

Florence sat on her front porch rocking back and forth.

I parked Velma and picked my way down the rocky path. She didn't look up or acknowledge my presence in any way, so I sat in the rocker opposite her and waited. I wasn't sure if she wanted me there or not. But there I was. We sat for a few minutes, listening to the wind rustle through her apple trees, gazing across the adjoining meadow at Mr. Marsdale's goats.

"Can I get you a cup of tea?" I said. "I know you like it sweet with honey. Trude said she used to make it for you when you had a cold."

"Trude's gone."

"I know," I said gently.

"She's not coming back, is she?"

"No, Florence."

Florence's dark eyes filled with tears. "I never could talk sense into that girl. I worried when she hooked up with your father because he was so much older. Then I thought, maybe that's a good thing. She's never really had a father in her life. Someone with a few years under his belt might be just what she needs." She glanced at me. "How is Les? Is he taking Trude's death hard?"

"He's sad, of course, and upset about what happened—we all are—and so sorry for your loss. But he and Trude had broken off their engagement. Did you know that?"

"I figured. Did he find out about—"

"—the other guy Trude was seeing? Yeah, he found out."

"I knew she was sneaking around on Les. I told her to stop deceiving him. To make her choice and stick with it. Les is a good man. He didn't deserve to be treated like that."

"You don't happen to know who the man was, do you, Florence?"

She leaned back in the rocker. A wedge of sunlight swept across the porch, washing her gaunt face in pale yellow. She looked like she hadn't slept in days. And I, no stranger to grief, was reasonably sure she hadn't.

"Did Trude ever mention his name or where he worked? Did she describe him to you?"

"She never said nothing. Just that she thought she'd finally fallen in love." Florence closed her eyes for a moment. "I went back to Grayson House this morning. Just to look around and make sure I hadn't left anything that belonged to me. I wanted you to know in case someone saw me there. Since you own the house now."

"I don't own it yet. I may never own it if they can't find out who killed Mrs. Grayson."

"But you said you'd found her address book. So you've read the list of names."

"Yes." I didn't tell her I'd located the research papers as well.

"Then you know Sherman's—Mayor Nash's name is in there. He had something in his past, a terrible accident that was his fault. He's spent years trying to make up for it. But Mrs. Grayson would never let him forget it. She held it over him. Threatened to expose him." Florence's eyes met mine. "She was a terrible person."

"I'm not going to tell anyone about Mayor Nash, Florence. I promise."

"Mrs. Grayson cut my salary when she found out Trude was stealing from her. At first, Trude only took a few trinkets and some small Civil War artifacts. But later, I noticed several pieces of silver and some of Mrs. Grayson's old books were missing. I'm sure Stephen noticed it too. He didn't say anything, but he always watched Trude when she stopped by for a visit."

"Did you know about the storage unit she rented?"

"That's where she kept the stuff until she could sell it on the Internet. I never asked where it was. Didn't want to know." Florence blinked. "You think somebody found out she was hiding expensive things there and tried to steal them? You think that's why they killed my girl?"

"I don't know. Could Stephen have known about it and followed her there?"

"Oh, no. Stephen wouldn't hurt Trude. He has his faults, but he wouldn't hurt Trude." Her face crumpled. "But someone hurt her. Someone killed my baby girl."

Florence began to cry, heartrending and soundless. She grasped the arms of the rocking chair with both hands. Her thin shoulders shook, and she let the tears flow without bothering to wipe them away.

"Florence?" I said softly. "I hate to think of you being out here all alone. Do you have any family I could call? Someone who could come and stay with you for a while?"

Florence shook her head. "Sherman's coming over after the parade. He's bringing his little girl Holly with him. She's so sweet. She reminds me of Trude when she was that age."

"That's good." I stood up to leave. "If there's anything you need, please call. I'd be more than happy to—"

"I was thinking about Trude last night, and I remembered something she said about that woman— what's her name?—Irena?"

"What about her?"

"Trude was sure Irena and her boyfriend were about to split up. In fact, Trude said she'd bet her life on it."

"Why? Had she heard them arguing?" Mr. Giles certainly had.

Florence's eyes met mine. "I don't want to hurt your feelings, Maggie. But I know you and Stephen have parted ways, so I guess it's okay to say this."

"Say what?"

"Trude saw Irena and Stephen kissing one day. At Grayson House. Out back, near the kitchen entrance. Trude had gone upstairs for something, and when she looked out one of the guest room windows, she saw them in a clinch."

"Irena and Stephen? Are you sure?"

"Oh, yes. Trude said it made her happy that Stephen had finally found someone as selfish as he was. She couldn't stop laughing about it."

Had Trude been telling the truth? I supposed an attraction between Irena and Stephen was plausible. Inevitable, maybe. They were both gorgeous human beings—tall, handsome, beautiful, sexy. Didn't all the gorgeous people gravitate toward each other, then eventually become a couple and sleep together? They did at college.

Maybe one of them glanced up at the window and saw Trude watching them. Stephen wouldn't want his new squeeze Rocki to find out, and Irena wouldn't want Luke to know. Could one of them have followed Trude back to the storage unit and warned her to keep what she'd seen to herself? And if Trude had laughed at them, which is exactly what Trude would have done, did it make Stephen or Irena so angry, they cracked Trude on the head with the first thing they could reach—the bronze unicorn Trude had stolen from Grayson House?

Just thinking about it made my head hurt.

"Florence," I said gently. "When you were working at Attorney DePaul's office, did you read Mrs. Grayson's original will?"

She looked at me with her dark, painful eyes and nodded. "I overheard Mrs. Grayson talking to Mr. De Paul about wanting to make some changes in her will, and I had to know what they were."

"And you mistakenly thought my father was going to inherit the Grayson estate. Is that another reason you were so keen on Trude marrying him?"

"Yes," she sniffed. "But Les is a good man. I wouldn't have urged her to marry him unless I was sure he'd treat her right."

I said goodbye and left, eager to talk to Sheriff Conley about my newest theory concerning Trude's death. It was farfetched, I know, to believe that Irena or Stephen wanted to keep their secret kiss a secret so badly, they drove to a storage unit on the other side of town, confronted Trude, then took her out with an objet d'art. I wasn't sure about Irena, but Stephen would never risk damaging something he might be able to sell to an art dealer for money.

Was that why Irena had brought a sweater with her to Mrs. Grayson's in the middle of July? Florence had thought it was odd, but maybe Irena had done it on purpose. Retrieving a belonging she'd left in the house was a good excuse to go back inside then duck out the back door for her brief, clandestine meeting with Stephen.

I laughed. Who the hell were these people? Irena was getting shadier by the minute and Stephen Grayson had turned out to be a revelation. I had learned more about his life in the two weeks since his grandmother had died than I had in the three months I had dated him. And none of it was good.

I checked my phone. I needed to hustle if I was going to make the parade on time.

Before pulling onto the highway, I glanced in my rearview mirror.

Florence still sat on the front porch staring off into space, rocking her chair back and forth. Back and forth. Back and forth.

Chapter 20

"Hurry up, Maggie!" Mayor Nash shouted. "The Wrenhaven High School marching band is lined up and ready to go." He motioned for me to cross the street. "Where's your costume? I thought you'd wear something that made you look like an artist. Like a smock with paint smeared on it. Or one of those French beret things."

I stared at him. "You're serious, aren't you?"

"Well, at least you're here."

"Mayor Nash, after the parade is over, we need to talk. I'm a little upset with you."

"Oh, Lord. What have I done now?" He stretched his chin out and raised his jowls to adjust his red tie. "You're mad about the mural, aren't you?"

"You could say that."

"Jesse came down to City Hall to renew his business license and ran into Delores. She told him Eli Grayson was bankrolling your salary. Damn that woman. She couldn't keep her mouth shut if—" He pulled at his tie and coughed. "Look, Maggie, we were going to choose you anyway, and I can prove it. I've got the list of votes back in my office dated the day before the Art Guild Awards. You had already won by a landslide. I didn't tell Eli we'd already chosen you because the DWA couldn't afford to pay anything near what he offered. I was trying to get you more money. You understand, don't you?"

"I guess so. Thanks."

"Your float is down the block and around the corner." He stopped. "Hey, did you hear about the little deaf Grayson boy? He's gone missing."

My heart missed a beat. "Alex? Are you sure?"

"I've got a deputy out looking for him, but I don't think there's anything to worry about. Most of the streets are blocked off for the parade. Somebody will spot him."

I found the purple Art Factory float parked on the side street across from Jesse's restaurant. The backdrop—if you could call it that—was a huge blowup of one of the mountain sketches I had submitted for the mural, hastily thumbtacked to a vertical piece of plywood. Someone had lettered my name beneath it in black acrylic paint. At least they had spelled it right. That was a plus.

I climbed on the wide flatbed, attached to Marty Hanover's truck with a giant trailer hitch, and sat on one of the two large bales of itchy straw they had provided. Two, I guessed, in case I brought a date. Marty's truck lurched forward. I grabbed onto one of the railings as it edged slowly around the corner, barely missing the curb. Once we were on the main drag, things slowed to a halt again. It was always like that in the Founder's Day Parade. Stop then start. Speed up, slow down. I had ridden that float so many times, I could have done it in my sleep. Which wasn't a bad idea.

The crowd was out in full force. Almost all the shops, except the ones on Main Street that we passed, stopped work for an hour to watch the parade.

I slid my phone out of my pocket and checked my messages. Nothing from Eli. If Alex was still missing, Eli was probably out looking for him. I didn't think Eli would contact me since I had told him in no uncertain terms to back off.

I thought about calling Sheriff Conley to see if they'd located Alex and tell him about my conversation with Florence, but I knew he wasn't in the office. Everyone at the station would be on parade duty, rerouting traffic, keeping the citizens safe. Dispatch would take a 911 call and give him a message, but what would I say? That I strongly suspected Irena or Stephen was the murderer? And I had absolutely zero evidence to back it up?

And what about Eli? Had I been giving him a free pass for too long? Had he known Trude was stealing from Grayson House and selling the stuff online? Stephen knew. And even though the two cousins weren't very communicative, I couldn't imagine Stephen keeping something like that to himself. The day I sprung Eli from the locked attic room, he'd seemed genuinely surprised how many things had gone missing. If he'd known who'd been taking them, he hadn't let on.

The happy faces lining the street melded into a blur. Not sleeping through the night was beginning to show.

The parade came to a screeching, wobbly halt and waited for a group of saddled horsemen to take their places behind the last float. For obvious reasons, the decked-out parade horses always brought up the rear, heads proudly pulled up, long brushed tails flicking back and forth, wet balls of pony poop dropping like little torpedoes behind them.

My float jolted forward. I grabbed the wooden railing someone had the clever foresight to install, which kept me from tumbling off and crashing through the front window of the Sunset Art Gallery. I kept my eye out for

Alex but didn't see him. I hoped they'd located him by now.

Near the train station, latecomers were setting up lawn chairs on either side of the town square. The Wrenhaven High band struck up a jazzy version of "Never Gonna Give You Up" while they swayed their instruments over and back. Onlookers cheered the VFW float as it ambled by. A flock of starlings swooped and lunged in perfect formation across the bright blue sky. The hulking presence of Blue Wolf Mountain, never far away, usually centered me. But today, it made me anxious. I couldn't stop thinking about Alex, and how frightened he must be.

The parade inched along. And there were still two fire trucks, a group of kids in karate outfits, and an annoying candy-tossing clown waiting to get through the intersection. I gazed across the sea of faces, most of them familiar, some of them not. I was antsy to get off the float.

I scanned the crowd and did a double take. Wasn't that Luke Prichard walking behind the throng of people standing in front of the antique flea market? What was he doing jostling his way up the street? Had he seen me on the float? Did he know I could see him?

I took a shaky step forward and cupped my hand over my eyes to block the glare. That *was* Luke, right? It had to have been Luke. I grabbed the railing with both hands and craned my neck. Where had he gone? Was Alex with him?

I stood on my toes. Moments later, I glimpsed his shock of auburn hair, bobbing and dipping as he picked his way along the sidewalk around folding chairs and families. Where was he going in such a hurry? Was he looking for Alex? He didn't look like he was searching for a lost child. He looked like he was running for cover. What was he carrying under his arm? A pillow? No, not a pillow. A stuffed penguin.

Luke vanished behind a group of women pushing a brigade of baby strollers.

The parade crossed Hawthorn Street. I looked to my right and left, searching for him, desperate to see if he had left the main road. Was he alone? He was holding Alex's penguin, but I couldn't tell if the boy was running along beside him. I didn't see how a five-year-old could keep up such a brisk pace.

Did Luke know where Alex was and was taking his toy penguin to him? Or had he hidden Alex somewhere then gone back to find the penguin the boy had dropped on the street to cover his tracks? Was any of this possible? My mind was manufacturing so many crazy scenarios, I couldn't keep up with it.

I searched the crowd for a deputy in case I needed help, but didn't see anyone in uniform. A small troop of boy scouts with their dads in matching Jamboree vests marched on either side of my float, slowing it down even more. I stood on one of the straw bales and scanned the crowd until I spotted Luke elbowing his way through a herd of bodies as if the Zombie Apocalypse had begun. He was a man on a mission. But where was he going?

If Luke had something to do with Alex's disappearance, I needed backup. And I needed to know what was going on. I pulled my phone out of my jeans pocket and called Eli. He answered immediately.

"Have you found Alex yet?" I yelled. The float rolled forward.

"I'm out looking for him now," he said. "Where are

you? I hear trumpets."

"I'm in the parade. On a float. You sound out of breath. Are you running?"

"No, running is what *you* do. I lumber along and stop for breath every fifty feet."

"I can see Luke in the distance. He's ahead of me hurrying to get through the crowd. He's carrying Alex's penguin."

"He's what?"

"It looks—I don't know—fishy. He keeps glancing over his shoulder like he's making sure no one is following him. I don't have a good feeling about this."

Eli gulped in air. "Where are you now?"

"Past the four-way stop. Almost to the glass-blowing place. Luke's made it to the wide curve in the road. *Dammit.* I've lost him again."

I edged my way around the moving float and grabbed the edge of the paper backdrop. "How long has Alex been missing?"

"A little over an hour. Irena had brought him down to see the parade. She was standing in line at one of the food trucks placing an order, and when she turned around, he was gone."

"Did he have his penguin with him then?" Eli mumbled something unintelligible. "Can you speak up? The band's playing, and I—"

"Speak up? I can hardly breathe."

"I see Luke!" I jumped up and down. "He just crossed the intersection."

"Is Alex with him?"

"No, he's alone. But I'd bet the farm he knows where Alex is. Why would he take him? Why would he kidnap Irena's son? For a ransom? Irena doesn't have any money."

"She does now," Eli said. "I gave her everything she asked for in cash. And more."

"Why did you do that? You could have convinced the courts to give you permanent guardianship of Alex. I'm sure of it."

"Because it's my fault he's deaf. Don't you understand? It's my fault. And I know I can never make it up to him, but I have to try. I have to do my best for Alex. And I can't chance leaving his welfare up to the courts. Or Irena."

I lurched to the front of the platform. The truck pulling the float swerved left. "Slow down, Marty!" Luke's head shot up. "I see him. He's almost to Fairlane Road. It runs behind the—"

"I know where it is," Eli huffed. "I'm halfway through the park."

"I'm going to follow him."

"Maggie, no. Wait until I get there."

"If I wait, we'll lose him. If he has Alex, once he gives the penguin back to him, we might never find him. I don't think he's seen me. Don't worry. I'll keep out of sight." I banged on the cab of the truck. "Slow down, Marty. I need to get off this thing. *Now!*"

The band had stopped playing and was marching to the syncopated cadence of a snare drum. Marty slowed the truck while I waved to the men on horseback behind me, signaling I was abandoning ship. The float came to a rolling stop, and I jumped off.

I pushed my way through the mass of bodies, almost slamming into Mac from the diner. I sidestepped him with a quick apology then jumped again to miss a man with a black lab puppy on a leash. I circled behind the last row of onlookers and hurried down Main Street.

The street below the intersection was empty. The sharp rat-a-tat-tat of the drums began to soften in the distance. No sign of Luke. No sign of anyone.

Where had he gone? I was sure I'd been right behind him.

I paused in front of the wide trunk of a sycamore tree to catch my breath, looking frantically up and down the street. Where had Luke gone? Had he seen Irena kissing Stephen in the Grayson House backyard? Was kidnapping Alex a way to get back at her? Or was it just about the money?

I started running again. Luke couldn't have gotten far; he had to be in the next block over. Once I made it to the crest of the hill—gotta love those Tennessee hills—I would be able to see which direction he was heading.

The far end of Main segued into a small industrial common near the south fork of the river down by the train tracks. It was usually deserted. But today, because of the throng of parade goers, the streets were lined solid with parked cars. Which worked in my favor. If I caught up with Luke, I could crouch behind them and stay hidden. I paused for a moment beside the back entrance to Constance Grayson Park. Still no sign of Eli.

I topped the hill, panting like the neighbor's basset hound, and gazed across the square. The two buildings that had housed the now-defunct printing company stood to the right. Could Luke have ducked inside one of them? Or had Scotty beamed him up to the *Enterprise*? He was nowhere to be found.

I slunk down the hill to the rear of the first building, then hunched beneath the tall windows to keep from being seen. I climbed the concrete steps and tried the rear door—locked. The second door—locked. I darted down the alleyway between the two warehouses, skirting trash cans and stacks of empty cardboard boxes. The sour stench of rotting garbage coated the back of my throat.

I scanned the upper windows. If Luke hadn't gone inside the building, then where was he? There was nothing at the end of Fairlane Road except a rusted-out caboose sitting on a weed-infested railroad track. Mr. Giles said Luke had worked at the printing company before it closed, so Luke would know his way around the building. Possibly even know a secret way in or out.

The printing company had been closed for months, but I was optimistic I could find a way in from the other side—an open window or a door left unlocked. The plan I had generated in my head was to find an opening, get inside the building, sneak through the corridors in the non-squeak running shoes I'd worn on the float because no one could see my feet, and find Alex. Or Luke. If I ran into Luke, perhaps I could convince him to let me take Alex back home to his mother. The kid must be terrified by now.

A good plan.

Unless I was looking at it all wrong.

Perhaps I should give Luke the benefit of the doubt, and not be so quick to judge the person who had come to my rescue when I was speeding through town like a maniac in a van with no brakes. Luke had followed me, called 911, and let me know someone had my back. He had put his arms around me and let me shake until the adrenaline subsided. I had no evidence he was guilty of stealing a child away from his mother. What if he'd discovered the child's mother was guilty of murder and taken him from her to keep him safe? What if he'd suspected Irena was meeting Stephen then followed her to the storage unit? Once there, he might have heard Irena warn Trude not to tell anyone what she'd seen, watched her pick up a bronze unicorn head, and strike Trude dead with it.

I had always thought of Luke as one of the good guys. Someone who'd taken care of his dying mother and scratched his way out of poverty to make a better life for himself and his family. But then, my judgment of men, and their characters, had never been too reliable.

So maybe Luke wasn't so innocent after all.

My gaze fell on a path of tamped-down weeds beside a partially overgrown basement window. A fresh set of fingerprints smeared the light film of mud on either side of the beveled glass. As I leaned down to inspect it, my phone rang in my pocket.

"Is there any flat ground in this town?" Eli said. "I'm lost. Where is Fairlane Road?"

"Off Main Street beside the bagel shop. I'm at the first warehouse down by the tracks. I think I know how Luke got in."

"Wait for me. Don't you dare go inside by yourself."

I pulled the low rectangular window open. "I'm going in."

"No."

"If Alex is in there, he's frightened. I've dealt with a lot of irate parents, and I know how to stay calm in a volatile situation. If Luke's got the boy, I might be able to talk him into letting Alex go home."

"You're very stubborn. Did you know that?"

"But you like that about me, right?"

"Be careful, Maggie."

I ended the call, switched my phone to vibrate, and took a deep breath. I balanced the toe of my shoe on the dusty window ledge, lowered my backside to the ground, and slipped into the opening.

It took a few seconds for my eyes to adjust to the dim light. I could just make out a row of metal shelves lining the cinderblock walls and identify the dark hulking presence in the corner as an empty soft drink machine. Two desks covered with office paraphernalia sat facing each other in the middle of the room. So this is what a bankrupt printing company looked like when their employees jumped ship in the middle of the night. I flipped a light switch on and off. The electricity had been cut off, so no elevator for me. I would have to take the stairs.

I moved silently into the adjoining hall. A shaft of filtered sunlight fell from a window at the top of the stairs, lighting my way. I held onto the banister and gazed up into the stairwell.

Everything was quiet. Too quiet.

At the top, I pushed open a large door leading to some kind of production room. I stepped across the threshold. Afternoon light poured in through the tops of tall windows blocked halfway down with black opaque paint. Four huge metal printing presses sat evenly spaced in the middle of the room, flanked on either side by wheeled wire baskets full of paper rolls on metal spindles.

I pulled out my phone to call Eli. It had been foolish to sneak into an abandoned building alone, but I'd had no choice. For Alex's sake, I needed to find him as soon as possible. And it wasn't going to be easy. There were hallways and offices and more rooms than I could count.

I punched in Eli's number, but nothing. No signal. No anything. I was on my own.

A muffled clatter echoed from across the hall.

I grabbed a five-foot metal spindle and held it down by my side. If I needed to defend myself, the best I could hope for was to whack my attacker on the head when they weren't looking. And even that was a stretch.

I moved silently down the hall, one non-squeaking foot in front of the other. My heartbeat pounded in my throat as I pushed the door open.

The room was set up for meetings: tables and chairs lined the walls, an empty water cooler was shoved into the corner, portable computer desks had been stacked on top of each other like lawn chairs stored for the winter. I moved toward the raised platform in the center of the room. The air went out of my lungs.

Luke Prichard sat on the platform with his back against a wooden podium, watching me. He crossed his arms over his chest and grinned. "Hello, Maggie MacGill."

Chapter 21

"Where is Alex? Is he here?"

"Why would Alex be here?" Luke genuinely looked confused.

"He's been missing for several hours. I saw you walking through the crowd on Main Street holding his stuffed penguin. I thought—"

He reached behind the podium and held up the toy. "This penguin?"

"Yes." I tightened my grip on the spindle.

"And you thought—hey, wait! Didn't Mr. Giles take him home? I stopped at the market to pick up a six-pack and the lady behind the counter said Mr. Giles found Alex wandering down Main street looking for Sam and Dan's. He kept licking a pretend ice cream cone so Giles would understand what he was trying to say. Pretty smart, huh? I texted Irena and told her." He laughed. "Kids! They'll drive you crazy, won't they? Sorry for the misunderstanding."

"But you have his penguin."

"I found it on the street. He must have dropped it. Poor little guy can't sleep without it."

"That's good." I took a step back. "Good to know Alex is all right. A lot of people were worried about him."

He tucked the penguin under his arm. "I heard you discovered another dead body. You didn't mention that when I found you stranded on the courthouse roof."

"Well, technically, Eli found me on the roof. You were sitting in your car in the parking lot, remember? I tried to flag you down, but you didn't see me. Then you shared your umbrella with me while Eli looked for my phone."

"That's right."

"I wondered at the time why your hair was so wet when you had an umbrella."

"It was a bad storm," Luke said, stepping toward me.

"Yeah, it was. You never asked what I was doing trapped up there."

"Didn't I? I guess I just figured something had happened to your ladder."

"Good guess. It fell to the ground. The wind must have knocked it over."

"Yeah, that's probably what happened." Luke smiled. "But if somebody moved it on purpose, you'd never be able to prove it. You can't get fingerprints off a wet surface."

"Well, actually, you can." I forced a laugh. "But don't listen to me. I watch way too many *CSI* reruns." I was trying to sound cool and unruffled, but lightbulbs were going off in my head like the Eiffel Tower on New Year's Eve. "My mother used to hide money in the back of a pillow. It didn't have a zippered pocket like Alex's penguin, but it served the same purpose."

His ruddy cheeks darkened.

"That penguin's tummy is too lumpy to be filled with a pair of pajamas, so I'm guessing you stuffed it with the money you stole from Irena. The money Eli gave her today. Am I right?"

Luke's eyes narrowed. "Irena promised me half of that money for pretending to be her boyfriend. She knew if there was a stepfather for Alex waiting in the wings who looked like a gold-digger, it would drive Eli crazy. And he would pay anything to be Alex's guardian and keep me out of the picture."

"Eli never mentioned having any qualms about you being Alex's stepfather. It was only Irena he objected to. He didn't believe she cared enough to give the boy the kind of special education he needs."

"So that's another lie Irena told. After Eli paid her today, I asked for my cut and she pretended like she didn't know what I was talking about. But I've earned every penny, and I'm keeping it. I've put up with Irena and that brat of hers for four weeks. And besides, it's Grayson money. And the Graysons owe me big time."

"Is that why you brought the penguin here? To hide it until you could leave town?"

"There ain't nothing left for me in Wrenhaven. I can get a job anywhere moving other people's crap."

Of course. Luke worked for a moving company. Mr. Giles had told me that, but I hadn't connected the dots. Was he employed by Family Haul Movers? The same company that had gone to Trude's storage unit, picked up her boxes, and stored them in my father's garage?

If Luke had moved the ladder while I was on the courthouse roof, then he'd probably thrown the stink bombs in Jesse's restaurant too. And cut the brakes on Pop's van. Had he left Comfort and Joy and gone straight to the storage unit to meet Trude? Then what? Picked up a bronze unicorn and—

My arms suddenly felt cold.

Why couldn't I have figured this out earlier? Like

before I'd climbed through a basement window into an abandoned building to confront the man I thought was a kidnapper. I'd been so sure he'd taken Alex. But all he'd taken was Alex's stuffed toy full of Irena's bribe money.

I glanced around. If I had to make a run for it, I needed to know what my options were.

As it turned out: they were shockingly limited.

The only way out of that room was through the door I had come in, a sealed window I would have to climb on a chair to reach, a narrow closet, and a three-foot square HVAC vent near the floor with its hinged, louvered door standing slightly ajar. Maybe that's where Luke had planned to stash Irena's money.

"Whatcha thinking about, Maggie McGill? Are you wondering if you're strong enough to hit me with your little spindle and run away?"

"Not at all." I kept my voice steady. "I was wondering what your sweet mother would think about all this."

A soft crash echoed from the stairwell.

Luke swung around. "What was that?"

"Sounds like cardboard boxes falling over. I must have knocked against them on my way in."

"I don't think so." His eyes shifted to me then back to the door. "Someone's in the basement. And I'd bet half of what's in that penguin that it's Eli Grayson. Aw, how sweet. He's come to your rescue again. Well, at least, this time it isn't raining."

Luke pulled a sheathed knife from his back pocket. In a move so fluid it fascinated me, he slid the leather cover off, snapped it open, and held the six-inch blade out in front of him.

I opened my mouth to shout to Eli.

"Don't do it." Luke pointed the knife at me. "Sit."

I sat on one of the folding chairs grouped near the wall. Another crash sounded in the stairwell, this time followed by a muffled curse.

"What is that bozo doing?" Luke started to go then turned back. "Do not move, understand? Stay right where you are or you and your family will be sorry."

He went out into the hall, and shut the door behind him.

I didn't hesitate a nanosecond. I ran to the door and banged on it. *"He's got a knife!"* I screamed. *"Eli! He's got a knife!"* My voice bounced off the walls like cannon fire.

Luke's footsteps clattered down the stairs then stopped. Was he coming back to shut me up for good? Or had he found Eli? It had to be Eli. No one else knew we were there.

I slid the spindle under the chair I'd been sitting on and scrambled toward the air conditioning vent. I opened the grillwork and dove inside the duct. The sour stench of mildew assaulted my nose. The narrow tunnel of metal panels stretched in front of me like a long gray coffin before veering off to the side. If I could make my way through the wall duct to another part of the building, it might drop me near an exit.

I raised up on my knees. My hips brushed against the metal walls, making me painfully aware of how small my world had just become. I kept my head down and began to crawl. My breath huffed warm against my chest. My knees ground into the metal floor through my jeans.

The HVAC looked outdated and inefficient. This warehouse had housed many different businesses over the years. Most of them unsuccessful. Companies probably didn't even install ducts like these anymore.

As I crawled, the palms of my hands burned. I reached into my back pocket to pull out my phone. Still no signal. I turned on the flashlight app and held it in front of me. All I could see was a long silver box that seemed to go on forever.

I pulled in a deep breath. Perspiration trickled between my breasts. Was I going to run out of air? How long would air last in a tunnel without a fan moving it forward?

Had Luke found Eli? Were they fighting on the stairs? I stopped to listen for Eli's deep voice, a sound that had become so dear to me. But all I could hear was my heartbeat thudding in my ears. The wedge of light from my phone glared hot against the silver walls. A dark padded surface loomed in front of me, the sides tufted white with insulation.

Which way to go? Left or right?

A sudden movement darted across my line of vision. My heart slammed into my throat.

I held up my phone, praying it was not a rodent. I really hated rodents. And coming face to face with a giant rat in a passageway the size of a Pez dispenser would be a childhood nightmare come true. I swallowed and backed up a few feet. Whatever it was, skittered away.

I stopped to rest and sighed. What the hell was I doing? The tunnel was a warren of channels and shafts getting narrower and more difficult to navigate with every foot. I needed air. I needed to be on a beach. I would never complain about the wind in my face again.

It was time to change plans and retreat. Find a better

way out of the building. Retrace my steps and rethink my escape route. I was desperate to know if Eli was safe. I hadn't heard a sound behind the grillwork since I'd escaped into the duct. I worked my way back down the long passageway, one butt-length at a time, stopping every six feet or so to rest.

"Maggie!"

I looked behind me.

At the end of the duct, the shadow of a man bathed in the blue-white light of a phone screen crawled toward me. I heard Eli before I saw his face, panting and gulping in air like he was suffocating. He moved slowly, one hand in front of the other, his broad shoulders brushing the narrow walls, his head knocking against the ceiling. It had been tough for me to travel through the small confined space, but I wasn't claustrophobic. How was he even managing?

Every few feet, he stopped to shine the light in front of him, as if to reassure himself that he wasn't trapped in a place he couldn't get out of. I imagined I could hear his big heart hammering against his ribs. Or maybe it was mine.

"Maggie!" he cried hoarsely.

"Up here!"

Eli shone the light on me. "Hey, you look familiar."

I laughed. "We've got to stop meeting like this."

"Fine with me," he rasped. "But if you want to get my attention, there are easier ways of doing it." He leaned against the wall, holding his hand to his chest, waiting for me to crawl toward him. "And thanks for the heads up about the knife."

"Anytime." I backed a few more feet. "Where's Luke? Are you sure he isn't—"

"Luke is gone," Eli said. "We scuffled for a few minutes until I kicked the knife out of his hand, then he took off. He left the penguin behind. I think he dropped it by the podium."

"He'll be back then. That's where he stashed the money he stole from Irena." I came to a wider cross-section that allowed me enough room to turn around. I put my hand on Eli's arm. "Are you okay, Beach Boy? Dark scary tunnels aren't exactly your thing."

He grinned. "So how about we get the hell out of here."

We crawled the rest of the way down the long vent until we reached the opening. Eli kicked the door open and backed into the room. I stepped out, faltering on my right foot.

"You're hurt," Eli said. "What happened to your shoe?"

"I lost it when I took that last corner a little too fast." He held onto my arm. "At least Luke is gone." My gaze shot over Eli's head to the platform. "Or not."

Luke held up the penguin. "Did you really think I'd leave without my money? Or a hostage? I don't think I'd get very far alone, do you?" He brandished the knife in front of us. "How about you, Maggie? Want to go on a road trip?"

"Well, she has always wanted to see the ocean," Eli said.

"Does Irena know you stole her money?" I said. "Or is that going to be a lovely surprise when she takes Alex home and discovers it's not there?"

"Oh, she knows," Luke said.

"And does she know you were getting it on with Trude Claussen?" I said. "Before you killed her and stuffed her in a trunk?" Eli's grip tightened on my arm.

Luke sucked in a long breath of air. "That she doesn't know."

"Why did Trude have to die?" I said.

"I didn't mean to kill her," Luke said, "it was an accident. I met her at the storage unit to tell her it was over. That Irena was getting suspicious. But Trude wasn't having any of it. She was so angry, she tried to hit me with that bag of hers and missed. Then she tripped over a box and hit her head when she fell against that iron horse thing."

"Unicorn," I said.

"She was dead before I could reach my phone. Like I said, it was an accident."

"Was it an accident when you tried to smother Mrs. Grayson with a pillow?" I said.

"You killed my grandmother?" Eli asked incredulously. "But why?"

"Yes, why?" I said. "You and Irena already knew she'd changed her will. Florence told you. Why risk killing a woman who only had weeks to live?"

It occurred to me it was probably not the best time to be having this conversation. My right foot had begun to throb and Luke had a long shiny knife he wasn't afraid to use. If Eli and I had to run for our lives, I wasn't sure I could make it to the door without falling on my face.

My gaze fell on the spindle I'd shoved under the chair. Not the ideal weapon to fight a man holding a knife, but better than nothing. I tried to catch Eli's eye, but Eli's eyes were on Luke, trying to anticipate his next move.

The best I could do was try to diffuse the situation.

"I know your mother was sick for a long time with

cancer, Luke," I said gently. "That must have been hard on you."

Luke lowered the knife a few inches and stared at me.

"You said the Grayson family owes you," I said. "Is it because you needed help when your mother was so ill? I know Mrs. Grayson had set up a charity fund with the city to assist families in need. Did you feel like it didn't offer enough help to your family?"

"Offer enough help?" Luke scoffed. "Constance Grayson took everything my family owned. She bulldozed our home to build that stupid park named after her. She pushed us out of our house with nowhere to go. My mother was in the last stages of ovarian cancer and getting weaker every day. She begged Mrs. Grayson to spare our house and build the park somewhere else— begged her! But the old witch wouldn't hear of it. Then Mama pleaded with her to at least stop construction on the park until after she died. She only had a few months left; it wouldn't have been that hard. But Mrs. Grayson wouldn't do that either. She didn't care that the house had been in our family for four generations. All my mama wanted to do was die in her own home. That's all she wanted in this world. But your grandmother was too selfish to give it to her."

"Wasn't your family compensated?" Eli said.

"Compensated?" Luke said. "They were *screwed*. Mrs. Grayson got the mayor to rezone our property two weeks before the sale went through. It sent the property value into the toilet. We barely got enough to cover moving expenses."

"I'm sorry," Eli said.

"Like hell you are," Luke said. "Your family owes

me, Grayson."

"I wish you'd talked to Mayor Nash," I said. "His wife died of cancer too. He might have been more sympathetic and tried to buy you more time to stay in your home."

"Mayor Nash would never have stood up to Mrs. Grayson. We all knew that."

"How did you get inside Grayson House that night?" I asked. "Did you steal Trude's key?"

"Yeah, I took it. I didn't plan to hurt the old woman. I just wanted to talk to her alone after everybody left. Once I found Mrs. Grayson's room, I begged her to help us. I'd had an idea, see. I thought maybe she could give us enough money to fly Mama to a cancer specialist. But when I told her Mama was dying, you know what she did? She laughed. She laughed and said, 'We're all dying, son.' Then she picked up her book and started reading. She just dismissed me. Like she was some rich queen or something. It made me so angry, I—"

"—smothered her?" I said.

Luke smiled. "Nah. All I had to do was pick up the pillow and stand beside the bed. She knew what I was going to do. She grabbed her heart and in five seconds, she was on her way to hell. I knew she was dead, but it felt so damned good to push that pillow into her ugly face."

"What about the brakes on Les MacGill's van?" Eli said.

"Well, now, that was just fun," Luke said. "Almost as much fun as pushing Maggie's friend into her painting. And the stink bombs…oh, man. I felt like I was in high school again."

"Why did you want to hurt my father?" I said. "He

didn't even know you."

"It was all Irena's idea," Luke said. "We thought he was going to inherit the Grayson estate—that's what Florence said." He looked at me. "Because of the initials being the same, we didn't know it was you and not your old man. Irena and I didn't want to hurt him. We only wanted to scare him into giving the inheritance back so Alex would get a cut. But she didn't leave it to any of you Graysons, did she?" Luke laughed. "Which must just chap your ass."

"Yes, my ass is definitely chapped," Eli said.

"Didn't look chapped last night," I said under my breath.

"It was dark," Eli whispered. "You only let me light one candle, remember?"

"What are you two saying?" Luke said.

Eli cleared his throat. "Maggie is wondering why you think I'm going to walk out of here without taking back the money you stole from Irena. Paying her such an exorbitant amount nearly wiped me out. And she won't agree to let me be Alex's guardian without it."

"You're a Grayson," Luke said. "You've got money stashed everywhere."

"Who told you that, Irena?" Eli laughed. "She always did have an inflated view of my finances. The truth is: for all intents and purposes, my grandmother cut me loose a long time ago. I never made more than any other second-level grunt working for the firm. Probably less. So no, I do not have money stashed everywhere. Or anywhere." He looked at me and shrugged. "Sorry, babe. In case you thought you had an offer last night to make the earth move with a millionaire."

"Don't feel bad, Luke," I said. "You could still

marry Irena. I'm sure she'll forgive you for stealing her money and sleeping with Trude and scaring Alex's great-grandmother to death. Of course, you might have to tie the knot from prison."

"You're hilarious," Luke said, raising his knife in the air. "And you're coming with me."

Eli lunged in front of me, grabbed the spindle, and spun it around. He held it with both hands and smacked it against Luke's arm. The knife flew out of Luke's fist and bounced across the floor.

"What the—" Luke sputtered.

"Ten years of bringing in blue marlin with a fishing pole." Eli pointed the spindle at Luke. "Besides hiding Irena's money, is this where you hid some of the more expensive things Trude stole from Grayson House? Leaving them in a storage unit would be a little risky."

Luke's dark blue eyes flashed. "You know about that?"

"Not really. I just guessed. Stephen warned Trude about filching our family's possessions weeks ago. We should have known she had a partner."

"You knew the sheriff was closing in on you for killing Trude," I said. "So you waited until the parade started then came here to pocket the rest of the stolen jewelry and clear out."

"I told you, I didn't mean to kill her."

"Then you need to tell that to the sheriff," I said.

"It's too late for that," Luke said. "No one will believe me. No one's ever believed me." He jumped to his feet and in one deft movement, kicked the spindle out of Eli's hand. "Six years of karate at the Wrenhaven Boy's Club." He laughed. "I want the two of you to get back in the HVAC duct. And this time, I'm locking the door. You first, Maggie. And hurry up, before I wallop your boyfriend with this stick."

"He's not my boyfriend," I said.

"I'm not?" Eli said. "Does this mean you're giving back my class ring?"

"That's right," I said. "And I'm not going to the prom with you, either."

"Shut *up!*" Luke slammed the stick against the podium.

Eli turned on a dime and shoved Luke into the podium, toppling them both like bowling pins. Luke lay motionless, holding his arm.

I picked up the knife.

"There he is!" Stephen yelled from the doorway.

My head whipped around.

Mr. Giles stood beside Stephen pointing a shotgun at Luke's chest.

"I should've known you were in on this, Giles," Luke said. "You never liked me."

"No, I never did," Mr. Giles said. "Are you all right, Maggie?"

I nodded. "Did Alex get home safe?"

"Oh, sure," Mr. Giles said. "After I found him wandering around Sam and Dan's in the middle of the parade, and saw Maggie jump off that float and start running up Main Street, I left him with my sister and went to find the sheriff. I flagged Stephen down in that fancy car of his. It took a little time to track down Conley, what with the parade and all, but he's right behind us."

Luke scrambled to his feet, grasped the spindle with both hands, and pulled it behind his head ready to swing. Stephen went for him and missed, catching the brunt force of the metal pole on his shoulder.

"On the floor!" Sheriff Conley burst into the room, flanked by two deputies. The deputies threw Luke against the wall and cuffed him, then hauled him out of the room before things could get nasty. The sound of a siren echoed in the distance.

After that, things happened quickly.

Eli unbuttoned his shirt and wrapped it around his cousin's bleeding shoulder. The EMS workers loaded Stephen on a stretcher and wrapped an elastic bandage around my foot. Sheriff Conley jotted down our statements then hurried off to the station, eager to get Luke's photo to the witness for identification and compare his fingerprints with the ones they'd found on the bronze unicorn and Mrs. Grayson's pillow. Mr. Giles, clearly the hero of the hour, and one who could never pass up an opportunity for free publicity, shook hands all around then took a smiling selfie with a deputy for the *Wrenhaven Gazette*.

The room finally cleared except for Eli and me. We both looked a little bedraggled. Stephen's blood was smeared across the front of Eli's shirt, and I looked like a hedgehog who'd fallen off a tractor and been drug through the Kesterson's hayfield.

"Well, that was fun." I sat on a folding chair and propped my throbbing foot on the platform. "I should go home. One of the deputies said he'd give me a ride."

"He also said there's no rush. He's in the car logging things into his computer."

I tried to put my weight on my swollen foot and stumbled.

"Let me—"

"No." I limped to the window. "It's not so bad. I'll

be out jogging again in a week."

"Why won't you let me help you?"

"Because I'm annoyingly independent." I raised my eyes to his. "And because this is where we part ways, Beach Boy. We caught the bad guy, we cleared my name, you'll get to be Alex's permanent guardian." I stopped and took a deep breath. "I want to thank you for crawling into that vent to rescue me. It can't have been easy."

"I'd have crawled into hell to make sure you were all right." He managed a laugh. "I'm not going back for your shoe, though. Maybe a repairman will find it one day and wonder what the hell went on in that air duct."

"My lips are sealed."

He ran his hand back through his hair. "So this is it, then?" He waited a moment. "Look, Maggie, I know there's a lot to forgive me for, but I'd like to make it up to you. Come to Kitty Hawk with me. Let me show you the ocean. While I'm crushing numbers for work, you can sit on the shore and paint. I'll wear a Percy DePaul bow tie. I'll rent you a cabana boy."

"I can't leave. I have responsibilities."

"Then bring them with you. Pack them in your carry-on with your toothbrush and sunscreen. Bring your father too. Les and my mom would hit it off great. They can have wheelchair races up and down Kitty Hawk Pier." He searched my eyes. "Please, Maggie. I'm throwing myself in front of a bus here." He threaded his fingers through mine. "What we hold on to isn't what shapes us into who we are. It's the things we're brave enough to let go of. Please let go of your doubts and come with me."

"Sounds good on paper."

"I wish you believed me. Maybe someday you will." He reached into his wallet and handed me a blue business card. "If you ever end up at the Outer Banks, I hope you'll check out my mother's shop. Gull Cottage Gifts sells the kind of artwork you don't think you're talented enough to market. But you're wrong." He grinned at me one last time and shook his head. "I'm gonna miss you, Mountain Girl."

My heart pressed hard against my chest.

A week ago, I wouldn't have given Eli Grayson one chance in hell of ever making me feel something other than hatred for him. But things can change. Even when you don't want them to. And miracles can happen when you least expect it.

I was going to miss him too.

Probably more than I realized.

Chapter 22

The wind from the sound blew against my face.

A dozen black pelicans, all in perfect V-formation, soared across the cloudless sky. Sunlight sparkled on the water like shards of green glass. The soft roar of the sea wasn't audible from the sound side of the barrier reef, but I knew it was there, behind the live oak trees, just waiting for me to introduce myself.

I followed Stephen's directions, parked Velma, and walked across the grassy lot to the small building. Two open safari trucks with blue and yellow striped awnings sat parked beside the curb. Families wearing sunhats and windbreakers stood in groups near the entrance.

Inside, the walls were covered with framed photographs of local landmarks: the dunes at Jockey's Ridge, Bodie and Hatteras lighthouses, the Wright Brothers National Memorial, the wild horses in Corolla.

I picked up a brochure. *OBX Wild Horse Tours*. "I'm looking for Eli Grayson."

The tanned blond guy behind the counter glanced up. "He'll be right back. His tour starts in five minutes."

"His tour?" I laughed. Stephen hadn't told me Eli was a tour guide. "Can I buy a ticket?"

"Absolutely." He made the transaction and handed me a receipt. "Weather's perfect. Should be great today."

"That's what I'm counting on."

I waited outside beside the safari truck, hiding

behind a boisterous family of five that reminded me of the Kestersons. A few minutes later, Eli sauntered out the door wearing a black T-shirt with the *Outer Banks Wild Horse Tours* logo emblazoned across the front. His brown hair, sun-streaked and wild, whipped across his forehead in the wind. His aviator sunglasses hung from a black cord around his neck.

"Afternoon, everybody. I'm your guide, Eli Grayson. Climb in, and we'll get started. Sit the little ones in the middle. Hands and feet must remain inside the vehicle at all times." He grinned at the elderly lady seated beside him. "They make me say that."

I found a seat in the back row and pulled my billed cap down.

"The wild horses in Corolla are descendants of the original colonial Spanish mustangs," Eli said. "We have over a hundred in the sanctuary and over 7,500 acres for them to roam." He guided the open-air truck off the main road onto the sand. "Are you guys ready for some fun?"

"Yeah!" the kids screamed.

Behind the sea oats, the distant crash of waves crested and slapped against the shore. The truck jolted over the last dune, and there it was: the ocean, spread across the horizon like a dark blue blanket glittering in the sun. The salt air blew my short hair back from my face, caressed the bare skin above my white tank top. I had waited for this moment most of my adult life, imagining that when it arrived, time would stop until I could evoke every sound, every smell, every heartbeat.

But now that I was here, I barely glanced at it.

All I could see was Eli Grayson.

"This is one of my favorite places," Eli said, as we rumbled along the wide expanse of beach. He glanced in the rearview mirror. "Is this anyone's first time seeing the ocean?"

I raised my hand.

"The lady in the back," Eli said. "Where are you from?"

"Tennessee," I said.

"Yeah, that's super landlocked. And you've never seen the ocean before this trip?"

"Not until three minutes ago, Beach Boy."

Eli's gaze shot to the rearview mirror. He lowered his sunglasses. Our eyes met.

"I see four horses!" one of the children shrieked. "They're standing in the water."

Eli steered the truck onto the hardened sand and cut the motor. "Take all the time you—" His voice caught. "All the time you want."

When the truck emptied, he walked back to where I was sitting and grinned. "Well, look what the wind blew in."

"I thought it was time I saw the ocean. You know, find out what all the fuss is about."

"The view is better up by the sea oats."

He helped me out of the truck and led me to the top of the dune. Clouds swept across the sky like brushstrokes. White tops crashed in the sea, unfurling as they rolled toward the shore. Four dark chestnut horses, who didn't look so wild standing knee-deep in the shallows, shook their manes and snorted while the tourists snapped their pictures.

"So what's up?" Eli said. "Anything new happen in the four weeks since I've seen you?"

I laughed, unable to contain the happiness I felt just seeing him there.

God, I'd missed his face. The strong square jaw. Those strange eyes that could turn either gray or green depending on the light. The way his grin flashed, revealing just a little preview of what was to come, until I'd do anything to make him laugh.

"How is Alex?" I said. "Stephen said he left with Irena after Luke was charged with attempted murder. The security camera video from the storage unit proved it was an accident. I'm so glad Luke wasn't responsible for Trude's death. I think Trude really loved him. At least that's what Florence said. And Florence—"

"—knows everything," we both said in unison.

"I think this Luke business shook Irena to the core," Eli said. "She returned the money to me and we're trying to compromise where Alex is concerned. I've enrolled him in the Tennessee School for the Deaf in Knoxville like you suggested. For now, he'll attend the day school, but they also have a residential school if we want to sign on for that when he gets older. He'll be with Irena until school starts in the fall, then I'll move back to your neck of the woods at the end of the summer, and he'll live with me. And Stephen."

"You'll be in Wrenhaven for the school year?"

"Thanks to my PC, I can work from anywhere. If I need to travel, Stephen's agreed to step up to the plate and watch Alex. The little guy has become quite fond of Stephen's girlfriend, Rocki. She lets him squirt paint onto her giant canvases and roll around in it."

I wasn't sure quite what to make of all this.

"Stephen sent me a photo of the new sign in front of Grayson House," he said. *Future Home of the Wrenhaven Art Factory.* I like that."

"Now that Kath has left with Dr. Harold, I'll be

running the place. And teaching art classes. Now that Jules' hand has healed, I may even add a music department. I have a lot of plans to make it more inclusive for special needs kids."

"That's amazing. And you've been very generous including Alex in the inheritance."

"I'm not sure your grandmother would approve."

He shrugged. "We gave her a proper funeral, did Stephen tell you? The morning I left for Kitty Hawk, we buried her ashes in Constance Grayson Park under the big sycamore tree facing the mountain. Reverend Lyon said a few words."

"That was nice of you."

"We didn't do it to be nice. We were afraid she'd haunt us if we didn't."

"Well, we don't want that," I said, laughing.

"Stephen also sent me a picture of the finished mural. Very impressive."

I glanced at him sideways.

"And very ballsy of you not to paint any people in it. I'm sure Mayor Nash was expecting his face to be immortalized for eternity. Although, there is an uncanny resemblance between him and that fat bear crouching in the corner."

"If you ever tell him, I'll deny it."

"Thanks for shipping the iris desk to me. You'll be glad to know the walking cane Grandmother left Stephen has been authenticated. I don't think anyone else would have had a clue it belonged to Toulouse Lautrec. Stephen's putting it up for auction in the fall. He doesn't want to keep it—too many bad memories." He laughed. "And he wants a new car."

"Of course, he does."

We stood in silence for a few moments, listening to the gulls. And the children's laughter. And the soft, never-ending roar of the sea.

"I have something else to show you." He took out his phone and pulled up Photos. "Scroll through those for a minute, then we'll talk."

In the first shot, a middle-aged woman with short gray hair and Eli's dimple slashing the side of her thin cheek sat smiling in a wheelchair. Behind her, on a gallery wall, hung a large group of seascapes. My seascapes.

"I don't understand."

"These are your paintings," Eli said. "The ones you threw away."

"But how—"

"Your father called me that night. I brought Big Blue around at the crack of dawn and loaded them in the truck, then I stored them at Stephen's." He scrolled to a photo of a bookkeeping sheet. "I was going to text this after I got up the courage to spill the beans about what we'd done. This is a record of the sales as of last week. Not bad, huh?"

"You've been selling my paintings? For this much?"

"It was your dad's idea. And only the prints. Mom would never sell the originals without your permission. Although people are clamoring for them." He pointed to a bank routing number. "All your earnings go into this account. So if you want to part with the originals, just say the word, and Mom will slap some obscenely high price tag on them and sell them."

I shook my head, trying to wrap it around what he was saying. "I'm a little blown away."

"You're also exceptionally talented and wonderful.

See? I do notice things." He nodded toward the horizon. "So what do you think of the ocean?"

"Better than I could have ever imagined. I didn't want to see it for the first time alone."

His dimple deepened. "Then I'm glad you chose to share it with me."

"Actually, I chose the blond guy I bought the ticket from, but he turned me down."

"Idiot." Eli's gaze dropped to the front of my low-cut tank top. "Where's the turtleneck?"

"I took it to Goodwill. Something else I've decided to let go of." I looked into his eyes. "Now that I'm flashing my very interesting bare chest to the world, I'm thinking of getting my scar tattooed. Maybe a giant butterfly. Or a zipper."

"How about a treasure map? The Outer Banks is very big on pirates."

"And wild horses." I touched the logo on his shirt. "Looks like you've let a few things go yourself. Like your tie. And your former job. And—" I glanced down. "—the rest of your pants."

"I'm going to spend the rest of the summer following my bliss." He took my hand and brought it to his lips. Then he grinned at me, full force, turning my cynical, mended heart into mush. "I was starting to think you'd written me off."

"Not a chance."

"Can I please hang out with you, Maggie MacGill? Like maybe for the rest of my life?"

"I guess that wouldn't be so bad. I mean, we are friends now."

The wild horses drifting past the shoreline stirred as the wind picked up. They snorted softly at the tourists, kicked up the sand, and turned into a blurred swirl of flying manes and tails as they raced beside the sea.

I laughed. "And you are my favorite person to find a dead body with."

A word about the author...

Rebecca lives with her husband and a dog named Wilbur in the beautiful, misty mountains of East Tennessee, where the people are charming, soulful, and just a little bit crazy. She's been everything from a tax collector to a stay-at-home-mom to a professional actor and director. She loves to travel the world but her Southern roots and the affectionate appreciation she has for the rural towns she lives near inspire the settings and characters she writes about. www.rebeccaleesmith.com

Other Wild Rose Press Titles by Rebecca Lee Smith

A Dance to Die For

A Shadow on the Ground

The House on Crow Mountain